SKIN CURSE

KRISTIN JACQUES

Midnight Tide
PUBLISHING

Edited by Mithlia Karnik, Rebecca Milhoan, & Aimee Bounds

Midnight Tide Publishing

www.midnighttidepublishing.com/

To those who pushed themselves to keep going, to survive, when they could not see the light.

SANCTUARY

 I 

AZURE

Azzy was safe. Through the thick glass of her bedroom window lay a city of monsters, both hidden and seen. The streetlights flickered, sparks in the haze of twilight as the denizens of Avergard choked the throughways, far from where she stood in observation.

It was a bewildering sensation, one she struggled to accept as she twirled the feather between her fingers. She wasn't fleeing from creatures of the Above or Below. She'd survived the Snatcher's caravan. Ensconced behind the walls of Lord Wallach's estate, she was beyond the reach of those elegant, hungry-eyed monsters.

Azzy pinched the feather between her fingers so tightly her bones whined, her mouth pressed into a hard line as the image replayed through her mind. The boy with wings, the vacant storm-shrouded eyes so achingly familiar and so very empty of recognition. She sucked in a breath, broken by a withheld sob. She was here, she made it to the city, and everything she'd lost to reach this place left the taste of ash in her mouth.

What had she gained but an insurmountable set of tasks? A tremor ran through her limbs, and Azzy wondered if it would ever stop when she heard the soft trod of footsteps approaching down the hall. She looked up as her doorway filled with a figure swathed in a swirling contrast of white smoke and shadows, curling around the feminine curves of her body like living cloth even as it obscured her face.

"Hello, Azzy, will you come down to dinner?" Her voice emerged as the smoke receded around her lustrous dark eyes. They seemed to glow through the wreath of smoke.

Azzy tucked the feather into her frayed sleeves, wishing to

keep it close to her skin, comforted by the contact. A sanctuary it may be, separated from the city by glass and stone, but her brother was out there somewhere. And who knew what other secrets these foreign streets held. The whispers plucked at her mind, delicate notes that made the barest ripples across her thoughts as she rose to follow the woman of smoke. She hesitated, listening, but the inaudible voices that had carried her so far continued to slip away, receding beneath the surface of her thoughts with each beat of her pulse like retreating waves in a surf. It left the world around her muted, and apprehension settled heavy on her shoulders.

"Please, you need to eat. A stiff breeze could tip you over," said the woman, misinterpreting her hesitation.

Azzy offered a tentative smile. "My apologies. I'm simply tired."

"You'll be given plenty of time to rest this eve," said the woman. "Now come, the others are waiting to meet you before we dine."

"Oh, they don't have to—" Azzy began, but the woman of smoke took her hands, the contact solid, the woman's skin cool as silk.

"It's tradition for all new additions to the household," she said, her voice warm. "Normally, we would have fed you immediately, but there was the other one to settle, and you looked so lost we wanted to give you a moment of privacy."

Azzy stared into the woman's dark gaze, at a loss for words. The gentle burr of the whispers shifted, an internal crackle as the lens of her altered eye pierced the haze, revealing the remarkable features of the woman beneath. Her features were rounded and delicate, but for a wide scar that scrawled over the bridge of her nose. One end tugged at her full lips while the other marred the slanted arc of her brow, her beauty shone despite the mark, but for the ghost of sadness and shame stamped in her expression. Azzy's grip unconsciously tightened on the woman's hands as the smoke billowed forward, obscuring her features once more. She strained to recall the woman's name from the rapid introduction they'd received upon arrival.

"Cherise, yes?"

The head servant bowed her head, a smile conveyed through her gaze. "Well done. I'm certain you shall adjust quickly here." She didn't release Azzy's hands as she gently tugged her from the room, tucking one hand beneath her arm as she led her charge down the second story of Wallach's vast home.

The house was dazzling, a sumptuous visual feast a world away from packed dirt and roughly chiseled stone. Azzy drank in the pristine white marble columns. The main wall boasted a tile mosaic of exquisite detail, a frothy, animate sea, backlit by a wild storm that framed a woman rising from a massive shell, her ethereal body scantly covered by ribbons of vibrant blue-green tiles. Azzy realized they had to be individual shards of turquoise. Hints of real gems shimmered in the figure's red hair, so very reminiscent of her mother's that Azzy's gaze snared on the mural as they walked. She could have stopped and stared at it for hours if Cherise's insistent tug hadn't pulled her along. Polished wood floorboards slid beneath her bare feet, broken by plush floor coverings softer than the thickest moss, in shades of color and intricate design far beyond anything that graced the grandest homes in the Heap. Elder Prast would choke on his own spit at the mere glimpse of so much splendor. If there was anyone in the Heap left. The thought burst the small vindictive swell that rose as she took in the overwhelming opulence, a reminder of the cost, the precarious position in which she'd left the Heap.

"Here we are. Told you I'd ferret her out."

She stiffened as Cherise pulled her into a very different space from the outer grand rooms. It took a moment for her eyes to adjust to the dimmer lamplit room. A handful of people stood around a rough-hewn wooden table like any she'd find in the Heap, with half a dozen place settings of quality but plain plates and utensils.

Azzy's gaze was immediately drawn to the man across from her, his slate gray vest and pants offset by his crisp white shirt, rolled up to the elbows. He could have been the age of her missing guardian, but it was difficult to determine due to his dark brown skin, cracked and curling like ancient tree bark. As Cherise spoke, her words appeared in luminous handwritten script on his bared arms before they dispersed and soaked into his skin like water into parched dirt. The close-cropped hair on his jaw and head reminded her of the thread moss she once gathered for Brixby's supplies, pale in color, with a faint green hue. His eyes were the same color as his skin, alight with warmth and curiosity as he looked her over.

Beside him stood a man who couldn't have been much older than Azzy herself, his servant's garb rumpled but clean except for his frayed, stained gloves. His nervous gaze never settled, bouncing from surface to surface, never once looking directly at her. Azzy found she could not look at him either as he began to blur and fade if she stared at him for more than a few seconds. She couldn't form a concrete mental picture of his appearance beyond a pale, anxious face surrounded by unruly dark hair.

Unsettled, she shifted her gaze away and found Morglint's familiar lopsided face at the far end of the table. The knot of nerves loosed at the sight of him, allowing the taut pull of her muscles to finally ease. She almost missed the final occupant at the table, her appearance startling for its normalcy. The young woman hovered in Morglint's shadow, the drab color of her dress and hair blended with the dim recesses of the room.

Cherise brought her to an empty chair and hovered nearby within a plume of smoke. "My dears, may I introduce our lord's latest acquisition, Azure Brimvine."

"Hello," Azzy bowed her head, uncertain of the formalities. The feather quill lightly scratched against her skin, an anchor that kept her present as the others nodded and murmured greetings as Cherise introduced them in turn. These introductions were vital, to people she hoped would be her allies here as she sought out her family.

"Lennon is our lord's manservant and personal butler." Cherise gestured to the older gentleman with tree bark skin. "Petyr takes care of household affairs and parlays with the House of Lords." The blurred young man with stained gloves snapped into sudden sharp focus as he held Azzy's gaze for a long tense moment. The room rocked and spun, and the faint scent of decay teased her senses, but Petyr's intensity failed to stir her internal whispers. The effect snapped off as his gaze darted away, leaving her faintly dizzy.

"I'm the Maven," said the woman in Morglint's shadow, with a voice that slid over Azzy's skin like snake scales. There was a hard smile on the woman's face and a keen interest in her gaze that belied her mundane appearance. Winking at Azzy, the Maven sat down, though the others remained standing. Curiosity pricked at Azzy, but Cherise continued as if the other woman hadn't spoken.

"And our new gardener and apothecary, you already know."

Morglint's smile banished the final snag of uncertainty. She looked him over as they finally sat, relieved her friend appeared far more relaxed than when they first arrived. The former Snatcher looked ready to bolt when Cherise took them in hand. They'd dropped off Morglint first in what appeared to be a hastily cleared out storage room, still half stacked with crates and thrown down pallets large enough to accommodate his frame. The space was dusty and dingy, but Morglint's eyes fell on the workbench and rack above it, built for the drying and storing of plants.

The other appealing feature of the room was the door, an ornate construction of iron curlicues and fluted rods. Cherise presented the Snatcher with an equally elaborate key. Azzy stayed to watch her friend open the door to reveal a glimpse of the Eden beyond, his expression of delight enough to let Cherise pull her away.

As the others set covered platters on the table, Azzy curled her fingers around Morglint's wrist.

"Are you—settling in?" She watched his features, relieved by the peace in his countenance.

"Oh, little one, the garden is wondrous. You come visit after dinner," said Morglint. The excitement in his eyes convinced Azzy she'd made the right decision, urging Wallach to take in the former Snatcher, that he would have a better life here and her choice wasn't borne of the simple selfish desire not to be alone.

Azzy nodded. "I will, I promise."

Lennon and Cherise removed the coverings with a flourish. Steam billowed across the table, carrying the scent of unknown spices that made Azzy's mouth water. The contents were unrecognizable, an array of ingredients sauced and diced, but she allowed Cherise to fill her plate with a hearty portion of everything. Eager as she was, the flavor and texture still caught her off guard, soft and savory, with more than a hint of salt and black flakes that made her tongue tingle. She ate half of the serving before her stomach clenched, unused to the intake of so much food.

"Slow down, dear, there's plenty to eat," said Cherise as she poured a dark red liquid into Azzy's cup.

"I believe I'm full," said Azzy as she sipped the tangy substance. It had to be wine though unlike any she'd tasted in her life, certainly better than anything traded from the Foragers. Caught up in the flavor, she nearly missed the glance between the head servant and Lennon.

"Would you like to bring some up to your room, in case you are hungry later?" The manservant asked; his low, rich baritone a pleasant rumble.

"No, I'll be fine until the morning," said Azzy.

Petyr's gaze fell on her like a physical weight. He had glanced at her throughout their meal with mounting consternation. Now, his gloved hand tightened on his fork as he gave her his full focus. "She doesn't taste like the city. She must have been brought in from the outside."

"Petyr!" Cherise set her cup down hard enough to slosh wine onto the tabletop.

"I can't place her. It unsettles me." The dark slash of Petyr's brow raised as he studied Azzy. "Her coloring is off for the swamps, and she looks too delicate to hail from the North."

"I—" Azzy stopped, bewildered. There were other settlements in the Above? Other regions? Why hadn't they guessed she was from Below? The whispers pulsed. Azzy looked up to find the Maven watching her as she lazily moved the food around her plate without eating it. The scrape and squeal of the fork tines across the porcelain surface filled the sudden silence, a drawn-out winch of sound that broke with a snap.

The three main servants stood so fast their plates bucked.

"My lord," said Cherise, bowing her head.

"At ease," said Lord Wallach. His presence pressed against Azzy's back. He radiated heat with the intensity of a blacksmith's forge. "Azure, have you finished eating?"

"Yes, sir—" she flinched as Cherise gave a sharp shake of her head. "Yes, my lord."

"Join me in the study then," said Wallach. She knew by the cold rush of air he'd left before her answer. The others were all watching her now with varying degrees of worry and curiosity.

Azzy didn't understand their expressions until Cherise shuffled her seat closer and leaned in, her silk-smooth voice low as she spoke. "Do you wish me to accompany you?"

She frowned, uncertain of the motives behind such an offer. "If you could show me to the study, I'd be grateful."

Cherise's dark eyes flashed; her expression obscured and inscrutable. "It takes time, adjusting to a place like this, to someone like our lord. Are you certain you don't want someone there to act as a buffer?"

"I'll be fine," said Azzy. She wondered if perhaps she should take the offer, but she knew Wallach wouldn't hurt her. That was the only certainty she had as the two of them rose from the table. She nodded to Morglint, intent on finding him after, before scurrying after the head servant.

A hallway stretched before them, lit by lamps that fluttered and buzzed as they passed, far brighter than any torchlight. The light hurt Azzy's eyes if she looked directly at them. Plush carpeting absorbed the weight of her steps, turning her into a wraith haunting the lord's hall. She trailed her fingertips along the cream-white walls, a physical reminder the house around her was real. This was real. Cherise paused outside a deep reddish-brown wooden door that matched the color and polish of the floor.

"I'll be in the servants' dining quarters if you need anything," Cherise said. She drifted away, and Azzy suddenly wished she hadn't been so quick to brush off the offer of company. The knowledge of safety didn't lessen the imposing presence of Wallach; a great, terrible presence, one the whispering voices in her mind acknowledged when they first met in the woods, but her desperation and fear had muted the intensity. She swore she could sense him beyond the barrier of the door, wondering if the closed walls of the house magnified the potency of his presence.

Azzy was stalling. She knew what he would ask of her— what he had to ask of her. The truth of it sat bitter in her mouth. *I lied to enter this house.* Had it been a full lie? Was it a lie when she meant every word? She wanted to help the Witch of the Wood, but she wanted many things, and she had little idea of how to achieve them.

The door swung open. Azzy startled, her gaze locked with Wallach's as he frowned down at her. She was close enough to follow the long seam of his mouth, partially concealed by facial hair. She wondered what purpose it served, irritated when she realized she waited for the whispers in her head to provide the answer, and worried when they didn't.

"What were you waiting for?"

Azzy focused on his words. There would be time to mull over the consistently inconsistent muttering in her head later. "I was thinking."

Wallach leaned back against the door frame, crossing his arms. The movement pulled the suit jacket he wore tight against the breadth of his shoulders. "What were you thinking of?"

Azzy fidgeted, tapping the feather in her sleeve against her forearm, the physical reminder of her purpose here enough to make her press on, though she couldn't look the lord of Avergard in the eye. Instead, she stared at the jeweled pin on the lapel of his jacket. "I know that I can't answer your question."

Wallach went utterly still, but his presence coiled around him, a trap set to spring. "What question would that be?" His tone was deceptively light.

"How I will help you save the witch." Azzy braced herself as all that pent-up energy that surrounded Wallach coalesced, a physical tension of a blade to the neck, poised to dig in.

The whispers kicked up at the sour hint of fear. *He wouldn't hurt her.* Wallach sucked in a breath, and the tension popped, the void of so much energy enough to make her stagger. He caught her and steered her inside, setting her down in the receiving chair that faced his desk. Wallach's steps were slow as he circled around, bracing himself on the desk through great gusting breaths as he fought for control. He composed himself faster than she expected, settling across from her in a winged high-back chair that rose like a shadow behind him.

"This foresight, is this how your magic works?" He rested his steepled hands against his chin.

"I don't—" the denial died on her lips. She'd denied the presence of magic for so long it came as second nature, but she had to have something, even if her understanding of it was paltry at best. She knew it was more than gut instincts and luck. That she'd convinced herself the whispers were a benign effect for so long was her own willful ignorance. The truth was worse. "I don't know." Her voice wavered. It hurt to draw breath, a vise of shame and embarrassment a crushing stone on her chest as she spoke. "I don't know how it works. I—I didn't think it was magic. I don't know how to use it."

"But you knew who I was," said Wallach, tapping his gloved fingers against his bottom lip.. "You called me by name. By title."

"Yes, and no," said Azzy. "I knew... pieces, an incomplete story. I can't—" she pressed her lips tight, biting the insides of her cheeks until she tasted blood in her mouth. "There's nothing now." The whispers remained silent, gave her nothing as Wallach watched her.

"Azure," he said, but the stone grew ever larger until she couldn't breathe. "Azzy!"

She choked out the words. "I'm sorry."

"You were so confident when you approached me. You took my hand without fear. What happened between then and now?"

"I'm not afraid of you," she said. Her words rang true. She didn't fear Wallach, but she was in a panic, unable to explain the stifling weight that bore down on her.

"You're afraid of something," said Wallach.

"I don't know what to do," said Azzy. There it was: the core of her dilemma. She'd made it this far with a single goal in mind, to reach her brother, but that focus had changed, shifted, with each loss.

Wallach's jaw flexed. "Why are you here? I know it's not for Safiya. You were as shocked by her capture as I, but I don't think you are here by chance. You were leaving that caravan when I encountered you, yet you came here willingly."

The words welled up against her lips. Did she dare tell him? Did she trust him? It was different, admitting her own ignorance of her magic, something she couldn't hide from him. What could she tell him but the truth? How could she gain his confidence if she lied now? She needed his trust, the safety of Wallach's domain if she were to have a chance.

"I came here for my brother," said Azzy. "He was brought here by Snatchers."

Wallach's lip curled in distaste. "Yes, aside from your rather unusual companion Morglint, the Snatchers willfully ignore set laws when it comes to acquiring their merchandise. If the auctions weren't so successful, the restrictions would be easier to enforce." Wallach sighed as he rubbed the bridge of his nose. "What region were you taken from?"

Saliva filled her mouth. A chill pervaded through the overwhelming warmth, cooling the sweat on her skin until she shivered. This echoed the assumption his servant, Petyr, made. From what Azzy had gleaned, she thought those cast out from the Below regularly wound up in the city, but something about Wallach and his servants made her wonder. What was she missing? For the first time since their conversation began, the whispers fluttered, but their inaudible words failed to give her a direction or warning.

"We came from Haven. From Below."

Wallach jerked as if she'd struck him. "That's not possible."

Her mouth filled with dust. Azzy licked her lips. "There were rumors, the Snatchers took those who were cast out by the Elders. I didn't know it was true, that they were real, until we—I followed Armin into the Above."

Wallach clasped his hands together. "It is an ill-kept secret the Snatchers often acquire the castouts among the territories, but not from the underground. Were you taken together?"

"He wasn't in the same caravan you bought me from," said Azzy. She stared at him. She didn't need the aid of the whispers to deduce that her brother's abduction wasn't a fluke, or a random occurrence for the Snatchers. They took not one but three people in one go, her brother, her guardian, and the infected Bethel, ready with rope and chain, and leashed wolves in the shape of men to chase down those who fled. Azzy remembered those terrible whispers as she stood across from Windham, and heard the cries of those weeping ghosts, the ones he'd sold to fill his coin purse. Did Wallach honestly believe the Snatchers didn't have a frequent supply of 'goods' from the Below? The idea unsettled her more than if he had lied about it.

"What happened?" His question pulled her from her tangled thoughts.

"I ran. And I lost the one who came with me," said Azzy, unable to speak her guardian's name. Her heart ached as she wondered what happened to him. Had he survived the journey with her brother? Had he lived past the moment she ran? When she glimpsed her brother through the crowded streets, she hadn't seen her wayward guardian.

"You were alone?"

She nodded, trying to stifle the lingering pain of her loss. She couldn't think of that, not now, not when she had to make it through this first hurdle. *One task at a time, Azzy.*

Wallach's lips parted, an unconscious moment of shock that revealed the full seam of his mouth. "How did you survive?"

"I wasn't alone for long," she said. Moisture gathered on her lashes. "There were others who helped me get here, including Safiya." She brushed a finger beneath her colorless eye, where her skin was dry despite the press of grief.

"When we met, I sensed the touch of other magics on you," said Wallach. "Some almost familiar. She truly helped you?"

"Yes." For a price, though at the glimpse of longing in Wallach's eye Azzy kept the witch's mercenary side to herself.

He rubbed his thumb along his bottom lip, a markedly nervous gesture. "What is it like, your Haven?"

"It's a dying city," said Azzy. "Probably a dead city now."

The color drained from Wallach's face. "What?"

"There was never enough food, never enough medicine, and the Rot, the Rot festered at its core." Azzy's fingers curled at the surge of memory. What she left in Haven was bad, and nothing compared to Caletum, which invaded her nightmares, but his reaction surprised her as if he expected a different answer.

Wallach surged to his feet. "I'm afraid I must send you off for the night. Cherise will escort you back to your room."

The abrupt ending of their conversation left a note of unease between them.

"I'm sorry," she said, the words inadequate for what she needed to convey. "I didn't want to lie. I will help however I can."

The lord sighed through his nose. "Self-preservation is a difficult path to navigate in our world, Azzy. You are safe here. Rest, and we will discuss this further in the morning."

Azzy searched his face, trying to glean the truth of his assurances. Frustration pricked at the silence in her head. "Thank you."

She found Cherise waiting for her at the dining table with a steaming cup beside her.

"Before I lead you to your bed for the night, drink this," said the woman of smoke. "I promise it's not poison."

"It would be a waste of Wallach's coin to poison me now," said Azzy, though she hesitated to take a sip. The dark, fragrant liquid had another unfamiliar scent.

"The tea will help you sleep," said Cherise, "I added a touch of honey."

The warm liquid held a touch of bitterness under the cloying sweetness that coated her mouth, at odds with the floral scent that wafted from the cup. She decided she liked it more than the wine served at dinner.

"I promised Morglint I would visit tonight," said Azzy.

"The garden will be there tomorrow," said Cherise, her voice gentle. "You look ready to drop."

Did she? She'd pushed and pushed herself for so long, she wondered if she now recognized her own physical limits. Azzy glanced down. The liquid in her cup shivered with the fine tremor in her hands. When was the last time she slept free of fear and pain? When had she given her body the chance to rest without straining it to the breaking point? Until she woke in Morglint's tent, her journey was one long endless run, her lungs burning for a breath she never drew. She could feel the toll on her body, the bone-deep ache in each step, but she dreaded lying down in a bed with nothing but her ghosts for company.

"I just want to say goodnight," she said.

"We can do that."

Azzy ignored her shaking hands and sipped the tea. The lamps in this room flickered with natural flame, a few of the bracketed candles extinguished so that Cherise was a looming, wavering shade beside her.

"Why is this room so dark?"

"Hmm, Petyr's uncomfortable with the electricity," said Cherise. "Says it makes his teeth itch."

"Electricity?"

Cherise straightened in her chair. "But that's—what region are you from?"

"I'm done with my tea," said Azzy. She presented the empty cup, unwilling to enter another conversation concerning her origins. There had to be plenty of people in this city from Below, not just forced here by the Snatchers. The Foragers must have come here, or others. Wallach's incredulity unsettled her.

Cherise tried to wait her out, but years of dealing with Elder Prast perfected her stone-faced expression.

"Very well. Let's say goodnight to your friend,"

Azzy hesitated. "I could find the way on my own." She was pushing an unspoken boundary here. Despite Wallach's evident kindness, she was not only a stranger in this household but also a newly acquired servant, bound by rules she wasn't familiar with yet.

"I am certain you can, but you will not until you've proven trustworthy," said Cherise. Azzy appreciated the blunt words, and the woman's concern appeared genuine.

Azzy regretted her insistence on bidding Morglint goodnight as she trudged after Cherise. The woman of smoke glided forward as Azzy struggled to force one foot in front of the other, her legs leaden weights as exhaustion hammered at her with sudden ferocity. She leaned against the wall to catch her breath and found herself nodding off, barely able to keep her eyes open until the sensation of cool smoke drifted across her flush face.

"The tea?"

"I didn't expect it to hit you so hard," said Cherise. "You've strained yourself more than I thought. I will apologize to the Snatcher for you."

"He's not a Snatcher," insisted Azzy, her voice muddled in her own ears. "He's a healer. He's good."

Cherise pressed a hand to her forehead, her touch an icy balm against Azzy's fevered skin. "An unusual acquisition indeed."

Azzy tumbled forward into a solid fog. A sigh stirred the fine filaments of her hair. "You're too thin, little one," murmured Cherise. "Far too light." She floated on the edge of sensation in a shroud of smoke, barely aware as Cherise settled her into bed. She'd worried that sleep wouldn't come, plagued by her ghosts, but they waited for her in her dreams.

S he walked through the empty streets of Caletum, leaving a trail of footprints through the dust in her wake. The silence wrapped around her, thick and cloying. It itched against her skin, while the crawling sensation of unseen eyes pricked at her senses. The silence was absolute but for the harsh beat of her heart drumming in her ears.

Azzy stopped in the space between two buildings, their doors carelessly left open, rocking on soundless hinges. Through the shadowed crevice, she could see the ledge where the city of Caletum ended, as if sheared off by a giant blade. And in the pit, it waited.

I see you. The voice crept into her mind, an insidious whisper that wound through her skull in a serpentine fashion, seeking a way into her deepest self. *You are a flame in the dark. Come to me.*

Azzy dug her nails into her palms until they bit through her flesh, bloody crescents that wept red drops into the dust. Drip. Drip. Drip.

The dust wicked the blood as it fell, a growing stain that drew her eye as it began to spread in deliberate threads, an unclear image. She had to see.

The silence buckled beneath the rustle of wings.

Azzy's head snapped up, her concentration broken as she searched for the source of the invasive sound. A name rose and caught against her closed her lips, afraid and unwilling to whisper it where the listening presence of the pit could hear.

We hear him, sweet flame. We listen. We yearn.

Azzy shuddered as the voice slid through her mind. A figure moved in the corner of her vision. She turned to see him, only for him to move out of sight once more. Her heart stuttered as a feather drifted through the dust at her feet, caught in the web of drying blood. She tracked the figure without turning her head, watching as he entered one of the empty houses.

The city began to unravel around her, the stone crumbling away with sudden deafening sound as she rushed for the doorway he had gone through. The presence of the pit leeched away as she walked through the opening, the air woolly and resistant as she pushed through before it burst into brilliant light.

Her surroundings were an unfamiliar grandeur, a labyrinthine opulence that made her certain she stood in the dwelling of a lord of Avergard. She caught the figure as he turned a corner, where the familiar flash of his jawline wrapped her chest in a vise. His magnificent wings dragged on the floor where they wept a trail of feathers that withered and faded seconds later. She longed to chase after him, though her legs were wooden and stilted, each step increasingly difficult. She ignored her surroundings, focused on his back as he led her through the house, even as the shadows began to writhe at the edges of her vision.

He ducked through another doorway. Azzy followed after him; the air shifted again. Her breath clouded the air as a stinging cold nipped at her face and bare feet. This room was an icy tomb. Her steps slowed as she entered after him, drinking in the details, committing them to memory. The floor and walls were oddly grooved, the texture distracting as she peered down at the uneven lines. Azzy crouched down, tracing her fingers through the grooves as if the room was carved out by a thousand scraping hands. She followed the tracks to their end, a hole in the center of the floor.

He stood at its edge. Azzy rose, reaching for him.

"Rise."

She opened her mouth in a silent scream. Warmth trickled from her nose, the taste of blood invading her mouth as the whispers surged in her skull. A riot of warnings banged against the cage of her flesh and bone.

We listen. We yearn.

Azzy dropped her hand, forcing herself to the edge. She needed to see. The icy air seized in her chest as she looked down into the gaping maw. It blasted her with the foul, chill breath of the Below. She swore she could hear the distant scrape of claws on stone.

There was a gasp at her back. Azzy spun and saw a woman gaping at her from the doorway. They stared at one another, locked in mutual shock until the woman's face began to split down the middle. The grisly seam parted to reveal a pulsing mass of flesh. In the center of that red, wet mass, an eye flashed open. Azzy fell back a step and her foot found nothingness.

Her body tilted, unbalanced, a scream caught in her throat as she fell. The world rocked around her as deep within the pit, a hungry howl rose to meet her.

Azzy's back slammed into the unyielding floorboards. She lay there, tangled in her blankets, as she gasped for breath. The chill lingered in the cold sweat coating her back and face, shivering through her bones, while the skin beneath her nose was tacky with drying blood.

The floorboards quivered beneath her body, the tremor slowly coming to a halt, but for the aftershocks. Her head ached with the echo of screams. Azzy waited for the world to settle and dug the feather out of her sleeve. Pieces of it were stuck together from her perspiration, but it was real. She wondered why it hadn't faded like the others. Or was that a trick of the dream.

"Was it a dream?" She whispered. She turned her head.

The Maven watched her from the doorway. Through her fractured gaze, Azzy could see another face, terrible and monstrous, lurking beneath the woman's human mask. The whispers remained silent and still, a null space in her mind, as the Maven left without a word.

 2 

AZURE

She never knew there was so much green in the world. Lord Wallach's estate was what Azzy imagined a true Haven would look like, a pocket of paradise in the middle of the city. The high walls were obscured by living trellises of flowering vines that created the illusion of endless space. Azzy sat with her knees tucked up against her chest, surrounded by a circle of flowers the same shade as fresh split blood, the dark hearts reminiscent of the yawning pit from her dreams. She stroked the velvety petals, lost in thought as Morglint bustled in a patch of herbs. Green stained his skin to the elbows. He hummed an unfamiliar song as he worked. The melody soothed the shivering creature huddled inside her skin, but it was unable to banish the lingering specters from her nightmares.

Morglint plunked down his basket and settled beside her, his large hands nimbly plucking the unwanted rough bits of his harvest. She rested her head on her knees, content to watch him work, but her friend had other ideas.

"She just left?" He watched her as his hands kept moving, concern creasing his face. "Are you sure you weren't still dreaming?"

"I was awake. And you felt the shaking too," said Azzy. She sought him out once she trusted her legs to hold her weight. Her friend had the same idea, wandering the dark halls looking for her room while the rest of the household slept despite the tremors.

"I did," Morglint admitted. His jaw worked. "Who was this again?"

Azzy frowned. "The Maven. She sat next to you at dinner."

He shrugged. "Honestly, little one, I was so hungry and

relieved to see you, I could have been sitting next to Wallach himself and not noticed."

Her frown deepened. It wasn't that Morglint dismissed what she saw, but it was as if he didn't believe her either. Or, at least the part about the Maven. She could feel his attention slide back to his meticulous work. Azzy had trouble believing it herself, each time she tried to recall the Maven's true face, the memory grew hazier each time. Frustration pinched at her, and worse, inside, the silence remained. "Morglint, I think something's wrong with me," she said.

He caught her hand as she pinched the flowers around her too hard, shredding the petal with her fingernails. "Easy, poppies are spiteful, little one," he said. "Why do you think there is something wrong with you?"

She shook her head and rose to her feet, pacing the stone path that cut through the garden. "I don't know," she said. Her fingers twisted and twined with the hem of her shirt, expressing the writhing, raw nerve that spiraled inside her. "It's just—ever since we got here—it's too quiet in my head."

Azzy reached up, rubbing her temples as she spoke. In the absence of the whispers, the sounds of the world filtered in too loud—too much. The distant bustle of the crowded streets with their mix of shouts and shrieks – of both fear and delight— all of it mingling with the rustling vegetation, Morglint's movements, and the sound of her feet slapping over stone. The cacophony of sounds blended and bled into one another, overwhelming her until two large hands settled on her shoulders. Azzy looked up into Morglint's uneven gaze.

"Breathe," he said, his voice gentle.

She inhaled, suddenly aware of her burning lungs. "I don't know what's wrong with me," she gasped out.

Morglint released her, rubbing a hand over his jaw. "I've never seen anything like your magic, little one, but from what you told me, it's the reason you've survived."

"Except it's gone," she said. "And it isn't." She clenched her hands into fists as she remembered the burst of warning from her dream. "I never had to think about it or force it, but now I can't find it."

She fought to maintain a steady breath through the panic that beat in her veins. "I've spent years denying it, Morglint. I never called it magic. I don't even know what magic is supposed to be," she said. Not when magic was synonymous with being tainted in the world Below, something to be hidden and reviled. Pain flared through her sore palms. She'd woken to find scabbed crescents from her fingernails, where fear had carved its mark in her skin. She wondered what would have happened if the fall hadn't woken her. What waited for her at the bottom of the pit?

"There's something else," said Azzy. She hadn't told Morglint about the dream, only her eerie encounter with the Maven after. It was a private, surreal experience, one she wasn't sure she could successfully put into words, especially when what she had seen left her equal parts terrified and confused. The gaps in her knowledge aside, she knew that pit was real, in the deep instinctual part of her brain ruled by the quivering animal that hid from the predators of the dark. "I saw my brother. In my dream."

Her friend met her gaze and looked away. "When you were feverish and hovering at death's door in my tent, you called his name. You muttered...constantly." He glanced down at her. "I think you do more than see him."

"What do you mean?"

"In the market row, there are specialty shops where some of the healers dream share. There are extracts and tonics that let them explore a patient's subconscious mind. It looked a little like that, yet not the same." Morglint sighed. "I don't know how to explain it."

"We have the same problem," said Azzy.

"You've lived under threat for most of your life. It's no wonder your magic has gone quiet. You've only used it while in danger." Morglint leaned back, folding his arms over his chest. "But here, you've been given a moment of true respite. It's a shock to the system. You might just need to adjust, little one. You have time to properly rest and recover here."

The poppies brushed against her ankles. She remembered the cold, serpentine whisper, calling to her from the trench in Caletum. *We yearn.*

Time was not a commodity here.

"Morglint, I—"

Smoke billowed through the garden door. It curled off the woman in dark black plumes that telegraphed her sour mood. Azzy flinched. Disappearing from her room before dawn probably had not curried any points in her favor when the head servant had kept such a close eye on her since her arrival. Cherise was still feeling her out as the newest addition of the household.

"There you are." Cherise drew closer. Her dark eyes darted between the two of them until she appeared satisfied they weren't conspiring in secret. "Breakfast will be served within ten minutes." A ripple of movement carried through the smoke as if Cherise had smoothed her concealed skirts. "Azure, Lord Wallach has requested I assess your skillset and assign you to a household task. You'll be accompanying me to the market later."

The prospect of stepping foot outside the walls of the estate so soon was as thrilling as it was terrifying. Her pulse jumped with anticipation. This was her chance to get a more comprehensive scope of the city without Wallach's overwhelming presence, and to test Morglint's theory. He wasn't wrong; her life had been a series of swords poised over her neck, the looming threats of the Rot, of exile, of starvation. She followed Morglint to the servants' dining room where a much more modest fare of bread and various jellies and spreads were laid out for them. The other servants were there, though the Maven was absent, much to her relief. There was an accompanying bowl of fruits, some of which she'd never seen fresh. She chose an apple because she recognized it, startled by the sweet, crisp flesh beneath the waxy skin.

If those who dwelled Below knew the bounty of the Above, she wondered, *would they risk the wilds and monsters rather than huddle in their stone dens?*

Azzy finished her meal fast, observing the others as they ate. Cherise maintained her shroud of smoke as she ate, the movements of her mouth hidden so that her food seemed to vanish from her plate. Azzy wondered if the head servant had control over its appearance, as it currently existed as a light gray haze, the lines of her body vague but semi-visible. Her auditor didn't keep her waiting long, leading Azzy out the door as the ninth hour chimed from the ornate standing clock in Lord Wallach's front hall.

A long stretch of gravel road fed from the house to the main stone-paved street. The front green possessed the same well-maintained growth and scattered pathways as the interior garden, soaking the air in a fragrant floral perfume that masked the reek and refuse of the surrounding city. A true sanctuary, one Azzy was hesitant to leave so soon, but she needed to carve out a niche for herself in this house, in this city, if she hoped to save her family.

"What happened this morning?" Cherise's voice dragged her from her anxious thoughts.

"A nightmare," said Azzy. It was a simple truth and explained why she sought out Morglint. "I woke up to the ground shaking."

"I'm surprised you felt that," said Cherise, stretching her body. "The others slept through it."

"Except for the Maven," said Azzy.

"What was that?" Cherise held open the front gate as Azzy stepped into the living stream of the city street. She forgot the woman's question as her senses were assaulted by the alluring mix of foul and fair. Raw, butchered animals spun from strings of thick twine while women fluttered from stall to stall, in elaborate, brightly colored dresses, collecting hunks of bloody meat in neat brown parcel packages. The muck strewn alleys, choked with waste, were offset by displays of uncut jewels that flashed in the sun. There were tables full of intricate hand-crafted wares where the merchants bellowed and shouted over one another to get the attention of passing patrons. The hint of putrefaction lingered beneath the mouth-watering scents of spit roasted meat and sweet sticky treats. Azzy absorbed it all, her wide eyes still watering from the glare of the searing morning sun. It was far too much after a lifetime of grimy street lanterns and dark tunnels in rock. She hugged herself, trying to contain her heart as it pounded against her ribs, like a fist that knocked on the back of her bones. Azzy longed to flee back to the confines of her room and bury her head beneath the blankets until the world stopped being so bright and loud.

The quill of her hidden feather lightly scratched against her forearm as she clutched her elbows. Azzy closed her eyes, focusing on the sensation. She could not run. She had to do this.

An arm settled around her shoulders, cool smoke curling against her cheek. "It's a tad overwhelming at first," said Cherise. "Do you need a moment to adjust?"

"I'm fine," said Azzy. And she was. The feather wasn't merely a reminder of why she was here, it was a connection to Armin, somewhere in this city, as concrete as the string she once wrapped around his finger. She would find him.

The corners of Cherise's eyes crinkled in the smoke. "Excellent control of your senses," said the head servant. "Now, let's see what you can see."

She propelled them forward into the thick of Market Row, the main thoroughfare that Morglint told her stretched the entire length of the city, chock-full of merchants and traders with every ware in existence. He had insisted one could find anything among the sprawl of stalls and booths, for a price. Tucked beyond the stalls were established shops, a clear path to their doors no matter how crowded the area as if it were an unspoken rule of the market. Her curiosity burned to explore those hidden interiors, wondering if she could find one of the healers who read dreams that Morglint told her about, but there was no chance of that now.

Azzy didn't know what Wallach told his head servant about her, but as she strolled over the stone streets in the fresh boots Cherise fitted her with, she began to pick up on the undercurrents of the churning crowds. Women hovered at the edges, posed at alley mouths, their sinuous bodies clad in threadbare silk and worn velvet. They watched the passing stream of people with hungry eyes, while their skirts billowed in odd places, the mark of their transformation concealed by voluminous layers of fabric.

Children darted through the mass, slipping dirty fingers into pockets and purses, grinning with too sharp teeth. One strayed close to Cherise, blinking up at the woman with two sets of eyelids as her wreath of smoke thickened into a contained, impenetrable black mass, a clear warning. The street urchin concluded the head servant too difficult a mark, wandering over to a woman in a violet silk gown. Azzy watched as the child dipped a hand into the folds of her skirts, only to jerk back with a squeal and bloody fingers. The woman in violet grinned as her skirts writhed, a hint of extra appendages peeking out from beneath the hem.

Azzy moved forward, intent on intercepting the child before they came to further harm. Cherise caught her by the arm and yanked her close as the other woman's gaze slid over her. The woman in violet tilted her head, scenting the air with a frown as the head servant steered Azzy away from her.

"Wallach was right. You're far too empathetic," murmured Cherise.

"But the child—" Azzy whispered.

"Will be fine," said Cherise, her tone patient but stern. "If you want to survive here, don't draw attention to yourself, ever." The head servant glanced back to make sure they weren't followed, her grip too tight on Azzy's upper arms for a mere word of warning.

"Did you draw attention?"

"Far too much of it," said Cherise. "Come, the kitchen spices need to be restocked, and I need to see if you have a knack for haggling."

"I don't," Azzy said. She pressed a hand to the hidden feather to distract herself from the sharp pang of loss. Brixby was the one who had the skill for bartering. Her chest was too tight. She wiped away the tears that gathered in the corner of her eye. Between the search for her brother and her separation from Kai, she hadn't processed the loss of her guardian. If he had survived the journey to the city, she didn't even know where to begin looking for him.

Azzy startled as Cherise's cool fingers carefully brushed a stray tear from her cheek. "We've all lost someone to the cruelties of this world, even my lord. The pain will ease in time," she said.

Contrary to her own warning of empathy, it was clear Lord Wallach's head servant cared for her charges. Azzy kept close to the lady of smoke as they entered a pungent corner of the open market. Herbs hung in drying bundles, while ground spices sat out in piles atop wax-sealed cloth where customers scooped portions into pouches and glass bottles.

"Wait here," said Cherise, smoothing a hand down Azzy's arm. "I'll talk to the seller, see if we can cut a deal on the salt."

Azzy wandered closer to the piles of various spices, teased by a dozen scents she'd never experienced, wondering what flavor each created as she read the handwritten labels, rolling the unfamiliar words over her tongue.

Awareness prickled at the nape of her neck. Azzy looked up to find a boy watching her from the far end of the stall. His golden-brown eyes were too large for his face. It gave him the appearance of innocence, enhanced by the dusting of freckles across the bridge of his nose. The effect was ruined by the feral gleam in his eyes, bordering on violence. Her gaze dropped to the familiar ugly collar that gouged the tender skin of his neck. The sight of it filled her with loathing while serving as a reminder of what she'd lost. She caught his gaze again and went still, his pupils blown wide the longer he stared at her until the black nearly eclipsed his iris. He lifted his hand and pointed. She followed the direction of his gesture—the enshrouded figure of Cherise.

The smoke around Cherise was soot black, streaked with even darker inky patches that pulsed, in a visualization of her fear. The head servant backed away from the spice booth, her usual grace absent as she stumbled and scuttled, seemingly unaware of the dead-end alley at her back. A figure peeled off from the crowd, following her with unhurried steps. A predator in a well-tailored, dark blue suit, he flowed forward, his movements punctuated by the silver-tipped cane that cracked like thunder each time it struck the stones. None of the other patrons paid any attention to the two, either oblivious or consciously turning a blind eye to a lord of Avergard stalking his prey.

Cherise backed further into the narrow alley between a tannery and butcher. Azzy stood there, paralyzed by uncertainty. She could *almost* see the power wafting off of him, not as potent as Lord Wallach's, but daunting. A flicker appeared at the corner of her vision, tantalizingly out of sight, but when she shook her head she could see how it flared off him, eager golden flames that trailed from him in shimmering ribbons of heat. Cherise backed against a wall, her smoky cover evaporating as he bore down on her, revealing the frightened lines of her scarred face. He reached for her with a gloved hand, fingers curled like leather-clad talons.

The whispers stirred, muting the sounds and sights of the

market as her vision tunneled on the advancing lord. Her altered eye pulsed, her vision suddenly alight as the lord's magic shifted into tangible threads of fire. Azzy rushed forward as pieces of information filtered into her mind, her anger mounting as she drew up beside them. He had pinned Cherise there, snared by fear and magic, with a familiarity that spoke to the scars on her beautiful face. The smile he wore was all cold cruelty as his magic wound around her throat like a noose. Azzy sucked in a breath. Through the lens of her altered eye, Azzy could see the snare of his magic, the fibrous texture encased in a harsh luminescence, writhing like a tangible living creature of fire and thread. She could see the connective tissues of his magic; the whispers intensified as she dug her fingers into the weave and tore it wide open.

The lord stumbled away with a hoarse shout, too stunned at first to react before anger twisted his face into a monstrous visage. "What did you do to me, you vile—"

The boy suddenly appeared, shoving his slim body in front of the lord to snarl up at his face.

"That's enough, Howl," he spat, but the boy crouched in front of Azzy and hissed. She saw the lord's leg cock back and yanked the boy, Howl, out of range of the kick. She held him tight against her chest. His small body was ablaze with heat; he hissed and snapped his teeth at the lord whose face purpled with rage as he bore down on them.

"I believe that is quite enough, Lord Brusker," said Wallach. Azzy stiffened. Where had Wallach even come from? But if Azzy was startled by his appearance, Lord Brusker looked downright horrified.

"Lord Wallach," he said, his voice far too high to be sincere. "I didn't realize she was one of yours." Brusker only acknowledged Azzy as he spoke, careful to keep his gaze away from Cherise.

Wallach clasped his gloved hands in front of him. "Is that so? Then, I must inform you they are *all* of my house," he said pointedly.

Brusker reared back, his gaze darting nervously to the crowd. "But the boy—"

"Is fitting compensation for the harassment of my servants," said Wallach. "Unless you'd like to settle this slight in the House of Lords?"

Brusker went pale and vigorously shook his head. "No, you are quite right. Please accept my apologies." He gave Wallach a final bow, shooting a glare at Azzy before he disappeared into the milling market crowd.

Wallach sighed through his nose. "I feel the market has grown tiresome today, ladies. Why don't you head home?" Cherise murmured agreement. Azzy still didn't know how Wallach arrived so quickly until she saw Petyr hovering nearby. The young man nodded at some unseen cue from Wallach. Azzy gaped as he peeled off his stained gloves with a grimace, revealing the raw torn skin of his hands. She saw the reason for his wounds as his fingers twisted through unseen seams and ripped a hole in the air. Wallach ducked through the tear as Petyr slid his gloves back on. The air sealed itself as the young man followed his master.

Azzy turned back to Cherise, the boy still clutched in her arms. She released him, wondering if he would run away now that his master had abandoned him, but he remained, hovering by her side. Cherise gaped at her as fresh smoke rose off her skin.

"What are you?"

Azzy winced. "Did he hurt you?" She left the words 'this time' unspoken.

"You broke his magic," Cherise breathed, sagging back against the wall. "Snapped it like kindling."

Azzy swallowed around the pinch in her throat. "I didn't—I don't know—." Her voice drained to a whisper. She didn't know what to say, unsettled by her own actions. In the moment, the solution had appeared so simple, clean, and absolute. Her fingers were numb where she touched his magic, the skin faintly pink as if burned.

"I've never seen that kind of magic before," said Cherise.

Unease dug icy claws into Azzy's shoulders, leaving her chilled in the shadows of the alley. The city was brimming with men and women twisted by hundreds of variations of magic. She couldn't be such an oddity. "Who was he?"

Cherise licked her lips, still visible through the fresh vent of smoke. "Lord Brusker. You shouldn't have done that, Azure. He'll be gunning for you now. As you saw, not even Lord Wallach's reputation will protect you." The grim line of her mouth spoke volumes.

"Why wasn't he punished?"

The lady of smoke stiffened at the question, poised to snap and retreat to lick her wounds in her personal shroud. Instead, the smoke remained a light haze as she traced the scar that slashed her face, the bitterness shifting into a deep sadness that hurt to observe.

"He was," said Cherise. "He paid a fine to the Madame of the carnal house. But she had no use for damaged goods, and I declined her *generous* offer to be sold to one of the less discerning houses." The smoke coalesced, obscuring her once more. "Wallach found me wandering the gutters along the Way of Heavenly Delights."

Morglint had mentioned the name in passing during their journey to Lord Wallach's estate. "What is that?"

"The pleasure district of Avergard," said Cherise, her words bitten off as if she spat them from her mouth. "Carnal houses, gambling dens, fighting pits; every foul fetish and devious delight under the sun resides there. It's where the lords of Avergard come to play, and the law has little presence. The Snatchers take those who fail to sell at auction to its Flesh Markets."

Azzy shivered at the description. The Heap had no carnal houses, though there were plenty who bartered their bodies for whatever goods they could secure. Azzy truly couldn't imagine the misery wrought by an entire district built for such exchanges.

"Count your blessings that our Lord found you first," said Cherise. "That place chews through beautiful, bright, young things. Nothing but nightmares are found there."

Cherise could have been a wraith of her own past, a ghost of smoke and scars, marred by cruel hands and crueler masters, but she'd been given sanctuary in Wallach's house, same as Azzy.

She offered the woman a hand. "Come on, let's go home." The word fell flat in her mouth, but it was enough, for now.

"He did say to return, didn't he?" Cherise sighed. "Bother him, he's too bloody high handed." She jerked back as she realized the boy had waited patiently nearby through their whole conversation. "Who's this?"

"Brusker called him Howl," said Azzy. "I think Wallach claimed him as recompense."

Cherise raised a brow as Howl leaned against Azzy's arm. "I think he claimed you as well." The head servant blew out a breath, her features harder and harder to discern as the smoke shaded around her. "There's nothing for it. Let's get some food in him." She offered her arm. Azzy wondered if she should offer her own to the boy, but he stuck to her like a burr as they moved.

Cherise kept a grip on her arm as they retreated toward the shelter of Wallach's estate. The gates where in sight when a tug in the pit of her stomach demanded her attention. Azzy's unfocused gaze shifted to one of the many branching avenues that peeled off the main row.

"What's down there?"

The lady of smoke shuddered. "I told you. Nightmares."

SCENT AND MEMORY

3

ELEANOR

She remembered her name. She clung to it, a tenuous lifeline, as the choking collar snapped around her neck. Her body was weak. Newly formed, unfamiliar limbs wobbled and shivered as they dragged across the muddy ground. Her senses were clogged by the overload of new information, a swirling mass of sensory details that overwhelmed her with each breath. Her vision was different, the edges of objects sharper and more defined. Her hearing was better than it had ever been, but the things she now heard buzzed as a tangled swarm inside her skull. She'd go mad before long. The clang of the lock echoed in her ears, cool metal bars pressed against her cheek, the worn wooden floor of the cart rocked beneath her like a boat in a storm. Through the influx of sensations, her latch on reality fluttered, a dying light against the dark.

Eleanor, her name was Eleanor. Named after the great Eleanor of Aquitaine from her mother's precious brittle tomes. She hugged her elbows; her new claws dug into her skin.

They said the change burned away the memory, the fever scorched everything you were, all the bits and pieces of your humanity. Except Eleanor remembered everything: her childhood in the mud hut village to the north, her mother's long and drawn out sickness that left her too weakened to care for the rest of them. How they buried her sweet sisters, and, finally, the fever that ravaged her own body. She remembered the stones that cut her forehead as the others chased her out, her mother unable to protect her, straight into the hands of the waiting Snatchers. She remembered the climbing heat as if she'd charred on the inside, the ashes of her memories—her soul—peeling and flaking away to nothing. Then, hands—hands on her face, wiping her burning tears away while a girl's voice whispered in her ear. *'I'm here.'*

As her world spun out of control, she stared up into a shard of sky, her lifeline through the fever. The girl...who was she? The girl's face burned brightest of all her memories, branded there, the memory of her a balm over the endless stream of information pouring into Eleanor's mind. She could still feel those hands on her face, anchoring her, a tether she followed back to herself. She gasped in a sharp breath, the acrid scent of urine and old sweat burning her nose as she shifted her body into an upright position. The action alerted her to the new angles and hinges, places where her spine hadn't bent so before. She shuddered and moaned as she looked down at herself. Her familiar limbs were gone, replaced by monstrous parts: the dark claws that tipped her fingers, the extra teeth crowding her mouth, the tail.

The tail scared her the most. She traced the reticulated plates, smooth as polished stone, each joint tingled beneath her touch as her fingers followed the new curve of her elongated spine to the barbed end. Liquid beaded at the tip. Tears stung her eyes as she realized, *'I'm poisonous now.'*

The cart jostled beneath her, causing her tail to twitch for balance. She grasped the bars with her clawed fingers, squinting against the harsh daylight as she took stock of her surroundings. Her container was more cramped than she realized. She couldn't rise any higher, restricted to a hunched over position. The misshapen Snatchers walked on either side of the cart, filled with more than one too-small cage. Beside her was another woman, her black eyes wide and feral. There wasn't a hint of humanity there. Eleanor leaned as far away from her as the cage would allow, chilled by the smile that played on her blood crusted lips. The cart continued to lurch forward, taking them further into the milling crowd.

People. Some were visibly altered as Eleanor, their clothing made to accommodate their extra limbs and appendages. Others were more subtle, they wore their human skin as a thinly veiled disguise, betrayed by a glance, a gesture, that hinted what lurked beneath their guise.

In the bedtime stories her mother told her and her sisters, the monsters who dwelt in Avergard were wild beings; reminiscent of the fair folk from the old legends, baby snatchers, and cruel demons who used people until they broke. They were nothing like the jewel-eyed men and women who wove around the cart in more exquisitely cut clothes than anyone from her impoverished home could imagine. Fine clothing and empty stares, their glittering eyes blank like cut glass, ignoring the suffering that passed by them in those cramped cages. Eleanor wanted to snatch at their sleeves and beg for aid, but she feared what the Snatchers would do to her. She was all too aware of their proximity. She feared what those hollow men and women would do to her too.

The crowd peeled away, spilling the Snatchers and their cart into an open area blocked off with roped fencing. Several new Snatchers passed by, leading lines of men, women, and children in matching white shrouds. The unsettling gazes of the genteel monsters had nothing on these dejected creatures. Eleanor watched them pass, feeling the tremor start in her limbs anew. She knew where she was, the name passed around in fearful whispers from the time she toddled around at her mother's knee.

The Flesh Markets. The Snatchers were talking to one another. It took her a moment to register the words, to realize they were speaking of her and the other one, the feral woman, as chattel. Here she was, nothing more than an object to be peddled and sold off to the highest bidder. Eleanor clutched the metal bars to keep herself upright. Was that what happened to the blonde girl who wiped away her tears and nursed her through the fever. Eleanor took a breath and stilled at the fading whiff of the girl's scent. Her savior's essence still clung to her, something sweet and undefinable, like the dried wildflowers her mother bartered from the Foragers with sheets of handmade paper. Eleanor concentrated on that faint scent, trying to block out the abrasive sights and smells of the flesh markets that nipped at the precarious calm she evinced. She clutched to that mindset with everything she had until the bars were ripped from her grip.

The Snatchers opened her cage, their hands reached for her. She cried out, trying to back away from them, pressing her body into the furthest corner, but there was nowhere to go. They seized her round her neck and dragged her forward. She gripped the hand that wrapped around her throat. Her eyes watered, blurring the uneven features of the Snatcher who held her aloft. She could feel his critical gaze on her, examining her.

"Bit scrawny isn't she," he grumbled. He ignored the claws that gouged his forearm. "She seem off to you?"

Another Snatcher ambled up. "Most subdued scorpid woman I've ever seen. Not even snarling." One blunt fingertip prodded her ribs. The Snatcher sucked on his yellowed teeth. "Pretty enough, but far too skinny. She won't fetch but a handful of coin. Barely fit for meat."

Her body gave an involuntary jerk at his words. The Snatcher holding her chuckled. "She doesn't like that idea at all."

"She seems pretty lucid. Didn't she just transition?"

"Aye, but it was...odd." The Snatcher squinted at her. "Perhaps one of the Carnal houses will take her."

"Madame Murmur is always looking for new flesh," remarked the other Snatcher. "And she pays decent coin for the interesting ones."

The one holding her gave her an ugly grin that rose the hair on her arms. "Oh, I think this little darling just might fit her criteria."

'You want to take her? That woman's... unsettling."

The ugly grin widened. "Too many legs?"

The other Snatcher shuddered. "Try not to spend all your coin on drink and whores. Puts the boss in a foul mood. He might sell you like Morglint."

The one holding her snorted then tossed her up and over his shoulder like a rucksack. "Good riddance to that fool."

Through their whole exchange, Eleanor could do little more than gasp for breath and scrabble at the unyielding arm that pinned her at the waist. Her limbs hung limp and uncooperative, swinging in time to his footsteps. From this angle, she couldn't lift her head high enough to see more than the passing cobblestones, street litter, and polished boots. The world tilted and swayed as the swarthy Snatcher left the flesh markets behind them. She could only tell they reached their destination by the thinning crowd. It was quiet in this part of the city, at least at this time of day. The polished boots in the corner of her vision were fleeting and the garbage more plentiful. Her limited world came to a halt as the Snatcher rapped on wood. Eleanor could feel the vibrations of his humming as he waited, impatiently tapping one foot that jarred through her waist with each beat.

A door swung open with a muted screech.

"What's this, then?" A female voice, thick and slurred with drink.

"Got a potential scrap for your Madame. She in?"

There was a sniff. "Yeah, I'll get her. Not sure how much use she'll have for another bloody scorpid. Vicious little bitches," the unseen woman sneered.

"Not this one. I think it will be worth her while."

Eleanor tried to crane around to look at the woman, her actions stilled by the Snatcher's hand firmly clamped on the new hinge at her waist. She could only wait, her heart thudding hard and heavy against her ribs, for the Madame to arrive, to appraise her. And then what? The life of a carnal house slave? Fresh tears threatened, a reaction she detested in her current situation. Better a whore than dead. A small part of her wished the fever had seared her clean and blank, that it made her as feral as the other woman, unable to realize what was about to happen to her. She held her breath at the clicking thumps that approached, a rhythm that echoed like multiple footsteps.

They *were* footsteps. Eleanor saw the grotesque body first, built of the same reticulated plates as her own, massive and fluid as it flowed into her limited vision, the outer shell dark brown and crisp, polished to a faint glow in the low alley light. The legs were short pikes, sharp and pointed, dozens of them moving in harmony. So many legs. She stared at them, mesmerized until fingers slipped under her chin, forcing her neck up at a painful angle as her gaze took in more of the body, the unnatural transition where the brown shell melted into human flesh. Her gaze continued its upward crawl, over a feminine torso clad in an open robe of luxurious emerald silk, to the face, as beautiful as it was inhuman.

Dark brown eyes studied her, observing every shift in Eleanor's expression as *the other eyes* scrutinized the Snatcher who carried her.

"My, you are a timid one," the voice purred from red lips, giving her a glimpse of thin translucent teeth. Eleanor closed her eyes as the woman's black nails gently stroked her face. "Never seen one so docile. You swear on your caravan she is newly born?"

"Watched the boss haul her out himself," said the Snatcher. "She's too quiet and too small for the flesh market. Think you might get some use out of her?"

The Madame chuckled, reaching into her folds of silk for a slim leather wallet. Her dark fingertips plucked free several sheets of colored paper, offering it to the Snatcher as her brown eyes continued to study Eleanor's face. "Drop her there."

The girl wasn't prepared for the fall, landing painfully on her front. She flipped over, crawling away from them on her new awkward limbs. The Snatcher ignored her, already turning to leave with his pocketed earnings. The Madame continued her dispassionate observation of Eleanor, lifting the long-yellowed stem of a cigarette holder to her painted lips.

"A scorpid woman, frightened as a mouse, fair of face, and slight of form. Whatever shall we do with a little treat like you?" Smoke curled from the woman's mouth as she spoke, curling around her sleek black hair twisted up in elaborate braids. "Rose!" The word snapped out like a whip; Eleanor flinched against the filthy alley ground.=

She wanted to flee, somewhere, anywhere, but she was frozen, her limbs unable or unwilling to move. The hungry look in the Madame's eyes pinned her in place surer than a steel rod through her gut. Eleanor could only break it when the new figure emerged from the depths of the building, the girl's appearance so horrifying she couldn't stop the startled gasp that escaped her lips.

Half her face was simply gone, nothing more than a mass of scar tissue. A single eye, dull as ditchwater stared at the ground, empty, unseeing. She folded her hands, one mangled, one smooth but scarred, as she waited for the Madame's instruction.

"Get this one settled in," said the Madame.

"Yes, Mama," said the scarred girl. She turned back inside without confirming if Eleanor followed or not, but she found herself scrambling after the girl. It was a far better alternative than staying outside in the company of the Madame. The woman grinned at Eleanor as she scurried by. Smoke vented through her translucent teeth.

"Welcome to the Nightingale Carnal House, Little Mouse." Eleanor didn't think her mother's stories of demons were so far off from the truth.

The interior of the Nightingale Carnal House was filled with darkened corners and stank of the Madame's smoke. It seemed to hang in the air, circling the shadows in lazy swirls that feathered around the ghostly, faded figure of Rose as she led Eleanor through the narrow halls. Music filtered through the thin walls, grainy and heavy with drums, doing little to disguise the other noises of the house. Eleanor resisted the urge to cover her ears at the wet sounds of flesh on flesh, moans and cries, faint weeping, and short, sharp shrieks. The sounds of pain and pleasure tangled with the smoke and music until she stood, stunned, staring up at the stained ceiling. Rusted stains, as if the pain of this place seeped through from the floor above.

She'd walked into Hell.

The phantom of the broken girl appeared in front of her, her single dispassionate eye staring at the space over Eleanor's shoulder. Rose hadn't made eye contact with her once.

"Do not dally. Our patrons will not care that you are new and without instruction." There was no emotion to her words, but they dampened the swell of sensations like ice water. Eleanor hugged herself, shivering from a cold that radiated from within her chest. How long before her features and demeanor matched her broken guide?

Rose turned without another word, continuing on in silence. Eleanor followed the ghostly girl, passed closed rooms that contained dozens of unseen illicit acts. They passed a padlocked door. Something, no, *someone*, on the other side let out a mournful, agonized cry—more a howl than a scream that spoke to the primal core of her being. Eleanor stumbled to a stop despite herself, pressing her clawed hand flat against the locked door.

"What—"

Rose seized her wrist in an iron grip, far stronger than she thought possible from those scarred hands, yanking her away from the door and whatever creature it hid. A flicker of emotion crossed the scarred visage of her guide, at last, something Eleanor could almost swear was guilt.

"Do not linger," Rose rasped, not letting go as she pulled her charge to the end of the hall, up a set of stairs that creaked beneath each footfall. She did not release Eleanor's wrist until they reached the second-floor common room, filled with frayed upholstered settees and weathered low tables. A few girls lounged on them. Their features were hard to discern beneath their identical expressions. Each girl bore her time in the carnal house in tight red scars that marked their flesh. Eleanor glimpsed her future in their collective of listless gazes.

The source of the music sat on a side table against the wall, a strange contraption. The sound poured from the broad, fluted head of a metal flower as hollow as the occupants of the room. The music made it all that much more surreal.

Rose led her onward, until they reached a small empty room, with a narrow bed and clothes chest squeezed into the tiny space.

"You'll need a name," said Rose, gesturing to the shale tablet plate by the door, still smudged with chalk from the last occupant's name.

"My name is Eleanor." The words left her without thought. Rose blinked at her, another flicker of emotion crossing her features, gone so quickly it was difficult to decipher.

"You seem very sure of that," she said, her voice very quiet, barely audible above the grating music. She shook herself, the blank expression sliding back into place. "Pretty to be sure, but the Patrons like simple pet names. How about Hettie or Lacy?"

"My name is Eleanor," she repeated, firmer this time, her claws curling against her palms. This place was set to take much from her, piece by precious piece, but they would not take her name.

Rose pursed her lips, considering her for a long moment. "Ellie," she said. It was a compromise, but one she could stomach. Rose scrawled the letters on the slate with her good hand. Eleanor realized, watching her concentrate, it was not the hand Rose learned to write with. She itched to ask what would happen to her now, but dread made her tongue thick in her mouth. How long before they thrust a Patron on her?

"The Madame will be up to assess you later."

"When–"

"Meals for the girls are available in the kitchens at six-hour intervals. Be on time or starve. Eat what is offered or starve. If you please a Patron, they might bring you something sweet. Services are requested at all times of the evening, so get used to sleeping during the early morning. You will have a short grace period to acclimate to your surroundings. The Madame will determine the length. Until then, you will help me with the chores of the household."

Eleanor tried not to stare as Rose delivered her edict. Her toneless voice droned on as if she'd delivered this speech hundreds of times. She might have, given how smudged the shale was with old chalk. How many Hetties and Lacys were trapped in the specters of chalked lines before her? How many women slept in this bed? The room still smelt of stale perfume, as if its former occupant still lingered.

"I will come fetch you for chores and meals this first day. Then you are on your own." Rose left with those parting words. There was no door to the room. Not even a curtain for privacy. Eleanor slumped onto the bed, a lumpy, unforgiving mattress that smelt of old sweat. Her bottom lip trembled as tears threatened. Tears would do her no good in this place, but her eyes ached to release them, anything to quench the pent-up dread and dismay boiling inside her. A single hot tear tracked down her face, wiped away in a hurry as she heard the faint rhythmic clicking of the Madame's approach. Her shadow fell over the bed a moment later as pungent cigarette smoke wafted around her in a cloud, curling around Eleanor's throat.

The Madame's dark eyes did a languid study of their latest acquisition through the puffs of pipe smoke. Her eyebrows knit together as she traced the name on the slate.

"Ellie. A fine innocent name," said the Madame. The cigarette holder stem clicked against her teeth as she spoke. "Change took you young. I have a couple gentlemen who will love you." Her smile was almost kind, if not for the avarice flaring in her eyes. "However, both of them are away on business, and as I would rather not break you before their return, you shall help Rose with the household for the next few days."

Eleanor failed to completely stifle the relief she felt at her reprieve, knew her mistake as the Madame's hand snapped up her chin, her clawed thumbnail digging into Eleanor's bottom lip. "Learn quick and learn fast, Little Mouse, or you won't survive your first night on duty." The hand released her to stroke the side of her face. "And that would be such a waste."

She kept still, refusing to shudder at the Madame's touch though her body practically vibrated on its own from the effort. The smirk on the older woman's face told her she knew exactly how hard Eleanor struggled not to react. "Get some sleep. Your day starts early."

Alone, Eleanor curled up on the too hard bed. The new angles of her body made this difficult and she didn't know how to position herself comfortably, shifting over and over to find a position that allowed her an iota of rest. She wound up twisted in on herself, her arms over her head to block out the noise of the Carnal House. It never stopped, not fully, and she was certain she would chase sleep all night without catching it.

But the pull of exhaustion was stronger than she anticipated.

Eleanor woke with a start to silence. Her room was grey in the natural pre-dawn light that fought to illuminate the dim interior of the house. Rose would likely be coming for her soon. She shifted up, her body stiff and aching. What woke her? The lack of sound? Were the girls given a reprieve for the day? Or was it something else that woke her? She contemplated lying back down until she was forced out when she heard it again; that same mournful cry she heard last night at the locked door. As before, it pulled at her core, a haunting note she found herself drawn to, like the Willow o' Wisps in the old tales. She eased down the stairs, closing her eyes when it sounded again. It was muted by the close corners of the Carnal House, but louder than before. The reason was obvious when she reached the bottom of the stairs.

The door was open.

Eleanor flattened her body to the wall, holding her breath as she strained to hear something, anything. The door was open.

What did that mean? That the occupant was now free? Or that someone was visiting? The mournful calls that lured her down here were silent, but there was another, softer noise, a persistent murmur that made the fine hairs along her arms rise as it wormed its way in her ear. She resisted the urge to cover them and kept her eyes on the yawning mouth of the doorway.

What poor creature did they keep down there?

Eleanor froze as something moved from below, the familiar click, click, click of the Madame's spiked limbs ascending the stairs. She emerged from the dark as a nightmare being born, a creature shifting through smoke, her dark eyes heavily shadowed as she paused at the top step, worrying the stem of the cigarette holder so Eleanor could hear it chipping against her teeth. Lines of strain bracketed the Madame's mouth and pinched the corners of her eyes before she lashed out and slammed her open palm against the wall with a short shriek, muted by her clenched teeth.

"He should have broken by now." The voice emerged from the other side of the wall Eleanor hid on, startling her badly. She managed to keep herself still as Rose stepped into view, seeming to appear out of thin air, her presence entirely missed. How long has the girl been waiting on the other side of the wall? Did she hear Eleanor come down?

A new fear seized her, wondering if the broken girl would announce her presence to the distracted Madame, but both women continued to ignore Eleanor.

The Madame tapped her claws against the wall, her expression thoughtful. "This mysterious anchor is more powerful than I thought. Definitely not the witch. Our generous patron was correct in his assumption." A flash of awe flitted across the Madame's features. "I've never tasted magic quite like this. So delicate, so intricate, woven through the core of his being." She pushed away from the wall, taking a drag of her cigarette in a fresh gush of smoke. " Almost familiar. As if I've seen it somewhere else. I'll need to dismantle him to see it clearly."

Eleanor's throat felt tight at the Madame's words. The conversation was far over her head, but the implications slid under her skin like a blade. Rose shifted, her face blank, but there was an undefinable set to her body, a subtle stiffness to the clasping hands behind her back that gave Eleanor reason to believe the Madame's words sat ill with her too.

"Our patron desires him intact," said Rose, her voice soft, so soft Eleanor could barely hear her. The Madame's shoulders hunched a moment before she lashed out, catching the ruined side of the girl's face, knocking her off her feet in a spray of blood.

Eleanor shrank further into herself as the Madame reared over Rose, her beautiful features a mask of rage as she hovered over the fallen girl, her translucent teeth bared.

"You do not tell me the desires of our illustrious lord. You are no better than gutter filth, and you will do well to remember your place."

"Ye-yes, Mama," said Rose.

Eleanor pressed her hand to her chest at the tremble in the girl's voice, but she dared not rise, dared not give away her hidden position. The Madame's face cleared, smooth as silk once more. She relaxed, puffing clouds of smoke as she withdrew further down the hall.

"Close up," said the Madame, "and clean that up." She gestured to the spray of blood dripping down the wall.

Rose kept her head down, cowed, submissive. "Yes, Mama."

The Madame's clicking footsteps disappeared into another section of the house, leaving the two women alone. Eleanor fidgeted, uncertain whether she should reveal herself and offer comfort or retreat to the relative safety of her room when her skin prickled. She looked up, meeting Rose's stare, the girl's single eye calm and blank. Three slashes continued to bleed from her marred cheek, but she ignored them as if she didn't feel them at all. The two stared at one another, Eleanor's heart beating hard against her ribs.

"Why do you call her Mama? That woman deserves no such title," said Eleanor. The words slipped free before she thought better of it. She covered her mouth, eyes wide as she waited for the girl's reaction, but Rose remained little more than a bleeding doll, her expression empty. She wondered how long they'd stayed like this when Rose's single eye slowly turned to the open door. Eleanor followed her gaze, wondering if some other monster was about to rise from the depths, but nothing appeared. Frowning, she looked back to Rose, stunned as the girl walked away, leaning heavily against the wall for support.

She left Eleanor alone with the open door and whatever mystery it held. Why? The question plagued her, twisting at her conscience. She was torn between morbid curiosity and retreat. Whatever game the broken Rose was playing was a dangerous one, and Eleanor knew nothing of the rules. The Madame's expression of rage flashed through her thoughts, the suddenness of it, the ferocity of it. Her cheek throbbed at the sight of those horrid slashes on Rose's face. If the Madame caught her here, or worse, down the stairs, her punishment would likely be far, far worse.

Survival instinct tugged at her, to get away, to be safe, to hide as long as she could—

A pained groan rose from the below, breaking on a sob.

What creature deserved to suffer so, alone in the dark?

Eleanor inhaled a shuddering breath and crept forward, her steps slow and measured. She concentrated solely on keeping her new limbs quiet, not taking in her surroundings until she reached the bottom of the stairs.

The floor was packed earth, the air heavy with moisture and the musty scent all underground places held. She didn't see him at first, not until he shifted, a chain rustling over cloth. Eleanor froze at the sight of him, the conflict in her mind as confusing as it was terrifying. Her mind absorbed the sight of the raw flesh at his wrists, the oozing wounds at his throat where a cruelly spiked collar continued its slow torture. His swarthy skin was slick with feverish sweat. A long chain pooled on the ground between that awful collar and a solid bracket on the wall. One leg was straightened, a fresh-looking scar visible through the torn fabric of his pants. The other leg was drawn up to his chest, the position almost casual if not for the way his arms wrapped around his knee, hugging himself.

His suffering bruised the air with the scent of old blood like the rusting shrapnel from the ruins around her home village. There was something else, something that spoke to a deeper part of her brain where mindless instinct screamed at her to run, run far and fast.

His gaze shifted, noticing her for the first time. The bottom dropped out of her stomach.

The human visage he wore disappeared as their eyes met, the smoldering amber fire of his irises a window to the beast within, utterly insane. Whatever sympathies she harbored for this wounded prisoner were eclipsed by the wild fear throttling her in the presence of an apex predator. Eleanor managed only a choked gasp before he moved.

She'd thought him safely chained to the wall, thought him restrained without enough give to reach her. Both these thoughts proved false as nearly two hundred pounds of male crashed into her, and where she did not know how to handle her new body, he knew precisely where to strike to disable her completely. A knee pinned her to the ground at the juncture of her new tail, keeping the sharp barb from coming to her aid. Bewildered, overwhelmed, she stared up at him, eyes wide and frightened. He snarled and snapped teeth far too sharp for a human, forcing a shallow gasping shriek from her. His expression was a mask of pure menace as he pressed down on her.

The thought briefly crossed her mind that Rose sent her down here to die, to be savaged by the monster in the basement when he froze with a sharp intake of breath, a grain of sanity stealing into his feral expression. Eleanor didn't have time to understand the rapid switch when he pressed his face against her neck, breathing deep. She whimpered.

"Shhh, woman, shhh," he rumbled. His voice shocked her, rough as it was. Eleanor held still as she could, unable to stop her violent trembling. A different mood charged the air, a tentative one she dared not break as he took another deep breath against her skin.

He exhaled; his breath made the stray hairs at her nape flutter. To her great surprise, he hauled up against his chest, releasing a sob into her hair. Eleanor lay limp, confused beyond comprehension with her body plastered against a strange, dangerous male's chest. The fear was still there, lingering caution as she slowly reached up and laid her clawed hand flat against his back.

"Why are you doing this?" The words were as shaky as she felt, but they seemed to reach him as his tight hold on her eased so she could breathe. A beat of silence passed where Eleanor could only hear her ragged heartbeat keeping an uneven tempo to his panting breaths.

"You smell like her," he said, absently rubbing his cheek against the crown of her head. "But you're not her. Threads still connect you. Enough to find my way back."

His words shocked her anew. *Her, her, her,* the word tolled through her mind with the scent of sunlight and storms. The back of her neck prickled like goose flesh. Eleanor struggled against his hold, forcing him back to meet those half-mad amber eyes.

"You know her?" The mystery woman reared up in her thoughts, the memory of that phantom touch, soothing her, guiding her, protecting her being through the fire of the change. Eleanor gripped his arms, the sudden connection between herself and the wild male sizzling in her awareness. "Who is she? Will she come for us?"

The feral gleam returned to his eyes as he shook her. "No, no, no. She mustn't come here. *He* can't know about her."

"Who? Who is he?" Eleanor flinched as he snarled.

"You reek of her," he rasped, covering her mouth as he rocked forward and sank his teeth in her shoulder. Eleanor screamed into his palm at the pain, her mind sputtering to get a handle on the situation. She was going to die here, after all. He would tear out her throat for reasons she couldn't fathom.

The searing pain in her shoulder dulled to a persistent throb as his teeth released her. He ran his tongue over the wound. Eleanor shuddered and sobbed. "Gods, what are you doing?"

"Burying her magic," he whispered in her ear. Eleanor's tail twitched with the urge to strike at him, but he had kept her pinned through the whole encounter. He pushed her away, at last, setting her on her feet as he sank back against the wall.

Eleanor slapped a hand to her shoulder, reeling from the fresh memory of his bite. Her fingers met smooth, unbroken skin. As if it had never been. "What are you?"

He ignored her question, exhaustion clouding his gaze as his head lolled. The collar dug into his neck, releasing a fresh trickle of blood, but like Rose, he appeared mindless of his wounds. "Tell no one about her. Don't think about her, if you can."

She stared at him, hearing the dismissal in his voice. Questions whirled through her mind. Her fingers traced the spot on her neck where he'd bitten her, the lack of evidence shook her far more than the violence of the act itself. "What do I do now? How do I–" She stopped as his eyes turned vacant. Their highly unorthodox meeting was at an end, and she hadn't so much as learned his name. Eleanor backed away from him, refusing to take her eyes off him until she was nearly to the top of the stairs. Her legs wobbled beneath her as she left, the constant strain of adrenaline, leaving her weak and unsteady.

Rose waited for her, her back to the door as she scrubbed her own blood off the wall. She did not pause in this activity or turn to look as Eleanor crept by. Rose didn't seem shocked to see her alive, didn't acknowledge her presence at all. If the man in the basement confused her, Rose was an even greater enigma.

Eleanor thought the girl would ignore her entirely when her toneless voice carried through the silent hall. "Chores start in an hour. Go clean up and dress for the day."

Eleanor gave Rose a sharp look, but that scarred face gave nothing away.

4

ELEANOR

Eleanor woke in a panic, flailing off her narrow bed in a tangle of unfamiliar limbs. Hair plastered to the back of her neck by sweat, she shoved strands off her face as she lay on the floor, body askew. She gulped the stale air, shivering in the silent pre-dawn. Two days ago, she'd gone to sleep amid the moans and sobs of the Nightingale house in full service; the frayed, flat pillow did little to block out the noise, but she'd held it clamped around her head until exhaustion finally pulled her under. Struggling to catch her breath and slow her ragged heartbeat, she panted and stared up at the stained ceiling. The dream was one of teeth, tearing flesh, and snapping bone. At first, she thought she dreamed of the man in the basement; her neck throbbed where he'd bitten her, all to bury *her* scent. But as Eleanor turned the dream over in her thoughts, she realized it wasn't him. A faceless man stalked her dreams, clothed in the civil finery the patrons wore when they entered the house before they unleashed the monsters hidden beneath their fine silks.

The days that followed her arrival, Rose worked her from dawn 'til dusk, wringing every drop of energy from her body. The first day, she thought the scarred woman intended to break her through fatigue. She'd limped to the evening meal and slumped at the table in the backless stools made for those with tails and extra legs as she struggled to consume a simple stew. She froze at the thumping click of The Madame's footsteps entering the room in a stream of cigarette smoke. The Madame's unbound hair flowed down her back, a sleek black waterfall. Her robe hung off one shoulder, displaying the ornate ink tattooed there, so detailed it seemed to ripple over her skin. She observed the girls over the yellowed stem of her cigarette holder, eyes lingering over Eleanor as the girl hunched over her meal.

"Lord Harkham is in the mood for something...fresh," said the madame. Her offhand tone could have been describing slabs of meat at the butcher's stall rather than the assembled girls.

"Not her. Unless he wants his lady to nod off during service," said Rose. Until she spoke, Eleanor missed the pale specter hovering at The Madame's elbow.

The Madame scowled, baring her glass-like needle teeth at her head servant.

"You were supposed to occupy your charge with household tasks, not exhaust her beyond use."

Rose shrugged. "Her hands are soft. I doubt she worked a day in her life."

The Madame's hand whipped out, smacking the girl across the back of her head hard enough for her to stumble.

"Keep her hands soft." Her dark eyes lifted to look Eleanor over, studying every detail of her face for so long the girl wanted to scream.

"Yes, Mama," said Rose. She didn't look at Eleanor, not once.

The next day, Rose doubled the chores. Rose had been wrong. Eleanor was no stranger to hard work, but she wasn't used to the movements of her body, unfamiliar with the altered muscles and joints. A body that required study to function properly though she could hardly bear the sight of her new insectile limbs. The long, curved tail caught on every corner and edge, until she thought the dark brown carapace would crack like varnished clay. Her bulk was now balanced on hardened barbs, tottering on pointed ends less than the width of three fingers. The juncture at her waist, where her human skin shifted into hardened shell, was chafed raw and reddened, as if it were an infection her human side still attempted to reject.

The unsavory changes to her body added a great deal of complexity to the simplest tasks. A chore as easy as sweeping the stairs exhausted her as she struggled to find the synchronization to her limbs. Scrubbing the floorboards caused her to flinch every time her fingers made accidental contact with the carapace of her lower half in her awkward backward scuttle.

That evening The Madame found her passed out on the stairs, too exhausted to make it to the kitchen for her evening meal. A vicious snarl and smack woke her, though it wasn't Eleanor who suffered the blow. The Madame saved her abuse for Rose. Her eyes fluttered open to see the other woman slumped against the wall, a thin line of blood streaming from the corner of her mouth, but she didn't complain or even glance up from the floor in front of her. Rose merely picked herself up and went on her way. The experience made Eleanor's empty stomach twist.

When Rose escorted her to her room that night, Eleanor gnawed the inside of her cheek, struggling to find words as the woman turned to leave. "Thank you," said Eleanor.

Rose paused, not turning around. "For what?"

"For giving me an excuse," she said. *For helping me avoid service.* She didn't dare speak the words, wondering if she was wrong as Rose's shoulders tensed.

After a long moment, she responded. "It won't work for long."

Eleanor swallowed, the dread and exhaustion a dense sludge in the pit of her stomach. "I know."

A few days here, and she'd begun to lose track of time, and herself. Would this be the day the Madame placed her into service. The stain above her continued its outward crawl, marking the passage of time in a way the days and nights could not. It was only a matter of time before it began to drip. Eleanor released a long breath through her nose and slowly clambered to her feet. She tripped on her tail once as she stumbled to the communal bathroom, getting acquainted with her new limbs at last. In the cracked mirror, she caught a glimpse of her wan and smudged face. How could her body be so different while her face remained her own? The magic of this world made so little sense to her. She braced herself on the chill porcelain of the sink, staring hard into her reflection.

"One more day, one more pass," she whispered.

Her lip trembled, betraying the fear pressing in on her from all sides. She waited until it passed—until she could hold her face slack and serene—a trick she'd picked up from Rose, who must have spent years perfecting it.

Rose was waiting for her in the hall, leaning against the wall, arms crossed, and eyes closed. In the dim light of the hallway, her face looked smoother, giving Eleanor a glimpse of the woman she used to be.

"Time for chores," said Rose, jerking her head to the waiting mop and bucket. "I've got a list longer than my arm waiting for you, so don't dawdle."

It was enough to make her lips twitch. Eleanor threw herself into the task, grateful for the distraction. This time, she managed to bend her legs enough to settle into a comfortable crouch as she scrubbed the floor of the entry hall. The Madame approached at a rapid clip, her numerous legs thundering down the stairs, Rose trailing in her wake.

"Everything should be in order for this evening, but if any unscheduled patrons drop in, accommodate them with the full hospitality of the house," said The Madame as she tugged red satin gloves up her forearms. A brilliant red cape flowed down her shoulders, complete with a hood that framed her elegantly painted face. "I shall return by the morning."

Eleanor watched, wide-eyed and plastered against the wall, as The Madame drew parallel with her. She paused, peering down at the cowering girl. Without the constant stream of cigarette smoke, The Madame's face was a perfect porcelain masque, cold and emotionless. "Have this one cleaned up for this evening."

Rose's stony expression remained. If Eleanor could, she would have merged with the wall, her skin prickling hot and cold as The Madame's words roared in her ears. She continued scrubbing the floor, refusing to react. The thump-click of The Madame's footsteps continued out of the house; the door slammed, causing Eleanor to flinch. She finally noticed her shaking hands. She stared at them, willing them to stop. She still stared at them when Rose squatted next to her, gently prying the rag from her trembling fingers.

"Come, you must bathe," said the girl.

Eleanor's gaze snapped up to her face, closed and blank, despite the softness of her tone. She wanted to beg and plead for Rose to help her, to postpone her fate another night, to escape, anything, but that carefully constructed expression stopped her. There was no pity, no sympathy in that face. Rose would do her duty and prepare her under The Madame's orders, an innocent offering for the first interested client.

Eleanor's eyes slid to the front door, gauging the distance. How far and fast she could run before the guard caught up to her, or something worse? Her eyes were on the door when she heard a whisper of metal. A needle of fiery agony threaded up her spine as Rose drove a thin blade through the vulnerable exposed hinge of her tail, pinning her to the floor. Eleanor shrieked, her legs collapsing beneath her as pain unlike anything she'd felt in her life crackled and sparked through every nerve. Blood flowed from the wound, bubbling up in a grisly fount as Rose withdrew the blade in a quick, brutal pull. A breathless scream tore from Eleanor's throat, unable to give voice to the pain that stole her sight in a flash of throbbing black. Her vision cleared in patches, revealing the spasming wet smile of a wound. She looked away as shock threatened to knock her back under. Instead she looked back at Rose. The woman stood over her, calmly cleaning blood off her blade.

Blood loss made her head feel light. She struggled to get away, a tremor of weakness singing through her veins as she scuttled and clawed for the door. A pressure brought her up short; Rose pinned her in place with a foot on her tail, aggravating the wound. Eleanor cried out, the room spinning. Her cry ended on a sob, tears streaming down her face as the other woman kept her pinned and began to wrap the wound with a roll of clean gauze. She'd come prepared to do this? Rose expected she would try to bolt.

"You horrid bitch!" Eleanor screamed at her, digging her claws into the floor, vainly trying to chase away the dizziness that enfeebled her, gutting her resistance. Two days of exhausting chores made her muscles too watery to respond.

"Enough of that," said Rose. "Your body will heal the worst damage before the sun sets."

Eleanor glared at her, fiercely wishing for the strength to claw the vapid expression from the woman's face. "I pitied you," she said, her voice a low snarl. "I thought you didn't deserve to live like this. But you do. You do."

Rose didn't rise to the bait, her fingers steady as she finished tying the bandage. "You can walk like this. I will draw you a bath. There will be a fresh dress for you."

"You aren't human anymore," said Eleanor, hissing each syllable through her teeth.

The other woman looked at her then, her remaining eye vacant of warmth, soulless. "Neither are you. And the sooner you forget your humanity, the longer you'll survive."

The expression sapped at Eleanor's anger. It still burned, hot and fierce, but the deadened calm in Rose's face sent icy splinters of fear through her nerves. A wail rose from the basement, a guttural cry full of helpless rage, followed by the sounds of metal scraping on stone; the chained man struggled against his bonds. Eleanor's soul wilted at the tumult, the two of them trapped in this house. They shared a wretched fate, losing their humanity piece by piece.

"The scent of your blood upsets him," said Rose. "Come, let's get you bathed and dressed."

Too weak to flee, too weak to fight. Resignation sank into Eleanor's bones. Her tears were silent as Rose helped her rise off the floor. She braced herself on the wall and crawled toward the bath. Listing heavily, she tried to support her injured tail while she watched Rose fill the old stained tub with steaming water. Anger and fear warred for dominance as Rose helped her strip and ease into the hot bath, her first in months. The woman left her to soak, mopping up the mess of blood in the hall. That wretch of a woman, the dregs of humanity long wiped away by the Madame's brutal touch. Eleanor's nails dug into the side of the tub when Rose floated back into the room with a flimsy gown, a mocking virginal white, so sheer it would leave nothing to the imagination.

Eleanor's tempestuous emotions burned down to icy ashes of dread.

By sunset, there was no trace of the wound Rose inflicted to her tail, though it continued to twinge, healing beneath the surface. Still torn and bruised beneath the beautiful lie of smooth skin. Eleanor watched through her reflection as Rose rubbed scented oil along her neck and shoulders, preparing her for service. Rose twisted her hair into an elegant knot that exposed and exaggerated the feminine line of her throat. Eleanor debated snatching the glass bottle of perfumed oil and smashing it against her scarred face.

The fingers of Rose's good hand gently worked at a knot between her shoulders.

"You must relax yourself," she murmured as always, her tone matching her remote expression.

Eleanor's fingers twitched, small black claws edging out of her fingertips. Prime to rake across that mask-like face.

"You are stone," said Rose, "untouchable, impenetrable. Your body must be soft, yielding, they will paint their fingers across it, but they will never touch *you*." Her voice was soft, so very soft. Eleanor's gaze shifted to the scarred half of Rose's face, studying the old, ruined flesh.

"Untouched like you?" Eleanor hissed. She had to remind herself again, this woman didn't deserve her pity. Didn't deserve to feel pity or compassion for her 'charges,' not when the Madame pulled her leash. Rose's sole eye focused, their eyes meeting in the mirror. For a breath, the mask came down.

Eleanor gripped the vanity to steady herself.

"That will not happen to you," Rose whispered.

Her words were so close to a promise. Eleanor knew she would be a greater fool for believing them. Rose's fingers resumed their task, smoothing oil into her skin until she breathed the syrupy-sweet floral smell.

"Lavender, to soothe the senses," said Rose, "for both participants." She finished with a circular swirl of her index finger between Eleanor's shoulder blades. "Tonight, you are Ellie. Sink Eleanor deep, deep beneath the stone." Her scarred arm reached around, depositing a small metal cylinder on the vanity.

"One to numb the senses, two to forget," said Rose. She didn't make a sound as she left. Eleanor stared at the cylinder, wondering what poison it contained. She inhaled another cloying lungful of lavender-scented air and swiped up the container, listening to the soft rattle within. She unscrewed the cap and shook two black pills into her palm.

One to numb, two to forget. Eleanor's vision blurred. Her choice sat feather-light in her hand. Come tomorrow, she could be one of The Madame's blank-eyed pets, lounging in silk and sweat, her mind floating in a black fog. Did The Madame know Rose drugged them? Or was it her incentive to keep them willing and moaning, oblivious dolls.

Eleanor's hand curled, crushing the pills to fine black mist. She stared at herself in the streaked glass, a face both familiar and foreign, her human features sharper, her body wholly different beneath the waist. The last time she saw her human face was the day they came for her, dragging her from her home, marching her through the small village of mud huts and straw roofs before they thrust her beyond the safety of stone walls that protected them from the wilds. She hadn't wandered long before the Snatchers found her, as if they were waiting for her. Was this a better fate than falling into a predator's jaws? The only difference was these predators wore fine clothes.

"You survived," she said, running her fingers across the glass. Survived banishment survived being captured and sold. Her chest grew tight as her claws scraped. *"You survived."*

The murmur of male voices filled the house downstairs. A figure appeared at her doorway

"Come on, love, you join us in the parlor tonight." One of the women, an Annie or Mary, her glassy-eyed beauty marred by the old claw marks down both sides of her neck.

Anxiety squeezed her throat as she breathed hard through her nose. She left the container of pills on the vanity as she followed the other woman's uneven footsteps. This was her first evening present during service. The other women had arranged them-selves on the settees and couches like wilted flowers, welcoming the finely clothed lords with those empty porcelain faces. Roses hovered by the entrance, heralding in the evening's first customers, her scarred face one of empty civility.

Eleanor sat at the edge of their loose circle, in an ill-suited, curved chair that pinched the muscles of her lower half. She kept her back ramrod straight, hands curled loosely on her thighs as she stared at the floor. It kept her from staring at the others, from thinking of their vacuous eyes or Rose's surreptitious glances. Instead, she studied the freshly scrubbed floorboards with fierce concentration, sinking into the grainy whorls of wood, holding her breath at each pair of gleaming black boots that paused in front of her.

The lords didn't seem discouraged by her quiet intensity but were lured away by the beckoning purrs from the other women. She was grateful to them, even if their motivations were selfish or twisted, they gave her another hour, another minute, of feeling like Eleanor inside her skin. The Madame wasn't yet home, wasn't here to insist her service, to force her. Rose didn't stop the others from diverting their customer's attention from her. She listened to the clock, rolling over the hour, her mind drifting to the droning tick, tick, tick, still as a stone beneath a mirrored pond.

One of the lords reared up in front of her, undeterred by her stiff presence. He breathed in her face, the sickly-sweet smell of liquor and vomit thick on his breath. Eleanor froze, fear crackling like splinters of ice through her veins.

"Hello, sweet one. You're new." He swayed as he turned and beckoned to Rose. The scarred woman kept a watchful eye on Eleanor as she approached.

She gave the drunken lord a respectful bow. "Yes, Lord Harkham, what can I do for you this evening?"

"I would like a room with this one," he slurred. Eleanor wanted to sink into the cracked wall behind her. She fought to keep her body still as the lord ran a clumsy hand through her hair, pulling pieces free from their pins. She flinched as one hit her shoulder. Lord Harkham laughed. "Skittish. I like that."

Her stomach heaved, and a cold sweat flashed across her skin. Rose watched her with that terrible passive expression.

"I'm afraid young Ellie has begun to feel off since service began. I was just coming to dismiss her for the remainder of the night, so she doesn't dampen the mood."

Eleanor couldn't believe what she heard. Her head whipped to stare at Rose. She didn't know what had changed or why the woman decided to help her now. She was grateful despite what Rose did to keep her here.

"She looks healthy enough to me," Lord Harkham scoffed. He grabbed her chest and squeezed.

Eleanor didn't think. She reacted. It didn't matter that her new body was ungainly and hard to manage; it snapped with instinctual speed as her tail whipped over her head and speared Lord Harkman's hand.

The spurt of blood splashed across Eleanor's face, leaving her awash in the scent of hot copper as the drunken lord bellowed in rage and staggered back. He cradled his bleeding hand to his chest. The sight of blood caused the other women to shriek, some of them with a hint of hunger, but they all fell silent at the cluster of sharp, staccato thumps.

Madame Murmur stood in the doorway; her silk robe slightly askew. Her nostrils flared at the scent of blood, but her expression remained smooth despite the rage burning in her eyes.

"My apologies for the incident, Lord Harkham, please allow Rose to treat your wound. Your next month's visits are on the house." The Madame scanned the room. The other girls shrank from her gaze, hiding behind the finery of their chosen lords. "Well, go entertain!" The women scattered like a cluster of disturbed insects, dragging their befuddled clients with them.

Rose shot Eleanor one last look, her expression unreadable as she led the moaning Lord Harkham from the room. The man's hand had begun to swell and turn purple. She hoped he lost the limb! Distracted by Harkham's wound she didn't see The Madame reach for her until the woman's claw-like nails were snared in her hair. Eleanor shrieked, her cry cut short as The Madame dragged her from the parlor and tossed her down the stairs.

Eleanor didn't have the sense or faculties to tuck her body. She landed hard, banging the bony angles of her hips and shoulders, knocking her head against a step, while her body kept a tally of the impacts with starbursts of pain that burned afterimages in her skull. She lay in a moaning heap at the bottom of the stairs, trying to regain her bearings when The Madame grabbed her by the offending tail and hurled her into the wall. The breath burst from her lungs. She was given no chance to catch it as she went airborne again. Her back cracked as she slammed hard into the stair railing. A low moan of pain slipped past her lips. The Madame's shadow loomed over her. Eleanor found she couldn't even bring herself to brace for more pain, her body one large agonizing bruise. But the woman appeared sated of violence, content to curse her out.

"Stupid, stupid girl," said The Madame. "You've cost me a valuable client. We'll be lucky if Harkham keeps his mouth shut about what happened. I should have left you in the street for the dogs." The Madame smoothed her mussed hair off her face. "Rose!"

The scarred woman appeared a moment later, wiping her bloodied hands with a rag. Eleanor couldn't see her reaction, but Rose's steps didn't falter at the sight of her battered body. She must have expected it. Now she understood why Rose offered her drugs. Because she knew what would happen if Eleanor reacted the way she did. When Rose realized Eleanor hadn't taken them, she made one last effort to avert this result.

Rose knew how to survive in this world, and Eleanor *did not*. She didn't think she would survive this night. The Madame seethed above her.

"Yes, mama?"

"What happened to Lord Harkham?"

"After lancing the wound, it appears he will keep the hand," said Rose.

The Madame drew a deep breath. "Good. Clean this mess up." She waved a careless hand, her gaze averted to the mess of Eleanor's body, but she failed to clarify what was to be done with Eleanor, and Rose did not ask. The Madame crawled away; her shoulders slumped as her lower half dragged along the group. Rose said nothing as she helped Eleanor to stand.

Eleanor winced in pain, but nothing appeared to be broken, a small miracle considering her tumble down the stairs. She hissed and gasped her way back up the stairs, leaning on Rose until the girl helped deposit her in a waiting bath. The hot water had an immediate effect, a soothing balm to her sore, already-bruised back. Rose didn't scrub the blood from her skin. Instead, she wrung out a cloth over Eleanor's back, letting the hot water do the work for her. Eleanor sat quietly through her ministrations until she couldn't stand the silence any longer.

"You knew that would happen?" Eleanor hugged her chest. The cloths of water paused. She could still feel the painful squeeze of Harkham's hands. As much as she wished it would cost him a limb, it was to her benefit that Rose had saved it.

"Yes," said Rose. She resumed her ministrations.

"Why help me?" There was a soft sob in Eleanor's words.

Rose huffed a breath through her misshapen nose. "You don't act like other scorpid women."

Eleanor swallowed the sudden lump in her throat. She couldn't tell if Rose meant that as a compliment or not. "That made me worth saving?" There was a self-deprecating undertone to her words.

"It makes you interesting."

Eleanor sniffed. Rose had moved on to washing her scalp, the woman's gentle massage soothing the ache where her skull took a knock. Eleanor hated the change, as if buried deep inside the wreck of her body, there still lingered a human side to Rose, a sliver of compassion. It would be easier to hate Rose if that piece was truly gone. Instead it haunted Eleanor, a contradiction to her harsh reality that made it that much harder to swallow.

"My mother used to do this," said Eleanor, her eyes drifting shut at the sensation. "Whenever I injured myself doing something stupid, she'd run her fingers through my hair like this. No matter the injury, it always seemed to help."

Rose's hands paused. Her fingers shook, tangled in Eleanor's hair. Eleanor opened her eyes and caught Rose's single eye in the vanity mirror.

The woman was horrified. "You really do remember," she said, a tremor in her voice. It was the strongest emotion she'd ever seen from the woman. "You remember everything."

"I told you," said Eleanor. "I—"

Rose ducked forward, covering Eleanor's mouth with her soapy hand. Both women stiffened at the clicking thump as the Madame approached. Rose jerked away and dried her hands. Eleanor sank deeper into the tub, ill-prepared to face the Madame's wrath without a stitch of clothing on.

The moment grew worse as the Madame tossed a burlap sack into the room. "Have her put that on. No use for frilly garments at the slaughterhouse."

Eleanor froze in shock.

"Mama, wait," said Rose.

The Madame whirled around; anger still etched in the lines of her face. "Don't disobey me."

"I think sending her to meat house would be a waste," said Rose. "She has fire. A strong will. Some of our patrons appreciate a spirited nature. Someone will pay a handsome fee to break it."

The Madame paused, considering. She tapped the stained porcelain stem of her cigarette holder against her painted bottom lip. "You have a valid point, Rose. I think I know just the one."

Rose's shoulders hunched at the Madame's words. She said nothing more, but Eleanor swore there was a spark of fear in the girl's ravaged face. Rose had just saved her life, but she wasn't sure if she should be grateful or not.

A PLAY OF LORDS

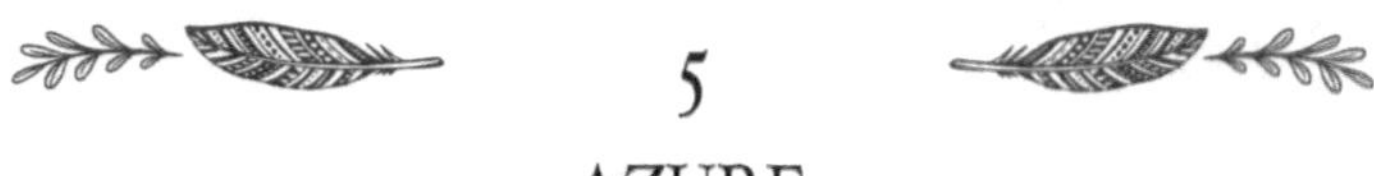

5

AZURE

The city quivered beneath her. Azzy curled on her side, listening to the creak and groan as the wood and stone foundations vibrated for several long moments—the second tremor since her arrival, only days apart. What could it mean? Through her lone window, the sky was a black mass, but the house would wake soon. Avergard operated on a strange schedule that was neither nocturnal nor diurnal, but some odd combination of both. Wallach's household was no exception, and Azzy discovered some of the house's occupants woke well after dawn while others stayed up through the better part of the night. Petyr was one such night owl, who hadn't made an appearance with the others at breakfast since her first morning. The whorled Lennon preferred the sun, while Cherise kept a shifting schedule that appeared to echo Lord Wallach's, though the reticent lord had been scarce since she'd returned from the market.

His absence worried her, and it seemed her encounter with Lord Brusker had spooked the head servant. Cherise had yet to give her a proper designated position in the household. Azzy began to frequent Morglint's room and the estate garden. The sunlight loved her friend, his skin even darker since their arrival due to his constant presence in the garden, while direct light seemed to scald her face after a quarter of an hour. His fingernails were permanently stained green while his workbench was now covered in plants in various stages of drying. The earthy scents soothed the hollow ache in Azzy's chest; if she closed her eyes, she could almost imagine Brixby at the workbench, sorting packets of herbs while she and Armin chopped and ground ingredients.

That ache hit her tenfold now, the crushing quiet dangerous for her wandering thoughts. An aftershock shivered up through the floorboards and saved her from her memories. Now Azzy was wide awake as a prickling sensation nipped at the back of her neck like she was being watched. The curve of her spine went rigid.

Twice she woke to find the Maven watching her in the middle of the night from the hall. She closed her door every night and woke to find it open, which would be unnerving enough, but the Maven, it seems, wasn't the only one who violated her privacy while she slept. Howl growled softly from the foot of her bed; his gaze fixed on the door.

Azzy held her breath as she rolled over. Her whispers had remained quiet through the Maven's visits, but she couldn't shake her unease, especially since Azzy and the feral boy seemed to be the only ones aware of her presence. It was a small relief to find Petyr hovering at her door, his hand raised to knock. He frowned at Howl who was lying in a tangle of blankets at the foot of her bed.

"I thought he had his own room?" For once, Petyr stood still, his features clear and unblurred to reveal his long, thin nose. His bottom lip was full, giving his frown a slight pout. Circles under his eyes, like half-moon bruises, made his dark irises stark in his pale face as if he were a confounded specter puzzled by the living.

"He does, but he won't stay there," said Azzy. It was a mild statement compared to reality.

Howl rarely left Azzy's side. She allowed it because her proximity seemed to soothe the boy, but he also made her feel utterly helpless. Cherise was quick to inform her that the laws of Avergard required his 'kind' to be collared, though the head servant had no suitable explanation as to why. The same day Howl followed them home, Wallach had exchanged the brutal collar for a much more humane bracelet, no spikes or thorns, only the runes to force him into human form. The bracelet angered her more, not only because it meant the use of the collar was a choice of casual cruelty, but the affect to Howl's mind appeared the same no matter how *gentled* the device.

Kai told her the collars drove them mad. How could Wallach

force them on a child, law or not? Not that she could ask the lord or argue Howl's case since he'd been avoiding her. Azzy didn't try to remove it as she had Kai's collar when she couldn't evoke a single whisper to guide her; the collar's magic was tied to its master, which meant forced removal could injure or possibly kill Wallach. Neither was a desired result.

Petyr continued to hover at her door, clearly thrown by Howl's presence.

"Is there something I can do for you?" He jolted at her words as if he'd forgotten she was there.

"Lord Wallach wanted me to see if you were awake," said Petyr. He shuffled from foot to foot, that near-constant blur over his features beginning to stir. She wondered if it was an effect of his nerves.

"And if I was?"

Again, Petyr appeared at a loss for words. "Then he would like to request your audience in his study," he said. It was Azzy's turn to frown as she began to ease from the bed.

Petyr's brows drew together at the sight of her simple night-gown. "Oh, you will want to change into proper attire," he said. He snapped his fingers at Howl. "Come along, give her a moment to freshen up."

Howl's response was a silent growl, his lips pulling back over his teeth. Azzy laid her hand on his shoulder.

"Just a moment, please," she said. The boy grumbled as he wiggled free from his nest of blankets, leaving her to dress. She did so quickly, wondering why Wallach wanted to see her *now* after avoiding her for days. Azzy emerged from her room to find Howl and Petyr silently sizing one another up, the latter once again managing to keep his body still under Howl's wary gaze. They shared a similar feral quality in their demeanor that made her curious where Wallach had acquired Petyr.

"I'm ready," she kept her tone soft, but Petyr flinched at the intrusion.

He regained his composure in a blink, tugging on the cuffs of his stained gloves. "We need to drop off the boy with Cherise. He can't follow you this time."

Howl had yet to speak a word, but he comprehended speech

well enough. He pressed hard against Azzy's side, a rumble of displeasure issuing from deep in his chest.

"I will come back," she whispered to him. Part of her wished she could take him with her, but she didn't know what Wallach wanted from her, and she refused to risk his safety. Despite her reassurances, he didn't move away until they reached the servant's dining room, where he went to Cherise with a soft whine that made Azzy's throat tight. The head servant gave her a tired wave as she set a bowl of porridge drizzled with cream and honey in front of the boy. Misgivings or not, Howl fell on the food, easing some of Azzy's guilt.

Petyr remained silent until they were close to Wallach's study. "I've never seen one of them latch on like that," he said. That contemplative frown continued to draw a line between his brows. "Or that calm."

'He'd be calmer if he could shift,' she thought, but bit down on the words before they left her mouth. "Do you know why Wallach wants to see me?"

"Yes," said Petyr, though he didn't elaborate further. She glanced at him sidelong; take away the bruised shadows beneath his eyes, and he was closer to her age than she initially believed. He had yet to grow into his height, a youth of ungainly limbs and bony wrists and knees, hidden beneath a rumpled, ill-kept suit.

"You asked where I came from," said Azzy, "Where were you from before you came here?"

A faint pink tinged his cheeks. He rubbed the back of his neck. "That was rather rude of me," he admitted.

"Oh," said Azzy. Which meant he likely wouldn't answer her.

"I was born here, in the city, but I came from nothing," he said, his voice raspy as if the admission cost him. Surprised by his openness, she itched to ask more, but the familiar deep red door loomed before them. Petyr rapped two knuckles against the wood in quick succession, not waiting for a verbal answer before opening it to lead her inside.

Wallach waited from behind his massive desk. Azzy swallowed her shock at his appearance, equally rumpled to Petyr's. His mane of sleek dark hair was mussed as if he'd constantly run an agitated hand through it.

"Thank you, Petyr. Grab something to eat while you can," said Wallach. The young man peeled off without a word, leaving the two of them alone once more. A swarm of questions buzzed in her mind, but she waited for Wallach to address her first. His deep cobalt gaze assessed her; gloved fingers threaded together in front of his mouth. At last, he sighed and dropped his hands, lifting a heavily creased paper from his desk.

"My apologies for not speaking with you sooner, Azure," said Wallach, "I'm afraid I've been engaged in an ill-fated mission."

She studied him, frustrated by the continued silence in her head, but she had an inkling. "You tried to reach Safiya?"

Wallach nodded, his mouth set in a grim line. "There was an order issued from the House of Lords that no visitors are allowed access to the prisoner without the written consent of the judiciary council." The paper crinkled in his grip, belying his frustration. "My request has been denied, indefinitely."

His tone remained calm, but Lord Wallach was seething. The rigid angles of his body telegraphed his tightly restrained anger. Azzy pursed her lips. "You expected a different result?" She feared she'd overstepped, but Wallach released a breath, forcing the tense line of his shoulders to release. Azzy had never encountered someone with such an iron grip on their temper.

"Not so long ago, I served as Lord Protectorate of this city," said Wallach, "the former position should have automatically granted me access, but it is fairly common knowledge that Safiya also came from my house."

They believed Wallach would attempt to free her, which was true, but it didn't help their chances to do so if the other lords were aware of it. "What do we do?" Azzy asked, worried this was why he'd requested her presence. She still had no answers to give him.

"We cheat," said Wallach, rising from the desk. "Ah, ready, Petyr?"

The young man barreled through the door, his mouth still chewing the remnants of his breakfast as he began to strip off his gloves. He hurriedly swallowed his mouthful. "Yes, my lord." Food seemed to have revived him somewhat as he lifted his ravaged hands in front of him, clawing at unseen seams in the air as he tore a hole. Without the cacophony of the market, Azzy could hear it, like ripping heavy fabric. Petyr grunted as fresh cuts sliced down his palms, his actions demanding a price of blood.

The scent of the underground wafted from the wavering hole. Wallach offered Azzy an arm. "It is very disorienting until your body adjusts," he said. "Hold onto me."

Azzy's hand shook as she slid it into the crook of Wallach's arm. Why did he wish for her to accompany him? Their interactions had been unusual, but she was only a servant in his house. Her thoughts a mass of questions and doubts, she stepped through the hole.

The world immediately shifted, revealing a tunnel just tall enough to accommodate Wallach. Petyr himself had to tilt his head to avoid brushing the ceiling, which appeared to be packed dirt, shot through with dangling tree roots. Azzy thought they were underground, but the air constantly crackled and spat around them.

"Where are we?" Her voice emerged distorted, echoing and wavering as if she shouted from a great distance.

"Nowhere," said Petyr, his voice affected by the same eerie delay. He moved around them to lead.

Azzy understood why Wallach offered her an arm as they began to walk. The throbbing air pressed against her eyes until the ground seemed to ripple beneath her feet. It made every step uncertain, though she could feel the firm dirt beneath her feet. Her head ached as her mind tried to adjust. Time seemed to stretch as they walked, but when they came to a stop, she realized they couldn't have gone more than a dozen steps. Relief flooded her system as Petyr lifted his bare hands to open the way.

He hesitated. "She's not alone, sir."

Azzy felt the muscles of his arm tense. "Can you open a window?"

Petyr's shoulders slumped, his exhaustion evident. "If I did, I couldn't bring us back, sir."

Wallach eased his arm free from her grip. "May I borrow?" The young man's eyes went wide, his expression pulled by taut lines of fear, but he nodded and extended his ravaged hand.

Azzy gaped as Wallach removed the glove of his right hand

and pressed his palm to Petyr's. The young man gasped once, his brows drawn. Wallach released him a few seconds later and caught him as his legs gave out.

"Easy, rest while you can," said Wallach, helping him sit on the ground. He beckoned Azzy closer. She almost missed the gesture, her gaze locked on the circular wound on Petyr's palm. "Stay with him and say nothing. There's no guarantee this visitor isn't preceptive enough to notice us."

Wallach raised his hand in front of him. The air strained and rolled as if he'd cast a stone into a still pond. Azzy watched, transfixed, as the air settled and revealed a window, an open one as a gust of cool wind ruffled her hair.

The prison cells of Avergard were chill and damp underworld. Condensation gathered on the stone walls; they continually wept moisture, creating a persistent dripping sound, as if a river waited to breach the ceiling and flood them out at any given moment.

Safiya sat cross-legged on the packed dirt floor of her cell, her eyes closed. At their first and only meeting Safiya seemed otherworldly, a powerful witch in her own domain. The confines of the cell did little to leech that vitality from her, her dark skin unlined by age, almost lustrous due to the moisture that clung to her, beaded in her hair the deep dark red of fire-raked coals.

Safiya opened her eyes at the sound of tapping, a familiar sound Azzy had heard before in the market. She followed the line of Safiya's gaze, listening to the sound of the cane before its owner finally came into view. He tapped it against the stone wall for effect since much of the lower level floor settled for dirt. The distain in Safiya's expression was subtle and vanished completely as the lord stopped in front of her cell.

"That bastard," Wallach hissed, a venomous whisper through the static air. Neither Safiya nor her visitor appeared to hear him. Wallach's free hand curled into a shaking fist. His anger made the air buzz around him, but he kept it tightly leashed. Petyr also tensed at the sight of the newcomer, a mix of fury and fear in his animate face.

The newcomer possessed the carefully polished look Azzy now associated with the aristocratic class of Avergard. The outer layers of his suit were soft dark grays, while his vest was a vivid red, almost the exact color of fresh split blood. Her gaze paused on his face, his appearance arresting. The carefully manicured scruff on his jaw was meant to seem careless, his long nose-tip tilted over a full, sensuous mouth. His eyes were the same shade and color of polished silver and blazed in his face as he settled in a waiting chair outside the witch's cell.

"Lord Vashon, what a pleasure to see you," drawled Safiya. Azzy jumped. Safiya's voice poured in, bright and unaltered. The witch didn't rise or bow to the lord, but when she inhaled sharply, Wallach rocked forward.

Azzy bit down hard on her tongue as the whispers slammed into her head. She moved in sync with Petyr, snaring Wallach's pant legs to keep him from moving forward.

"You taught her how to evade what is coming yourself, sir," said Petyr in an urgent whisper. "Trust her now."

Azzy said nothing, not fully comprehending the situation beyond the cries of alarm pounding inside her skull. She struggled to decipher the swarm of whispers, but after days of silence, she found the task impossible. Instead, she wrapped her fingers around Wallach's calf and struggled to focus on the scene before them. After a long moment, Safiya exhaled between her teeth. Lord Vashon sat back on the chair. Azzy could only see his profile from this angle, but she thought his expression amused.

"My, you have grown into a fine young woman, haven't you?"

The moment stretched and spooled, leaden by the intensity of Vashon's presence. Safiya bore it with a neutral expression that belied the concentration burning in her gaze. A bead of sweat trickled down the witch's temple, the only outward sign of her exertion.

Wallach stopped straining forward, his breathing harsh as he struggled to rein in his emotions. Petyr eased back, gently pulling Azzy with him. She wasn't sure if she should let go, until Petyr sagged against her, too exhausted to hold himself up.

"What did he do to her?" Azzy whispered, hoping to distract Wallach with questions, but it was Petyr who answered her.

"He can pluck memories from one's mind as easily as if you or I pulled a leaf from a tree branch," he said. "Unless one, like Safiya, has been trained against his methods." His nostrils flared white as he slumped against the wall, panting, his eyes half-closed. Wallach remained silent; his gaze fixated on the other lord.

The puppeteer. A single whisper came through loud and clear as a shout in her ear. The others writhed in her mind, a dozen mournful cries that sent shivers cascading through her body.

Vashon clucked his tongue against his teeth. "An interesting defense," he said, "I wonder how long you could keep that up?"

"Longer than your patience, Lord Vashon," said Safiya, her smile sweet.

Vashon's smile was anything but. "I will enjoy breaking you.".

Safiya rolled her shoulders. "Alas, my lord, it appears I am a temporary guest of this fine establishment until the fine citizens of Avergard see fit to give me a trial."

Something ruffled beyond Lord Vashon, hovering at the corner of their windowed view. Safiya glanced without turning her head. Azzy followed Safiya's gaze and forgot how to breathe.

A boy with wings stood further down the hall, watching Vashon with storm-shrouded eyes. A sob clogged her throat. Petyr suddenly gripped her arm tight, his bare skin fever hot. Longing tolled through her, so loud it muffled the whispers and shredded her common sense. Tears tracked down her face. Petyr tugged hard, pulling her off balance until she fell hard into his chest. He turned her face into his shoulder. A sharp, clean scent rose off him, unfamiliar but it somehow cleared her head as it tingled in her nose. She inhaled deep, fighting her own inner battle for control.

She chanced a glance up at Petyr, his somber expression one of understanding. His grip eased when she nodded, but he didn't shove her away, holding her up as she forced herself to look back at the scene.

Safiya picked at her nails, affecting an air of boredom. "I don't suppose you brought cards? It does get rather boring here."

"What if you didn't have to stay?" Vashon sat back, folding his arms over his chest. He looked her over, his expression bemused as he made a show of analyzing Safiya's body. "I would enjoy a jewel like you on my arm."

Azzy glanced at Wallach to see how their exchange was

affecting him. The man was so tense she expected him to crack in half.

Safiya's brow raised. "I'm afraid I have no desire to be an adornment, Lord Vashon."

He shrugged. "The food would be better."

"Very tempting, but I would like to abstain from your pissing contest with Wallach."

Vashon lounged back with a sigh. "What if my desire to take you from here had nothing to do with Wallach? You are a remark-able woman, Safiya Sabhayar."

Safiya tapped a finger to her chin. "Such compliments. You speak of desire, but men like you enjoy your toys, so much so you must constantly replace what you so carelessly break." She leaned forward. "And we both know this is all about Wallach."

"So what if it was? Wouldn't you enjoy seeing him unleash a little of that carefully bolted down rage?"

Azzy froze. The whispers surged as Lord Vashon's silvery gaze wandered in their direction.

"Hmm. I wonder how many stones are in this wall," said Safiya. Her ruse made Vashon chuckle.

"You should give my offer some thought, Safiya. It would be a shame to see the ax swing through that lovely neck," Vashon rose, straightening his clothes. "Come along, Lyre."

Lyre? The boy with wings followed Vashon, his limbs moving in a jerky pantomime as if he wasn't in full control of his actions. Azzy's heart ached at the sight.

Safiya let out a breath. The other lord was barely out of sight when Wallach surged forward into the hallway. Petyr held fast as Azzy tried to follow with a vehement shake of his head.

"He wanted you to observe their encounter," he said. "That was the whole reason we brought you along." *Observe? Why?*

Wallach sat in the chair left vacant by Vashon. Safiya froze at his sudden appearance, a veritable flood of conflicting emotions swept over her face at the sight of him. She threw up her hands.

"What are you doing here?" She hissed the words at him, surreptitiously glancing down the hall to see if Vashon had indeed left. "You just missed your dearest friend. Is the seat even cold yet?"

"Vashon will never see me come or go from here," said Wallach.

Safiya glanced around him. "You brought Petyr? He was still a boy when I left."

The 'boy' flushed at her words. Safiya let her body relax as she turned her attention to her second visitor of the day. The two of them stared at one another without speaking for so long Azzy began to feel like a voyeur. There was an evident longing in Wallach's gaze, though Azzy couldn't tell whether such longing was for a lost companion or a deeper bond. It was unclear if Safiya felt the same, her expression far harder to discern and carefully guarded, but her hands tangled together as if she fought not to reach for him.

"Why did you come here, Heinrich?" There was a catch in her voice more telling than her restrained demeanor.

"Would you let Petyr help you escape from here?"

Safiya closed her eyes and swayed.

"You know as well as I do that's unwise," she said.

"So is standing trial," he said.

"I can't leave here, Heinrich, not like this," said Safiya. "They would scour this city from the tallest tower to the sewers below. The entire House of Lords would turn against you."

The muscles of his jaw flexed, clearly conflicted by her answer. He touched the bars of her cell instead. "Dampening runes. Strong ones."

Safiya shrugged. "Not strong enough."

Azzy pursed her lips at the answer. Safiya stayed here by choice to protect Wallach? She only spent a few hours in the witch's company and knew the woman was far more cunning than that. Wallach wasn't smitten enough to miss that as well. Why has she returned to the city at all, with a death sentence hanging over her head?

"There's something else keeping you here."

Safiya reached up, pulling at her necklace. A familiar stone swung free of her blouse. Azzy stared as the witch rubbed her thumb over the shard of sky. "Is Azure settling into your household?"

A hum rippled through her senses as the witch stroked her

thumb over the smooth blue glass, the connection now faint and fading. Her lips parted as a whisper drifted through her mind, an errant thought given shape and weight. *The witch followed her here? But why?*

"I'd ask how you know, but I doubt I will enjoy the answer," said Wallach. He rubbed his hands together, one still bare.

"I don't know everything. She's often blocked from my view," said Safiya.

"I've never seen anything like her," said Wallach. He appeared to have ignored the Witch's words, but Azzy heard them. If the shard around her neck served as a link between them, what had the power to block it? Azzy clenched her hands as more questions mounted her already burgeoning pile.

"I don't know whether you should help her or kill her," she said, her expression troubled. Azzy tensed.

The witch's words cut through the writhing mass of questions. Her focus turned clear and cool as the whispers flooded in, building and waiting, a silent creature of hidden teeth and sharpest claw ready to defend against all comers. Petyr frowned up at her, sensing the sudden tension.

"I'm inclined toward the former," said Wallach. He was careful not to look in her direction. "Why suggest the latter?" The curiosity in Wallach's tone scraped across Azzy's nerves.

Safiya blew out a breath. "To keep her out of the wrong hands."

Wallach snorted at that. "I doubt any hands could hold that one."

She looked at him. "You think she's that strong?"

"I think once she unravels the mystery of herself, she could be," said Wallach. "She doesn't understand the basics of magic, so she doesn't follow them."

Safiya fidgeted with the loose threads of her skirt. "Then you must teach her quickly." She met Wallach's worried gaze. "The cities below are failing. The Children of the Gate have glut themselves. You know what that means."

"They'll be coming here."

The two of them fell into a companionable silence while Azzy's thoughts turned over. Safiya's words resonated in her mind.

Caletum has already fallen, Haven is not far behind. How many others had fallen? What were the Children of the Gate? She shivered.

We listen. We yearn.

"I have to go," said Wallach, his voice steeped in regret. "Is there a way for you to reach me if you have a need?"

Safiya hesitated. "A tooth," she said, pointing to his ungloved hand. "From that mouth."

He looked startled by the request but offered his palm to her. Safiya didn't appear unsettled by the mouth as it opened wide. She began to reach for it when Wallach shook his head. He gripped a tooth himself and pulled it free with a grunt to drop in her waiting palm. From her own experience, it surprised Azzy how willing he was to offer the Witch a piece of himself. She wondered once again, at the nature of their relationship, to the extent Wallach trusted Safiya, and wondered if she could bring herself to do the same in time to save her from her fate.

"If you feel an itching sensation, it's message incoming," she said.

Wallach's brow creased. "What will it do exactly?"

Safiya held the tooth to her mouth and whispered. Wallach gasped as the mouth of his palm dribbled ink, the word "this" flowing across his closed fingertips before it dripped to the floor and sank into the dirt.

"That is highly unsettling," said Wallach.

"I won't use it unless I have to," she said. She tucked the tooth away. "Train that girl, Heinrich. The faster, the better. Her task is far harder than you realize."

Safiya's words gained weight as another tremor shook the stones. Azzy tilted her head, listening to the beats between the shaking. There was something, just out of the range of her senses that she could almost grasp.

"I feel that time is very much not on our side," said Wallach.

6

AZURE

Wallach once again had to 'borrow' from Petyr to get them home. Azzy itched to speak with the lord, to confront him on what he planned to do with her after his conversation with the witch, but Petyr couldn't stand on his own. Wallach needed one hand free to maintain whatever magic kept the odd null space around them open. When Petyr's stamina failed, the crackling dark space around them shrank to brush against their shoulders. The roots on the walls tugged at her clothing, and the static air buzzed against the hum of whispers in her mind, the effect on her senses comparable to the time she and Armin stole a flask of Brixby's mushroom brandy. The further they traveled without Petyr consciously holding it open, the more the null space rejected them. Soon the air nipped and stung at her arms through the thin covering of her shirt. A sense of vertigo wrapped around her until Azzy had to depend on the grasping walls for balance, so that by the time they reached what Wallach claimed to be the study, sweat saturated her clothing from the exertion and the claustrophobic conditions.

Wallach wedged open an exit wide enough for their party to squeeze through, one after the other. He sent her through first. Azzy burst out of the null space, sucking in the clean, still air of the study in gulping, desperate breaths. Wallach emerged next, carrying Petyr on his back. She'd recovered enough to help catch the lanky youth as Wallach's own legs gave out. The two of them managed to ease Petyr onto the settee.

"Go, get Cherise. Tell her to bring the kit." Wallach knelt on the floor beside the settee as if he didn't have the strength to stand. She couldn't fault him; uncertain her own legs would hold as she staggered from the room.

Azzy thankfully found the head servant where she had left her in the servant's dining room, attempting to untangle the snarls in Howl's unruly hair. The pair made an interesting tableau, with her shroud of smoke little more than heat waves around her as she worked, Howl compliant at her feet. "Wallach needs you to bring the kit," she pushed out, hoping the vague statement conveyed enough information.

Cherise jumped up at her words. Her smoky aura coalesced into a panic streaked yellow, threaded with deep violet, the emotion was one Azzy couldn't gauged as she watched Cherise hustled around the room, grabbing supplies. The head servant's sense of urgency roused Azzy's flagging energy as she bolted from the room, Azzy a step behind her. Howl trailed after them as Cherise rushed to the study, her smoke plumed behind her like writhing gray serpents, their movements hypnotic to Azzy in her exhaustion. The streaks of violet deepened as Cherise shoved the study door open hard enough to bang against the wall, her arms laden with a bundle of packets and vials she set down on Wallach's desk without preamble. Azzy resisted the urge to slump against the nearest wall as she watched her work.

Immediately Cherise uncapped a vial of the same sharp, clean scent Azzy caught earlier. "Peppermint," said Cherise, noting her curious look. Despite her obvious agitation, her movements were steady and calm.

Petyr coughed, taking the vial from her to continue breathing in the smell as she set about creating a poultice in seconds. She grabbed his wounded hand, her scowl still visible through her agitated smoke, the violet eclipsing all other shades when she saw the coupling of bite marks. Petyr winced as she slapped the paste over the wound. Cherise's ministrations gentled as she wrapped cloth over his hand. She cinched the bandage tight and rounded on Wallach, her hands fisted over hips.

"Twice? Really?"

Azzy finally recognized the emotion behind the woman's violet smoke. Cherise was furious with them. Was it Azzy's imagination, or did Wallach lean away from the irate servant? He couldn't seem to look her in the eye. "It couldn't be helped."

"It could have waited a day," Cherise snapped. "You've run him ragged all week."

"He said he could handle this," Wallach muttered.

"Of course he did. He would work himself to death for you," said Cherise. "I hope she was worth it, my lord."

Azzy flinched as the head servant swept out in a huff. Wallach's expression answered Cherise's less than cordial question. *Safiya came from this house.* The encounter caught up with her abruptly. Azzy swayed on her feet until Howl leaned against her.

"Azure?"

She straightened her spine. Wallach's expression shifted once more to the same unreadable cipher he donned the moment they emerged from Petyr's null space. What she hadn't noticed until that moment was that the whispers had fallen silent once more. Her nerves frayed at the quiet in her head. It felt unnatural.

"Are you going to kill me or train me?"

Howl stiffened beside her. The cipher crumpled, revealing the weary and worn lord she saw earlier. "I thought I made it quite clear I preferred the latter," said Wallach.

Azzy mulled over what she'd heard in that cell—the measure of Wallach's feelings, what he'd exposed to the Witch, and not her alone.

"Lord Vashon knew we were there," she said. "He looked at us."

The moment still unnerved her, the ghosts of those shrieking whispers lingered, trying to impart their final warnings. She didn't need their insistence to know Vashon was dangerous. That evidence hovered only a few feet away, those beautiful wings dragging in the dirt.

"He likely knew before we saw him," said Wallach. "He knows the signature of my magic. It should have been enough to hide yours. But if you ever see him in Market Row, run the other way."

Azzy wasn't sure of that, but it didn't matter. She studied her master. He let Cherise chew him out for pushing Petyr past his limits. Wallach carried the young man by the time they made it home. There was genuine affection between the lord and his servants, but she didn't have that level of trust with him yet. Which was why, though he'd offered to help, she kept her final revelation to herself. She could not tell Wallach that his apparent rival had her brother, not yet.

"How do we begin?"

"We begin now." Wallach crossed his arms. "Describe to me what happened when you entered Petyr's tunnel."

"The whispers started again," said Azzy.

The lord's brows shot up. "Whispers? A voice that whispers, such as a familiar?"

Azzy struggled to find the words to describe what she'd never tried to put into words. She reached up to trace the scar on her chest, remembering how clear the whispers were, for the first time in her life.

"They used to be...soft, muddled, like listening to a conversation through a closed door." She closed her eyes, trying to tease the sensation forth. Her mind remained quiet, but she'd lived with the whispers for as long as she could remember. "They told me things, the outcomes of my choices, and—sometimes they were so sharp, like cut glass, when danger was close enough to touch."

"Was this your voice?"

"No," said Azzy.

She once thought so; that it was some innate instinct that guided her. That is until her encounter with Windham in the tunnels Beneath. Sometimes she still dreamed of the sobbing woman, begging for mercy in the dark.

"Maybe they're ghosts."

"Do you remember your first spell?" Wallach asked.

Azzy frowned, her eyes still closed as she strained. Had she ever created a spell? It was tempting to say Morglint's tent, where she'd pulled the girl, a stranger, through the fever. She hissed a breath through her teeth, her fingertips still pressed to her scar. Was that her first? It was the first she could remember, a mental tipping point before the change came thick and fast and consumed the life she knew.

She could almost feel the blood on her fingers, warm against the frigid air. The wolf hovered over her as she knelt in the snow beside the dead Winnowrook, and she sank into the moment, how she moved without thinking, smearing her blood across his snout. Her words tumbled free as she described her first encounter with the wolf, her wolf.

"I don't know what I did," she finished.

Wallach frowned as he tugged on his beard. "You tethered him," he said, his voice soft. "It's a complex piece of magic that should be impossible without any knowledge of how it works and doesn't make sense with these whispers you describe." He circled around his desk, jotting down notes on a scrap of paper. "Were there any other incidents like this one?"

Azzy swallowed. How many had she dismissed throughout her life as nothing more than instinct? When she tried to remember, she could feel the holes in her memory, gaps where her mother extracted those fluid events she intended to return. It was Azzy's fault those holes remained. What had she forgotten? Instead, she told Wallach what happened to her once she followed Armin to the Above. His pen paused when she told him about the necklace she wove for Kai. She watched his incredulity build when she described how she healed her chest wound from the Snatcher's hook.

Silence reigned. Wallach set the pen down and tore the paper to shreds. She drew closer to the desk, watching as he lit a match to burn the strips of paper to ash. His gloved hands tapped the varnished top of his desk as he watched the dissipating smoke. The silence stretched until Azzy thought she might scream from the weight of it.

"Azure, do you see anyone else in this office?"

She reeled, thrown by his question. "My lord?"

"Please answer the question," said Wallach, his voice tight.

"There is just you, me, Howl, and Petyr," said Azzy, the latter dozing fitfully on the settee. "Who else would be here?" Did he mean the Maven? Did he also sense her? Why did he act as if he hadn't?

Wallach looked up at her, poised to answer. She saw the moment his intentions slipped. He shook his head. "Sorry, another time," he mumbled. He clasped his hands in front of him. "You shouldn't exist."

Her mouth was too dry. Protests scraped against the roof of her mouth. "Why?"

"Magic is wondrous and flexible, but it's not a catch-all," said Wallach. "Even I have limitations to what I can do. What you described, I could do, but only if I borrowed the magic from another. The use would be limited, and both of us would pay for the exchange.

"Pay?" She'd seen the evident loss for Petyr. Wallach carefully pulled his glove down, revealing the dark bruising around the mouth in his palm. "I don't understand."

She'd been surrounded by magic her whole life, in the small miracles of the Heap, in the Rot that ate away at their numbers, in the monsters that swarmed the Above and lurked in the Below, but she understood so little of *how* it worked.

"Think of the body as a storage tank for magic. Every person contains magic, to a varying degree. It is the new nature of this world. Once a body tips over a certain holding point, the magic takes hold to kill or to change. That change produces a series of checks and balances of what a body can now do. Whether the change produces a physical alteration, a chemical one, or a mix of both, each body now holds its own currency. All magic comes at a cost, except I can't determine yours," he said. His brow creased as he mulled the situation over. "If it's an instinctual exchange, you might have paid with time."

"Time? As in mortal time? I paid with my life?"

"It's possible," said Wallach. "Though it still doesn't explain what you've managed to do. Or with what Cherise told me of your encounter with Lord Brusker." He rubbed his thumb along the seam of his mouth. "I'll need a demonstration to get a proper signature."

"I don't know if I can," said Azzy. The prick of shame burned the back of her throat. "I haven't been able to summon the whispers once since I arrived. They came unbidden when I left."

Wallach rolled his shoulders. "That is of no consequence, Azure. You lived this way for years. Control won't happen overnight, especially when you've only used it as a tool for survival. But that does give us a starting point," he said.

"It does?" Her hand pressed down against her scar.

"You seem to access your magic in a state of heightened adrenaline. We need to help you access that state of mind when you aren't in danger."

It sounded simple, but Azzy chafed at the time it might take. She couldn't shake the sense her time was rapidly slipping through her fingers.

Wallach dismissed her as soon as her stomach growled for food. They'd gotten no further than a few attempts at controlled breathing before the long morning caught up with her. She left for the servant's dining room close to midday, accompanied by her constant shadow as she fell into a chair.

Cherise set bowls of stew in front of her and the boy. "Is Petyr still resting?"

"He was when I left," said Azzy. He hadn't twitched once while she and Wallach spoke.

The head servant sighed. "I'll bring him a bowl later." She left the room, presumably to remind the others to eat.

Azzy was too hungry to wait on the others. She tucked into her food until the Maven sauntered into the room. Drawing a chair directly across from Azzy, she leaned forward on the table, chin in her hands as she stared with rapt fascination.

"Did you have an adventure this morning, little Azure?"

Azure stilled, her spoon halfway to her mouth. Aside from her singular introduction, the Maven hadn't spoken to her directly since that initial meal.

"You could call it that," she said, watching the Maven's face to see if she'd catch another glimpse of what lay beneath. The whispers remained silent, but the woman's presence set her teeth on edge.

The Maven leered at her. "Now you're to be Wallach's little pet project," she purred. She reached out, her fingers dancing across the table towards Azzy. Howl leapt to his feet with a snap of teeth. The Maven pursed her lips.

"Fierce little beast," she said with a pout. She was still glancing at Howl when her visage shifted, a second pair of eyes staring directly at Azzy. Howl hissed.

"Tick-tock," said the Maven. Azzy locked her knees to keep from jumping up and bolting out of the room. If fear was a trigger for the whispers, where were they now?

That terrible visage vanished as Cherise bustled into the room, dragging Lennon and Morglint behind her. "Sit, sit, I'll get your bowls."

"Hello, Azzy," said Morglint, "didn't see you this morning."

"I was helping Lord Wallach with something," she said, unable to look away from the Maven.

Lennon frowned at the empty seat. "Where's Petyr?"

"He's resting," answered Cherise. She balanced three bowls of stew as she entered.

"Can they even see you?" Azzy addressed the Maven directly, determined to prove something even if she looked like a fool to the others.

The Maven drew back, a hand on her chest. "How could you say such a thing, Azure?" She smiled at Cherise. "The stew smells delicious."

Cherise set the third bowl in front of the Maven and paused. Her expression was concealed by the haze of smoke. "I need to grab mine from the kitchen."

Lifting a spoonful to her mouth, the Maven took a bite. "Mmm, delicious. A meal one could *yearn* for."

Azzy's appetite evaporated. The play on words was deliberate, it had to be. And while Cherise placed the third bowl before her, the others didn't acknowledge the Maven. Or that Azzy spoke to her. The chair rocked as she stood too quickly. "I'm finished. Please thank Cherise for me," she said. Howl left with her, his own meal unfinished. The Maven didn't move from her spot, a small smile playing on her lips as she stirred her bowl of stew.

The hallway lights flared too bright. Azzy stopped to catch her breath, her pulse pounding in her ears. The whispers remained quiet, but she wasn't sure she could trust the silence. Howl whimpered beside her. She reached for him, tucking him against her shoulder feeling him tremble beneath her touch.

"I know. You saw her, too," she whispered. "But they don't."

The boy with wings followed Lord Vashon, his movements jerky and forced, tethered by invisible strings. Azzy wove through the market crowd in their wake, following the trail of feathers that wept from her brother's wings. The other denizens shied away from lord and servant, the stamp of fear on each of them. The scene shifted as they walked until Azzy found herself in the same opulent house from before. Lord Vashon's house, she realized, though she had not seen a clear path to the estate. Her brother was alone now, entering the room with the pit. Azzy hesitated at the threshold. A breeze gusted up from the hole like a giant's foul breath. She took a step forward, mesmerized, the pull tugged at her bones. Her toes curled at the edge, the yawning blackness drawing her in as she stared into the abyss.

*Armin stood beside her. "**Rise**."*

Deep within the pit, they gained another inch.

Azzy woke with a scream. Howl clapped his hand over her mouth, his expression stark. She shook violently, unable to banish the dream from her mind. It wasn't what she saw, but what she felt— the sense of longing, of a hunger, endless and insatiable, that filled her with vicious dread. Her cry broke off with a sob.

Howl moved his hand away, curling against her side as Azzy cried until her eyes could give no more. She reached for the feather, tucked beneath her pillow for safekeeping, and found nothing. It had evaporated, like the rest; she mourned the loss of that small connection to her brother as another tremor shook the house.

7

AZURE

"Again."

Azzy ducked to the left, forcing her exhausted limbs into motion. A faint crackle dusted her right arm. She sucked in a breath as she spun away, narrowly missing the gloved hands that reached for her. Her pulse throbbed in her ears and was drowned out by her gasps for air, her lungs working like a bellow. Her adrenaline was high and had been for most of the morning, but there was nary a whisper in her mind.

Her distracted thoughts cost her. She missed the crackle in front of her until she slammed into Petyr.

"Goodness, Azzy, I heard something snap." He gripped her shoulders with care as he peered with concern into her face. He winced. "Your nose is bleeding."

"I can fix it," she mumbled. She had before, but her head buzzed and spun. Her nose throbbed in time to her pulse, a fixed point of pain on her face. "It's not that bad."

"That doesn't mean you have to suffer through it," said Petyr. "Sir—"

She grabbed his arm. "I need to do this," she said.

"Exhaustion will do nothing for you," said Wallach. He appeared at her side, gently tilting her head to get a better look at her face. "Broken. Have Cherise set it. We will resume our session tomorrow."

Frustration bit at her. Azzy was exhausted, she had been exhausted for days, all for naught. Wallach employed several methods, trying to help Azzy evoke the state of mind he deemed necessary to access the whispers. They had gone through tactics of controlled breathing, meditation, physical exertion, and now he'd brought Petyr in to help create an imposed threat. It was a good tactic. Azzy didn't think the lanky youth could hurt her, but it was easy to trick the mind into thinking he was a danger when he burst out of thin air to grab her.

They'd been at this strategy for two days, but Azzy feared it was another failure. "Why can't I do this?"

"Consider it a muscle you've never used," said Wallach. She startled. Azzy thought Wallach had already left them. She chanced a glance at his face. He exuded nothing but warmth, his patience seemed infinite.

"It was never this hard," said Azzy. On the few occasions she tried to reach for the whispers, they'd come readily, their presence constant. The longer she stayed here, the more she felt like they had abandoned her.

Wallach folded his arms. "You've never asked your body to perform under its own limitations before. You simply let the magic work through you, taking whatever it pleased. A body cannot operate like that forever."

"What happens to those that do?" She needed to know this, a mental reprimand to remind her that her efforts here were necessary to reach her goals.

His expression turned sober. "Without limitations, a vessel eventually wears out," said Wallach. "Please, Azzy, let Cherise see to your wound. Let your body recover before we push it again."

He so rarely called her 'Azzy' that the gentle familiarity in his tone stopped her in her tracks, allowing Petyr the opportunity to sweep her out of Wallach's study.

Cherise was alone when they reached the servant's dining room, her smoke shimmering yellow at the sight of Azzy's face. "This is rich. Is his goal to train you with a boot to the face?"

"It was an accident," said Azzy, searching for Howl. "Where is he?"

She'd left Howl with Cherise. He'd come to her initial sessions with Wallach until Petyr began to chase her. Deciding not to risk Howl misunderstanding the situation, she'd asked Cherise to occupy him, an arrangement the boy appeared to tolerate, to a point.

"He got spooked. Ran to the garden," said Cherise. Azzy pursed her lips. Spooked meant the Maven was lurking about.

Petyr strong-armed her into a chair before she could leave, muttering darkly as Cherise swabbed the drying blood under Azzy's nose.

She winced as Cherise gently prodded her injury.

"Not quite broken, but definitely wrenched," said the lady of smoke. "This will hurt." Azzy held her breath as Cherise crunched something in the bridge of her nose that made her eyes water.

"Shouldn't be too crooked, now, long as you don't actually break it," said Cherise. "You should eat something."

Azzy's stomach rolled. "I'm going to make sure Howl's okay."

Cherise sighed. "At least sit until your head stops spinning." Azzy wondered how she knew. The head servant whirled on Petyr. "You. Sit. Eat."

"Yes, ma'am," he said, sheepish. Petyr slumped in the chair beside Azzy, letting his head fall back. He began to blur faintly at the edges.

"Does it take a conscious effort to keep from doing that?"

"Constant," said Petyr. "Worse when I was younger."

No wonder he looked so tired all the time. The sleepless smudges beneath his eyes appeared to be permanent fixtures. "Did Lord Wallach train you as well?"

"Yes," he turned to look at her. "He saved my life."

"What happened?"

"I trapped myself in the null space."

She shuddered at the idea, trying to imagine what it must have been like, alone in that dark crackling space. "How did he get you out?" From what she'd seen, he couldn't borrow the ability from Petyr without the physical contact.

Petyr gave her a wan smile. "The Lord of Seven Smiles is full of tricks."

Two steaming plates of vegetable mash slid in front of them, her portion considerably smaller since Cherise noticed that years of lean meals meant Azzy could only consume so much food at a time. The smell teased her aching nose, eliciting a growl from her stomach. She was hungrier than she thought.

"Eat," said Cherise, "Then you can bring a plate to Howl."

Azzy smiled around her mouthful. The head servant was short with them when she was irritated, bullying the entire household day in and day out to ensure they were properly fed and rested. "When you're finished, Petyr, fetch Lennon for me. He wouldn't eat for days if we let him."

"He could put down roots in the garden," said Petyr.

"Hush your tongue," said Cherise, but there was a glint of humor in her visible eyes. "Morglint would likely prune him."

Azzy nibbled on her food, soaking in their camaraderie. It soothed the constant ache in her chest that she couldn't be with her family like this. Wallach's servants were a family themselves, one that had absorbed her, Howl, and even Morglint with little fuss. The relationship between the servants and their master told Azzy more about his character than any of her whispers. The only outlier in the household was the Maven.

"No Maven today?" Her tone nonchalant as she watched Petyr and Cherise's reaction.

Petyr went still, his gaze unfocused. "Not today."

It hovered in the air between them, the fleeting reality of the Maven. The knowledge was viscous, thickening the air until it filled her lungs, a drowning pressure she fought to breathe though. The moment snapped, and the knowledge of the Maven evaporated like morning fog.

"Did you want more, Azzy?" Cherise nudged her empty plate.

"No, I'm full, thank you," she said. She wanted to push to see how deep the manipulation ran, but she didn't trust the Maven not to lash out. Dread suffused her at seeing that hidden face again. It vindicated her that Howl wasn't affected like the others, though she didn't know why.

He paced at the edge of the garden, treading so close to the way the rampant foliage bristled with each pass. Morglint remained nearby, feigning busy work to keep an eye on him. Neither he nor Azzy thought Howl would risk breaching the wall, but Cherise warned them one of his kind would be snapped up in a blink.

Azzy stopped beside Morglint, watching Howl as he prowled back and forth. "How is he?" The boy hadn't noticed her entrance, his actions mindless, punctuated by short snarling whines where he jerked his head to the side. Her proximity continued to have a calming effect on him, but she had noticed it lessened a little each day.

"He hasn't stopped pacing since he rushed in here," said Morglint. "Ran in like the devil himself was on his tail."

Azzy bit the inside of her cheek. She knew better now than to try and broach the subject of the Maven with Morglint. There was another subject she'd kept from him too, because she couldn't bring herself to disturb the peace he'd found here. She kept the apparent relationship between her brother and Lord Vashon from him as well. It wasn't important, not when he could do nothing.

"Azzy, he can't continue on like this," said Morglint. "I've seen the two-kind get like this. He's too young to be collared so long."

"They said it was a law to be collared in the city," said Azzy. The muscles of her jaw clenched, a helpless sort of anger burning in her gut. "Why is it a law?"

Morglint shook his head. "It's been a law for as long as I can remember. Free two-kind are not welcome in the city, but the reasons why are not privy to those below a certain rank and station."

Laws and reasons privy to the Lords who created them. Azzy bit her lip. She'd come to rely on what Morglint knew of the city to fill some of the gaps in her pitifully scant knowledge "I would remove that collar if I could."

"It's connected to Wallach. You could kill him, or both," said Morglint. "That wasn't fair of me, planting that idea in your head."

"Why hasn't Wallach taken him out of the city?" Every time she broached the subject, Wallach evaded it. She didn't understand.

Morglint sighed. "Lord Wallach is not what I expected Azzy, but he isn't a perfect benevolent lord. None of them are. He may have a history with the two-kind or a blind spot for them."

"That doesn't excuse it," she snapped. Or excuse why she let Wallach evade each challenge. She knew she owed the Lord of Seven Smiles for training her, for keeping her safe, and providing her a haven while she figured herself out, but had she let those factors cloud her judgment when it pertained to Howl?

"Why take him in at all? Was it merely to prove a point?"

"Azzy..." Morglint trailed off, staring down at his green-stained hands. "Benign neglect is a far better fate than that boy could hope for in Avergard. At least he has you."

A useless consolation, she thought. Howl suddenly dropped to his knees, rocking back and forth with his head in his hands. Her breath caught as the boy began to claw at his own face. She cried out, rushing to his side and gripped his wrists.

She froze as the whispers flickered to life. Howl's wild gaze shot up and locked onto her. The world slowed to a crawl.

The pulse and grind of the market murmured in her ear, just beyond the wall. Tendrils and leaves tickled against her back, the sweet scent of living green caressing her senses. The glare of the sun mellowed in the shade of so much green. Azzy stared into Howl's eyes and watched his mind fracture, piece by piece. Her breath shuddered as the whispers twined through her mind, softy and insistent. Her thumb brushed the bracelet on his wrist, the more merciful cage. Merciful? A less brutal construction than the Snatcher's collars, but far more insidious; it was slowly killing him. His agony beat against her. How could she have let him exist like this? How could she have done nothing?

"I'm so sorry," she whispered. She finally broke his gaze, tracing those familiar ugly runes with her forefinger. She knew why she had done nothing. Fear threaded through the whispers, a trap of uncertainty, confusion, and loss. She sacrificed so much to reach this place, left her loved ones behind with no regard for her own life, and now, at the first taste of safety and stability, her fears and regrets pinned her in place as self-induced mental shackles. Had she silenced the whispers herself out of selfish ignorance? Or was Howl's need great enough to break through whatever it was that silenced them?

Azzy closed her eyes, listening to those internal voices. She could see what had to be done, she had only to reach for it. In exchange for her life? Her ignorance of the cost had been a blessing. She hesitated, hovering on the edge of indecision. Howl whimpered, a soft broken sound. The memory of Kai's burning golden eyes, wide with horror, flashed through her mind. Her last sight of him, reaching for her, as the Snatcher's hook pulled her away. She'd failed him in so many ways.

Her fingertips grew hot as she traced the runes in reverse; the whispers grew in volume, drowning out Morglint's yell as Azzy followed their bidding. Smooth metal shifted beneath her touch. The magic winked out; Howl dropped on all fours as the bracelet fell to the ground with a clink, wobbling on the stones.

Howl's whiskers twitched forward as he padded around her in a circle, the tufts of his pointed ears flicking back and forth. His golden-brown eyes were unchanged except for the slit pupils, contracting in the sunlight.

Azzy's eyes rolled up in her head. She felt the world tilt, senseless if she hit the ground or not. She recognized the foul wind that stroked her bare skin. The pit breathed nearby. *Azure*, they whispered her name.

"Azzy!" The scent of bitter greens and damp earth teased her nose. She coughed, finally able to focus on the worried face of Morglint. Another face, furred and pointed, filled her vision as Howl nosed her cheek.

"Look at you. Not what I expected at all," Azzy murmured. She reached up to stroke his fur, somehow both coarse and soft, a grayish brown, mottled with black stripes and spots. The whispers shrieked and abruptly fell silent. Azzy turned her head to find the Maven watching her within the shadowed recesses of a cluster of trees. Her expression was rapt, the face beneath ravenous.

The wrought iron door slammed open hard enough to crack the glass. Wallach stalked into the garden, wide-eyed and panting.

"Where is she?" He bellowed. Azzy cringed, prepared for his anger, but his tone was panicked. He whirled towards them and froze as Howl dropped into a crouch and unleashed an angry hissing roar. Azzy grabbed Howl by the scruff of his neck, hauling him back as Wallach approached them.

His brows drew together in a tight knot, he said nothing as he looked them over. His gaze locked on something on the ground. Wallach bent down in all his finery and picked the bracelet off the ground, slowly spinning the smooth metal band between his fingers.

Azzy buried her face in Howl's fur; she clung to him, as much to hide as to keep him from attacking. "I'm sor—"

"Don't," said Wallach. He didn't snap at them, but something in his tone worried her. Frowning, he yanked off a glove, passing his bare hand over the metal. "Not a trace," he whispered.

She didn't want to confront him here, not with the Maven watching them so closely. "Did I hurt you?"

"No," said Wallach. "But it didn't feel like the magic broke." His gaze slid to Howl. "He can't stay like this."

"Wait, at least give him time," said Azzy. She could feel the nervous tension in the boy's muscles, quivering beneath her hands. "Can we give him the run of the garden?"

"No one can see him from the street," said Morglint.

Wallach huffed. "The two-kind are feral, Azure," he said. "He can't even speak."

"He understands every word you've said," she said. "They aren't animals."

The lord raised a brow at her. "I admit, I've never seen a lynx among their kind." He tucked the smooth bracelet into his pocket. "One hour. Then bring him to my study." His expression was distant as he left. When Azzy glanced toward the shadowy copse of trees, the Maven had vanished.

She released a shaky breath. The magic had left her drained before, but not like this. Her limbs were watery and weak. She couldn't stand if she tried. When she closed her eyes, she could feel the dank breath of the pit.

"Azzy?" Morglint's concern pulled her away from the edge.

"Go, run," she told Howl. The boy didn't need any more of an invitation, tossing his head as he pranced around the garden.

"I've never seen you faint before," said Morglint, "even after you healed yourself."

"Maybe I'm discovering my limitations," said Azzy. The sight of Howl frolicking in the sun soothed her shivers. The Maven made her feel like an insect pinned under glass. She let her body fall back against the wall that enclosed the garden from the rest of the world. A whisper slid through the cool, cunning silence in her mind, hot and incessant like a drop of fresh blood from an open wound. It was the first time she sensed the distinction as if there was a barrier squatting in her mind. In the absence of that internal sound, a high-pitched tone buzzed between her ears. The whisper threaded through it like a burning wire, connecting straight to her nerves. Heat flushed through her limbs, ending with a tug from the very bottom of her gut, an insistent pull outward and beyond. *To where, to where?* Azzy prodded the streak of heat in her mind, only to find it swallowed up by that chill block of silence.

Reluctance dogged her steps as she led the lynx that was Howl to Wallach's office. She had knelt before him minutes ago, trying to convey what would happen next. The words were inadequate and ashen on her tongue. Part of her yearned to take the boy and find a way over the wall. Azzy quashed the idea before it could take root. Avergard was not like the wilds, the monsters here possessed a darker, more subtle menace, one born of privilege and power she had no defense against. Or did she?

The seed of an idea tumbled over in her mind, taking root. Perhaps the sudden silence of her inner whispers went beyond her first taste of safety and the toll of exhaustion. Her gaze wandered as they walked, watching, waiting for the telltale flash of movement at the corner of her eye. How often had she missed the Maven watching her? What was more troublesome, was why hadn't she pressed anyone about the Maven's presence? A nudge here, a nudge there, but she never pushed further. The more Azzy dug and picked at the idea, the more she realized her own reactions were abnormal. Her body reacted to the Maven's presence when her whispers did not. Did she rely on them so heavily to ignore actual innate instinct? Azzy hadn't survived this long through stupidity.

A small ball of nervous energy squeezed at her throat. Her fingers threaded through the thick fur between Howl's shoulder blades, comforted by the shifting of muscles beneath the skin, the calm, steady gait beside her. She hated forcing him back into a shape not of his choosing. A rumble rose from his chest, through her fingertips. He leaned into her legs, the change in his weight and proportions knocking her off balance. She skidded sideways and released him to catch herself on the ground, face to face with Howl's whiskered muzzle. Her chest tightened at the intensity in his golden-brown gaze as the fur and whiskers rippled and receded, revealing Howl's freckled nose. He crouched in front of her, human and naked, the transition, so smooth and seamless she couldn't hide her shock.

He reached down to grip her wrists, pulling her hands up to frame his face. "Thank you," he whispered, his voice soft and hoarse from long disuse.

Azzy gasped. To their left, in the shadows between the wall lamps, the wall rippled. Howl's grip on her wrists tightened as he scowled at the yawning hole that appeared. Petyr stepped forward, shrugging out of his coat to drape it across Howl's naked back, his pale face tight. He kept a gloved hand on the boy's shoulder, his expression inscrutable as he stared down at Azzy.

"Don't say a word to Wallach," said Petyr.

Azzy gaped at him. "Why not?"

"Not you," said Petyr. The knuckles gripping Howl's shoulder tightened. "Him."

She stared at him, unable to understand the emotion in his expression. "For what purpose?"

Petyr hesitated. Guilt, was that it? Yes, Petyr looked guilty. He looked away from her, staring at a blank spot on the wall. "Our lord is a great man. He saved each of us from a terrible fate, but he's not perfect, Azzy," said Petyr. He sucked in a breath. Weary lines etched his face, aging his youthful features. "He doesn't understand the two-kind. To be honest, I don't either. I've never heard one speak before."

Howl's shoulders hunched at Petyr's words.

"That is a ridiculous excuse. How can he understand if he refuses to learn?" Azzy gently dislodged herself from Howl's hold. "Two bodies that occupy the same space, one and the same, but they can still talk."

Howl's lips parted.

Petyr gaped at her. "What do you mean *two?*"

Azzy frowned. "I'm not sure I can explain it clearer than that," she said. "It's as if they stand on top of one another, sharing the same heart, mind, and body, though I've never seen such a smooth change."

Howl's eyes widened. "You saw another like me?"

A pang shot through her chest. "Yes. A wolf." She swallowed hard, forcing herself to remember her interactions with the two-kind that haunted her dreams. "Though it seemed like he couldn't change without help."

The boy looked away from her. The muscles of his jaw flexed. "The longer we wear one skin, the harder it is to move between them, and we lose our thoughts." It was the longest sentence he had spoken, his raspy voice laced with an old anger, the sort inherited from others. Azzy knew it well, living in a population that carried anger and heartache through generations of misery. She touched the scar on her chest, the ache of her longing a palpable pulse through the healed-over wound.

Petyr appeared faintly horrified. "The collars break their minds?" It wasn't truly a question but an affirmation. The truth of it settled like barbs in Azzy's skin. Her stomach rolled.

"Wouldn't living in a cage formed of your own mind and body, day in and day out, drive you mad?" She whispered the words. Howl closed his eyes, leaning forward until his forward touched her shoulder. The tension went out of him at the contact. Petyr watched them both in silence, one that stretched for several minutes until Azzy was sure Wallach himself would come looking for them.

"You're right. Wallach shouldn't collar the boy," said Petyr. There was a ghost of anger in his expression. She wondered who he inherited it from.

This resolution was easier said than done. Petyr trailed them to Wallach's study, a nervous specter at their back, but he stayed with them. His long coat hung off Howl's slim frame, down to the boy's knees. Howl pressed so hard to Azzy's side that it was difficult to walk, her footsteps even more reluctant from the tremble in his limbs, but the door was open for them when they arrived. Wallach sat behind his desk, reading through a pile of papers when they entered. The lord of Avergard glanced up and froze.

It was clear from the startled expression on Wallach's face he did not expect a human Howl. His gaze shifted to Azzy. "Did you do this?"

How could she convince him? She shook her head, trying to piece her words together. "He did it."

His brows raised. "He shifted on his own?" The incredulity in his voice sounded far more condescending this time. A different sort than when Azzy told him she came from Below. "Azzy, I understand you have a calming effect on the boy, but the two-kind are simple-minded animals—"

"You're wrong." Her words ended with an abrupt silence. Wallach's mouth twitched, caught between annoyance and amusement. She'd thought him different from the other 'gentlemen' and elders she knew, but there was arrogance in him too, hidden beneath the veneer of the benevolent lord. Somehow, in the days she'd spent here, she forgot that Wallach didn't simply shelter her in his house. He bought her from the Snatchers. She couldn't forget Wallach owned her, that everyone in his household was ultimately a possession, no matter how kind he had been to her 'til now.

"Young Azure, I know you mean well, but I have had many dealings with the two-kind," he said, his gaze flicking over Howl.

"Free?"

Wallach tripped over his own words at the soft rasp of a question. His gaze flickered back to Howl, who straightened beside Azzy.

"C-collared," said Wallach. "The collar keeps them under control."

"It maddens them," said Azzy.

Wallach stood, a peculiar expression on his face as he crossed the room to them. He peered down at the two of them as he began to peel off the glove of his left hand, one Azzy had not seen him use before. "May I?"

Howl nodded, though he reached down and took hold of Azzy's hand in a painfully tight grip. She didn't say a word, as fascinated by another glimpse of Wallach in action as she was worried for the boy. The mouth on this hand appeared identical to the one of his right with the subtle exception of one unnerving feature, a forked tongue that flicked the air in a serpentine fashion as Wallach's palm hovered inches above Howl's skin.

The lord made a soft noise of surprise as he pulled back, hastily donning his glove once again. "It is illegal for the two-kind to go without a collar," said Wallach, his expression shuttered.

"You can't," whispered Azzy.

Petyr surged forward. "My lord, please—"

Wallach held up a hand to silence them. "Be that as it may, I need to further examine this situation. Petyr, take Howl to Lennon. Tell him we need a convincing imitation."

Petyr bowed. "Yes, my lord." He gave them an encouraging nod as he offered a hand to the boy. "Trust us," he said.

The pit of her stomach soured. It didn't matter if she trusted Wallach or not. Did a 'convincing imitation' mean Howl would be free from a real collar? For how long? Why would Wallach take such a risk for them? There was no choice, not really, but she feigned a smile for Howl, though it was clear he saw straight through it. He took Petyr's hand, his gaze lingering on Azzy as they left. Wallach sighed and stared down at his gloved hands.

"Tell me what you're thinking, Azzy," said Wallach.

"I find it curious you would ask," said Azzy, her words close enough to the truth to ring sincere.

Wallach huffed through his nose. "Spoken like one who's survived on their diplomatic wit."

A muscle in her jaw twitched. From the corner of her eye, she saw a flash of rustled skirts and dark hair. The Maven was watching her again. *Why now? What was she waiting for?*

"I feel I am failing you, Azzy," said Wallach, disrupting her train of thought.

She frowned at him, thrown by his change in temperament. "I don't understand. You told me this would take time."

"I caught a flicker of it, you know," said Wallach, his stare penetrating as he focused on her face. "Tangled in Howl's essence. Most would have missed it, so subtle and slight, like a fading memory."

"I-I'm sorry?" There was an ominous tone to his voice that made her body react despite the deadened lull in her head.

"Your magic, your influence was there, but faint, except no, I don't think that's it," said Wallach. "It will take you time to master, but it's almost as if your magic is muffled. As if I can't quite reach it."

He took a step forward, grabbing her chin when she began to retreat. His thumb pressed against her bottom lip, a hold not so much possessive as carelessly forceful. His manner was business-like curiosity as he examined every inch of her face, searching for something. She breathed in the scent of leather and ink, her pulse ramping up as their gazes connected. An ugly buzz filled her head. Azzy whimpered. Wallach abruptly let her go.

"I'm sorry," said Wallach, "that was not meant to hurt you." His brow creased. "You shouldn't have felt that at all."

With a mouth dry as parchment, Azzy tried to lick her lips as she cast about for the Maven, but if she was still in the room, she was beyond Azzy's perception. That possibility made her hesitate before she finally asked the question that had been niggling at her thoughts. "Is it possible there is something else at work here?"

Wallach stroked his beard. "Exhaustion, perhaps. Your body endured a great deal of strain for a prolonged period, which could be why your training has faltered thus far."

Another failure to breach the truth, and it vexed her. She itched to speak about the Maven's possible interference, but found the words stuck in her throat. Azzy looked past Wallach's shoulder to see the Maven perched on his desk, a hovering carrion feeder swathed in dingy taffeta and moth-eaten silk. She lifted a finger to her lips, the nail longer and blackened, as a wicked light danced in her eyes.

"I'll speak to Cherise about giving you an aide to sleep. Maybe give you an extra day to rest." Wallach turned to his desk, oblivious of the ghoulish woman perched there, even as he moved things around her. "About Howl."

Azzy swallowed, forcing herself to focus on Wallach's words as the Maven leered. "What will Lennon do to him?"

"It's illegal for the two-kind to go uncollared in Avergard. So, we must fool the eye," said Wallach. "He can't be the lynx anywhere but the garden, Azzy. I can't protect him outside this estate."

"Yes, master," she said. Wallach flinched back as if she had slapped him.

"Don't call me that," he snapped.

She froze, shocked by the vehemence in his voice. It was true that while Azzy thought of him as her master and the master of the other servants, they never once called him such. The Maven cackled from her perch.

"I'm sorry, my lord," she said.

Wallach tugged on his cuffs. "As am I," he said, his tone still brusque. "You are dismissed." Azzy didn't need the encouragement to leave, but she still hovered at the door, glancing back at Wallach's troubled expression as the Maven rocked back and forth on her heels on top of his desk, like his own personal demon.

8

AZURE

Her food had congealed to a wet, cold lump. Azzy moved it across her plate with her fork as the other servants ate and talked. Morglint, Cherise, Petyr, even Lennon, with whom she had scarce interaction sent more than one worried glance in her direction. She recognized the look on their faces and wondered to herself how and when they started to consider her part of their family.

Howl sat beside her, a rune etched bracelet identical to the one he wore before circled his wrist, but the metal was different. Azzy couldn't find the adequate words to describe it, except that the metal felt clean. His mood was somber to match hers, but he engaged the others. Now that Petyr knew he could speak, he pulled him into the conversation whenever possible, despite the boy's often monosyllabic answers. They left Azzy alone, sensing her disquiet even if they didn't understand the cause. She was grateful for the respite, her mind turning over her last sight of the Maven.

There was one good thing about this evening's meal; the Maven wasn't here. Azzy didn't know the logistics of how the Maven worked, and every time she tried to focus on it, her mind slid away without her realizing it until hours later. Was this how the other's perceived, or failed to perceive the Maven? The strange female seemed to evade even Wallach's alternate senses. How could she do that? Why could Azzy sense her at all? The headache from trying to decipher the mystery of the Maven wasn't worth it, yet, so her mind turned to another puzzle.

"Why does he bother training us at all?"

The others paused in conversation.

"Azzy?" Cherise loomed beside her, her smoke almost translucent today, revealing her smooth angular features, only slightly marred by the scar that slashed across her face. "What do you mean, love?"

"Why train us? Why ask us our opinion of anything?" She set the fork down harder than she meant to, the metal ringing in the quiet. She put herself in this situation. Followed the lead of the whispering voices in her head to be purchased by Wallach, but without their influence, her mind turned in circles around itself. It rankled her to be bought when she had worked so hard to maintain her autonomy in the Heap. She'd taken risks to keep Brixby's supplies stocked. She had endured Elder Prast's verbal barbs and the snubs of the neighbors when her mother was taken from their home. Kept her brother's burgeoning magic a secret. Fought monster and man to reach the city. The whole of her journey amounted to being purchased, a necessary evil to gain safe access to Avergard. Or was it necessary?

"Why does Lord Wallach despise the word master?" Azzy's confusion and pain wound into a tight knot in her chest. She was safe here, languishing in this house as she trained and rested; she realized with sudden cold clarity that she'd lost her way.

Morglint reached over and placed his enormous hand over her white-knuckled fingers. The scent of dirt and greenery rose off his skin, Azzy released a shuddering breath. Cherise leaned in, easing Azzy's full plate to the side to set a steaming mug of tea before her.

"He doesn't see us as property," said Cherise.

"Friends then? A family, bought and paid for?" The words were bitter in Azzy's mouth.

"He can only intimidate so many lords into coughing up their property," said Petyr, with a wink and nod to Howl.

"But why? We have no power here—"

"Don't we?" Lennon rapped his knuckles on the table. "Lord Wallach curates his allies with care. We may live as servants in this household, but we were given our freedom long ago. Each of us chose to stay."

"Tch, Lennon," Cherise hissed. "It's too soon."

Lennon waved her off, the bark-like skin of his arm creaking with the motion. "No, this one's like Safiya. Don't you see the intent in her face?"

"I'm not like Safiya," said Azzy. Safiya had power and the knowledge to use it. Azzy couldn't figure herself out.

"Would you stay?" Petyr watched her.

"Stay for what? You've told me nothing," said Azzy.

The room shivered as another tremor rolled beneath their feet. The older servants shared a collective glance.

"Things are stirring in this city," said Cherise. "Our lord is one of the safeguards that keep this city from dissolving into chaos, from without and within."

Azzy's skin prickled. Wallach told her himself he was once Lord Protectorate of the city, though she thought he meant in the past tense. What did that mean at present?

"That seems like a tall order." She hadn't come to Avergard for clandestine operations or world-altering fates. Her reason for being here had become muddled enough within the walls of Wallach's estate. "Why is he so different from the other lords I've seen?"

Lennon sat back, folding his arms in a posture so similar to Wallach, Azzy almost smiled. "Each of us has a past we are working to move on from; Wallach is the same. He doesn't hold himself above others."

Azzy didn't think that was true. Wallach clearly did hold himself above others, but not the same as the other lords. She kept that opinion to herself.

"Some of us would call it atonement," said Cherise, her expression unusually solemn.

She could only imagine what someone like Wallach would have to atone for, what temptations he'd entertained before becoming a benevolent guardian of Avergard. "I'm tired. I would like to go to my room."

Cherise and Lennon frowned at her abrupt change in conversation, but Morglint clambered to his feet. "Howl, I could use your help in the garden."

She hadn't known Morglint much longer than the others, but he remained tuned to her mood from their intense time together. "Thank you," she mouthed to him. Howl would find her later after she had time to clear her head. Azzy made her way upstairs, trying to settle her thoughts when she turned the corner to her room.

The Maven was waiting for her.

Each encounter with the Maven as akin to a first encounter. The memory of her appearance faded between each sighting of her, though Azzy had no trouble recognizing her as if the Maven were an old friend she hadn't seen in years.

Azzy clenched her jaw as she moved closer, unsure what sort of encounter she was walking into. She suddenly regretted letting Morglint lure Howl away. The boy was the only other person in this house that saw the Maven like she did, but she swore he made the disquieting woman nervous. She stopped a few feet away, meeting the Maven's gaze directly. A small defiance that made her head ache as her vision tried to focus on two faces at once. "What do you want?"

"I so love our little chats," said the Maven. She circled in close. Her hand darted out, long black nails snatching a strand of Azzy's hair and sifting it through her fingers. The contact crackled in Azzy's mind. The whispers spat and shrieked, jarring through her bones. Azzy tasted blood as if a knife lanced through the roof of her mouth, but the taste and sensation vanished the moment the Maven moved away.

She sucked in a breath. "What are you?"

The Maven tilted her head. "I think the more pressing question is, what are you, little one?" Another circle around, but she thankfully kept her hands to herself. Azzy fought to keep her calm. How had she ever convinced herself the Maven was harmless?

"I'm human," she said. Far more human than whatever the Maven was. She flinched away when the woman lifted a hand toward her cheek.

"You smell like family," said the Maven, "but you are a fox in the henhouse." A smile spilt her face, a mouthful of sharp white teeth that made Azzy's bowels tighten. "Such a surprise for my dear brothers and sisters when they rise."

Azzy forgot to breathe. Her thoughts shot to Armin, standing over the yawning pit, and of those unseen crawling things that haunted her nightmares. She stared at the Maven, a terrifying theory forming in her mind she didn't dare give shape. A thousand questions rose and died on her lips, fighting the effect the Maven had on her mind as much as her own fear. "What do you want?"

"Wallach can't teach you, you know," said the Maven. "Talented creature that he is, it's like handing a child an explosive. Only a matter of time before it blows up in their face."

The comparison sent another bolt of unease through her. It was as if she were privy to half a conversation, and the more she heard, the more dread pooled in the pit of her stomach. What would the Maven reveal if pressed? "He can't teach me because I haven't been able to summon my magic," said Azzy.

The Maven's lips curled in a smirk, confirming what Azzy already suspected. "But, you already knew that. The way you manipulate the perception of everyone around you—you're smothering it."

"Moi?" The Maven splayed a hand over her chest, her long nails digging into her own skin, leaving bloody gouges. "What an interesting accusation. I wonder, why would I do such a thing?" The Maven tapped her chin. Her nail pierced into her flesh, but the Maven appeared heedless of the wound. Blood spilled down her pallid jaw; the careless violence of it made Azzy's skin crawl.

"Ah," said the Maven, her mouth wide with feigned surprise. "*I* could teach you how to wield this marvelous gift you possess."

"No," Azzy gasped. Fear made her limbs watery. She took a step away from the Maven and found her back against a wall, unsure when she'd become turned around.

"We can start your training now," said the Maven, boxing her in before Azzy could evade her.

A plea to stop strangled in her throat as the Maven pressed her palm to Azzy's forehead. "Tell me, pet, what do those whispering ninnies tell you about me?"

Azzy couldn't draw her breath fast enough to scream. Her knees gave out as the whispers drilled through her, flooding her head with a frenzied cacophony that battered the inside of her skull. Her ears rang and popped in a gush of warmth, the iron tang of blood filling her nose as it dripped down the sides of her neck. It was a thousand times worse than the sobbing shrieks she heard Below, during her encounter with Windham.

Her consciousness slipped as the whispers cascaded in the echo of an achingly familiar voice.

Don't look, my heart, don't look. The hand on her face shifted, cupping her cheek as her mother's voice filled her mind. *Don't look. Don't let him see.* Her words to Azzy, before they dragged her from their home to burn, her last words. Azzy sobbed and sank down, falling through into memory as she lost consciousness.

It wasn't the day her mother burned. The memory wavered around her as if coated in an oily film. Her mother sat on a stool at the table, her arms folded beneath her as she hunched over, staring intently at the large bottle of swirling liquid before her.

The sight of her was a punch to the gut. Her vibrant red hair was pulled back from her face, tamed in a tight braid. Her bared features appeared wan in the flickering lantern light; exhaustion rimmed her eyes. Brixby sat across from her, a wiggling Armin on his lap. Through her own eyes, Azzy knew she was across the room from them, finger painting on scraps of paper with the homemade paints Brixby made for her.

The swirling liquid in the jar fascinated her.

"This is a dangerous gambit, Lia," said Brixby. He smoothed Armin's foppish blonde curls out of the little boy's face.

Her mother's pinched expression grew pained. "They can't ever know where the children came from. They'll destroy them, Oswin." She inhaled a sharp breath through her nose, her mouth set in a stubborn line. "They are my children now. I will protect them."

There was a deep sadness in Brixby's eyes as he looked over at Azzy, painting on the floor. "If Prast ever finds out about the contents of that jar, you'll burn."

Lia's smile was small and sad as she reached across the table to grab Armin's fingers. "Oh my sweet Oswin, one way or another, I will burn."

Her words hurt young Azzy, deep in her chest. She wanted to erase the fear in her mother's face. Take it away, make it go away. Her fingers curved over the paper, twisting into a semblance of a shape. The liquid swirled faster in the bottle, so quickly the glass rocked back and forth.

"Oswin," Lia gasped. Azzy ignored it, concentrating until her mother ripped the paper out from under her hands. She looked up at her mother's face, whiter than bone, and began to cry.

Lia dropped to her knees and pulled Azzy into her arms. It was safe and warm and was what Azzy sought for so long after the endless wandering in the dark. "My sweet girl, my sweet, sweet girl, you must never let them see."

Her temples tickled as her mother tugged the thread of memory from her, but it didn't work, not quite. Buried secret and safe, deep down, so mother would be pleased; Azzy could trick herself to forget.

Brixby watched her from across the room, Armin giggling in his lap, the now empty bottle gently spinning to a stop on the table.

Azzy sat up with a gasp. Somehow, she was in her bed. How long had she been out? Who found her? Had the Maven put her here? Breathing hard, she looked around the room. Howl sat on the floor by the door, eyes wide as he twisted a blood-stained cloth between his hands.

"I couldn't wake you," he whispered. Azzy flopped off the bed and dragged herself over to him, pulling him into a tight hug. She needed the contact as much as he did.

"I'm sorry," she whispered.

"You were on the floor, bloody," he murmured, shaking. She tucked his head to her shoulder, humming the lullabies her own mother used to hum.

The memory circled her thoughts. *What was that?* A faint murmur arose in her mind. Apparently, the Maven loosened the leash on her whispers, allowing a trickle through. Had the Maven planted the memory in her mind? It almost didn't feel real, polluted somehow, but deep down, Azzy knew it was true. She remembered those little bottles of 'memory' her mother left for her, how she felt no pull to drink them down, to reclaim what was taken. If the memory was real, then her mother never took them from her. But what did it mean?

Had she tricked herself into forgetting?

Far more troublesome was the piece that scraped at her nerves. *Where had she been, wandering in the dark?*

Wallach assumed his usual stance in front of her. "Are you certain you wouldn't rather rest another day?" He frowned down at her. "If possible, you appear more exhausted than yesterday."

Azzy bit the inside of her cheek. Petyr hovered nearby, while Howl ran free in the garden. Both had pushed back when she told them she planned to resume training at breakfast, but there was a new sense of urgency in her. She spent the remainder of the night, mired in an odd mix of hope and dread that the Maven would reappear. The tease of memory left her with too many disconcerting questions. The sight of Armin, so young and small, pierced her through the chest, a visceral reminder of her purpose.

"May I see your hand, my lord?" She woke to the whispers muffled but present, curious if the Maven was letting them trickle through or if she had broken through when the Maven forced contact between them. It gave her an inkling of an idea of how she might be able to focus the muted whispers.

Wallach's expression was hesitant, but he offered her a gloved hand, the leather warm and buttery-soft as she slid her fingertips across his palm. The touch sent a ripple through her mind. Azzy closed her eyes, teasing the trickle of whispers, tugging and plucking until bits and pieces began to shake loose.

"This one tastes, the other one takes," she tilted her hand, listening harder. Her free hand lifted, pressing gently against his chest. "this one devours." Her hand drifted lower on his abdomen. Wallach hissed in a breath. "This one shreds."

"Stop," said Wallach, pulling away from her. She opened her eyes to find his pupils blown. "There was something..." A knot of uncertainty drew down his brow. "It's like your shouting from far away." He blinked. "But you did it. What changed?"

How could she begin to explain this to him? Azzy didn't have the chance as the Maven blurred in the corner of her vision. Instead, Azzy smiled. "I woke with an epiphany," she lied.

Wallach seemed puzzled but his expression smoothed as the Maven came up behind him. Azzy wondered how much influence she had over the supposed Guardian of Avergard. "The others told me you safeguard the city," she said.

His expression soured. "Did they, now?"

At his shoulder, the Maven raised a brow. Her smile was all cold cruelty. "Still trying to make up for what you couldn't save, lamb?" She stroked his arm with her black claws. Wallach shuddered.

"That is a simple explanation for a complicated matter," said Wallach. "Avergard is one of the great bastions of civilization, but there are as many threats from outside the gates as there are within."

"What sort of threats?" She wondered about the tremors that shook the house on and off since her arrival.

Wallach pursed his lips. "The lords are a scheming mass, each with their own agenda. Some have higher aspirations than others." His gaze turned distant. "Incidents I once thought unconnected are proving to have deeper connections, and I'm learning certain individuals are capable of far darker deeds than I ever allowed myself to believe."

Azzy stared at him, her thoughts churning. *Don't ask. Don't dig. Don't get involved.* She came to this city to find her brother. To find her guardian. Then she could find Kai. Her list was already insurmountable, yet she agreed to help Safiya. She had agreed to Wallach's training. Every agreement brought her further from her goal. Even now, she couldn't see its end, couldn't see how she would achieve a single item on her list. Why should she add to it now? Why should she care about a city of monsters, full of flesh markets and carnal houses, where violent lords went free with a fee and cast out their scarred victims to the streets? That forced collars on the two-kind to control them and break their minds?

Heat built behind her eyes. How could she not?

"Tell me," said Azzy. The Maven raised a brow at that, an odd expression on her face.

Wallach drew her to his desk, tapping the pile of paper there, maps, and a stack of official-looking documents with so many stamps and seals the faded print was almost illegible.

"A dozen years ago, a group of Snatchers and mercenaries raided a village in the southern region. There are certain bylaws and protections afforded the other settlements, which meant their actions were illegal under Avergard law. However, nothing came to light until several years later."

Azzy peered at the maps, fascinated by the number of villages and settlements she had no idea existed. These were all people? Were they pure human? Or did they use magic? She traced the outline of a walled village with her index finger as Wallach continued.

"The responsible group of Snatchers was ultimately eliminated in an act that should have been filed as righteous retribution," said Wallach. "Instead, it was labeled a massacre, an offense punishable by death because it occurred within the outer boundaries of the city."

The connection clicked. "It was Safiya's village.

"Yes," said Wallach. "Unfortunately, the proof that would have supported a claim for righteous retribution was buried deep in city records. When documentation of the incident came to light, it was dismissed by the same person who lead the tribunal of lords when the charges were presented."

"I don't understand. Was the lord someone you know?"

"You know him too, in passing," said Wallach. "Lord Vashon."

The lord who had her brother. "Do you two have a history?"

"Oh, do they ever," said the Maven with a chuckle.

"You could say that," said Wallach. "We often find ourselves on opposing sides. I thought his interference with Safiya was purely personal until I saw the boy."

Azzy's ears began to ring, a low, ugly tone like the scrape of chains over stone. "The boy?" Her voice was strained. Fear coated her throat and a sizzling sting of bile and ropy saliva suffocated the words in her mouth. She'd held onto this secret, kept it from Wallach because their trust was so fragile and new. The Maven's predatory gaze locked onto her, sensing the secret like a bloody, dark offering.

"The servant he brought to Safiya's cell," said Wallach. "Power rolls off that one. It tastes foul and dangerous."

The lord sighed, bracing himself on the desk. "I thought he brought the boy to taunt me, but I think there is more to it."

"How so?" A confession burned on her tongue. Could she trust Wallach with this? The words were insistent as they were ruinous, and dug like barbs into her skin.

"Vashon needs absolute control. He might have been breaking

the boy in, which gave me an unexpected opportunity to sense his magic," said Wallach.

Dare she tell him with the Maven standing right there? The words continued to drown in her throat, a feat that had nothing to do with the other's presence and everything to do with fear. Wallach was a protector. He was training her, helping her, but what if Wallach considered her brother one of those threats within the city?

"We must find out more about this new servant. Vashon is a curator. He chooses his servants with care."

Odd, how close those same words were to how Lennon and the others described Wallach, with one exception.

"Are we allies, Lord Wallach?"

The lord's brows drew together. "You are sheltered under my roof. You eat at my table. I would consider us allies, Azure."

Behind him, the Maven huffed. "You are a fool, little pet, if you think his allies fare any better than his enemies."

Azzy swallowed. "How do we find out more?"

"*We* do not," said Wallach. "The others will report in as they can. In the meantime, tell me what else you can sense about my magic."

Azzy expected the Maven to trail her from Wallach's office, but once again, she stayed behind, absent from dinner. A thread of anxiety began to knot between her shoulders as she ascended to her room for the night. This time Howl was with her, and she knew when he dropped to a crouch beside her that the Maven waited for them in her room.

The ghoulish woman squatted on the corner of her bed. Howl snarled, the feeling mutual by the sneer on the Maven's face. "Lovely, you've brought the mongrel."

Azzy placed a hand on Howl's shoulder. She didn't like the Maven any better than her young friend, but a morbid curiosity pressed on her. Knowledge was a powerful lure, and the Maven, whatever she was, held a great deal. Knowledge that Azzy needed.

"Why don't you affect him like the others?"

The Maven grinned. "Not like you either."

"You do, to some extent," said Azzy. She could remember her, but there was a sort of influence at work. The admission seemed to please the Maven.

"Yet you recognized it was there," she said. She clicked her teeth at the still growling Howl. "Hush, the adults are talking."

The boy's voice vanished; his fingers scrabbled at his throat. Azzy grabbed his hands before he scratched himself bloody and glared at the Maven. "Let him go."

She flapped her hand at them in a dismissive gesture. "Once the lesson is finished. Or don't you want to know more about the minds of the two-kind? Could be useful."

The nonchalance of her wording gave Azzy pause. Howl stared at the Maven, wide-eyed and furious. "Release him," said Azzy.

"You really are a sap for their kind, little pet," said the Maven. Howl slumped down to the floor, a low rumble in his chest as he rubbed at his throat. "Interesting creatures, the two-kind. Somewhat impervious to mental manipulation and control. Slippery minds you see, two minds separate but not, occupying the same space. Grab one, and the other surges up to take its place."

The Maven's dark gaze held hers, a mysterious smile on her lips. "My siblings would call it an evolutionary balance, resilience, and a counter to the great predators that ravaged this world."

Azzy couldn't look away, pinned by her own curiosity. "Who are you?"

The Maven tapped a long black nail against her lip, the movement drawing attention to the misaligned planes and angles of her face, hinting at the features beneath. Azzy suppressed a shudder. "I suppose you could blame the Gate for their creation as well," she said.

Azzy recognized the line for the distraction it was, but it worked. "You think the same magic that made Winnowrooks and Snatchers made Howl?"

"Such a disparate comparison," mused the Maven. "Does one

really compare to the other? Does a predator compare to being of predatory actions?"

The question had Azzy shaking her head before she stopped, aghast there was something she agreed on with the Maven. "Not all predators look like monsters," she said. The jeweled lords and ladies of Avergard hid their monstrous natures beneath their silken suits, even those who bore more obvious alterations to their bodies had the shield of refinery.

"Ah, do you refer to the illustrious lord of the house?" The Maven chuckled. Azzy frowned. She hadn't thought of Wallach as a predator in any sense. The Maven stopped tapping her lip, her expression distant. "It is not the fault of the Gate. Magic, at its core, is glorious, chaos given form. It created such beautiful beasts for this world, but humans added their own taint to it. It fed on their fears, the secret wicked yearnings, and bloody dark secrets. Absorbed all those twisted thoughts that men harbor and spat out vile lords with pretty faces."

There was a beat of silence, both Azzy and Howl stunned by the Maven's words. The woman's gaze shifted to Azzy, who found it difficult to make eye contact without feeling dizzy.

"It is time for another lesson, pet," said the Maven. Azzy gasped as the woman flashed in front of her. Howl snapped at her, but the Maven ignored him as she pressed two fingers to Azzy's forehead.

A memory rose hard and fast; the same oil-slick feeling as before. On the heels of her fading consciousness, Azzy heard the Maven shriek.

Azzy ran in the dark. Her pace was slowed by the squirming bundle in her arms. Away, away, she had to get away. Her legs ached from the unending run. Sharp unseen rocks dug into the tender underside of her feet. Hunger clawed at her belly. The meager bits of food she'd scavenged had gone to the one she knew as brother. He was so very small, and his cries of hunger were so deafening in the dark. Her legs wobbled beneath her, threatening to buckle beneath their combined weight. But she couldn't stop. She had to get them away, far away from **them.**

She cried out at the sudden intrusion of light. It hurt her eyes after so long spent peering through the pitch black. She fell back to the ground, clutching her brother to her chest. The jostle caused him to wail, the sound high and thin in the close quarters of the underground. She tried to silence him, muffling his cries with her hand, an action that incensed him to a screaming mewl. So consumed by her panic, she didn't see the other, the source of the light, until arms filled her vision and pried her screaming brother from her weak grip.

She yelped, dragging on the arms that took him before the voice, a woman's voice, soothed her fears and panic. "Easy, little one, I won't hurt you, either of you."

A hand, warm and soft, pressed against her cold cheek. She leaned into it. Had she ever felt such warmth? Her eyes finally adjusted enough to peer up at the woman's face. It looked like home.

"Where are your parents?"

Azzy chafed at the inside of her skin, overwhelmed by a raw, ragged sensation, as if a dull blade scraped along her nerves. Her lungs were squeezed, an immense pressure pushed down on her. She glanced down, unable to cry out at the sight of the Maven kneeling on her chest.

"Your little mongrel bit me," the Maven seethed.

"Did you hurt him?"

The Maven snorted. "Hardly. But I strongly suggest you reign him in if you wish for these sessions to continue."

Did she want them to? "Get off me."

"There's the fire," said the Maven. Azzy gasped for air once the boulder of pressure left her chest. Howl was curled up against the wall, glaring at the Maven as his lip curled over bloody teeth. She was spitefully pleased though worried for his safety.

"If he agrees not to bite you, he stays," said Azzy.

"What's the matter, pet? Afraid I'll take advantage?"

Azzy didn't trust the Maven an inch. Her motivations were a mystery, but Azzy couldn't ignore the benefits, if she could call them that. The memories were important, she knew this, though they still confused her.

"He stays," said Azzy. She wondered if she demanded the compromise for his sake or her own.

The pattern of her days began to set. Urgency still spurned her, tempered by exhaustion and the need to learn what her teachers offered.

In the mornings, Azzy trained with Wallach. Though the Maven kept a tight leash on the whispers, the trickle she allowed gave Azzy a focal point for training, learning bits and pieces about what she could do. She worked with Howl and Petyr often, using her perception of their magic to evade physical attacks. In the afternoons, she began to sit with Cherise or Morglint as the two made medicines and tinctures, not only for the household but for the servants of other lords who needed them. The time she spent in their company was pure respite, a glimpse of the family she'd lost when she left the Below.

During these quiet hours, her anxious drive muted by the peace of the garden and Morglint's workroom, she learned more about the others. Cherise and Lennon had been with Wallach the longest. Cherise's past she knew in passing, abused at the hands of Lord Brusker in one of the city's notorious carnal houses. Lennon was bought off the auction block, his gift too obvious and unique to escape the pique of other lords. She listened to his story of the auction with rapt horror, though he assured her it was a better fate than the flesh markets. It was moments like these Azzy couldn't resolve the crueler aspects of Avergard with the wondrous side.

Nights belonged to the Maven. Each night, the walk to her room took longer. The heaviness grew in her legs with each step until she had to drag herself through the door. Howl came with her, though she tried more than once to convince him to go to Morglint. He looked so scared every time, Azzy couldn't help the pinch of guilt for allowing him to accompany her.

The Maven drip-fed her memories, forgotten moments she'd buried deep. She remembered incidents with the neighbors, small, impossible deeds that spooked the others. How her mother pulled the memories of each from them. Each episode was a tantalizing hint that dangled an answer just beyond her reach. No matter how many times the Maven pushed her under, her mind refused to return to the time before her endless run in the dark.

The tenth night, Azzy remembered the time she forced Armin's magic to subside, brought his fever down as her mother and Brixby scrambled to find an herbal remedy. How she looped a string tightly around Armin's finger, connected to her, and promised she would always find him. The memory made her chest ache and she woke with a sob.

"What is the point of this?" Azzy threw up her arm to cover her eyes, unwilling to let the Maven see how the memory affected her.

Her question was met with silence. She thought the Maven had left in her usual abrupt fashion, but when she peered beneath her arm, the Maven was still there her gaze remote. There was a somber expression on her face, her body quiet to the point Azzy could see the other face hovering beneath. The face stirred a more recent memory of something she hadn't quite seen, or thought she hadn't quite seen, in the yawning mouth of the pit.

"You're trapping me in this house," Azzy whispered.

"Yes," said the Maven, "and no."

"You know what's in that pit," said Azzy. She didn't clarify. The Maven didn't ask her to.

"You must train—"

"You told me Wallach could not teach me. You stifled my magic so he couldn't taste it."

"He can't know, not yet. But his training has a use, conditioning your body while I tap your mind."

"Why? What is the point of these little sessions?" Azzy sat up. Anger hummed beneath her skin. "I've been here for weeks, no closer to my family. Safiya's trial is coming. And my brother—" Her voice broke.

A tremor shook the room. They came with increasing frequency over the past few days, but like the Maven, it was a topic the others sought to avoid, though she often caught them sharing a glance if a tremor happened during a meal.

"Your mind is like a child's playroom," said the Maven, "a child who has buried pieces of gold beneath piles of trash. You must unearth those pieces. You must learn about yourself, as Wallach teaches you the finer points of control."

The Maven sighed, pinching the bridge of her nose with her knuckles, a gesture oddly human compared to her earlier macabre actions. "This city is a massive chessboard, pet. I've been moving the pieces into play for a long time."

Azzy didn't like the idea of being the Maven's pawn. "What is your checkmate?"

The Maven's dark eyes bored into her. "*They* hunger. *They* rise. And I will make sure this city survives."

9

ELEANOR

It took two nights for her body to heal from the damage of her beating. The Madame kept Eleanor confined to her room, leaving her with nothing better to do than stare at her despair-stained ceiling while dread suffused her system like bitter tea.

As the sun seized and sank below the hungry jawline of the city, Eleanor was convinced she'd be left to stew in her helpless boredom for another night when The Madame's rage flooded up through the floorboards of the carnal house in a series of furious shrieks. Her curiosity piqued; Eleanor wondered which of the girls managed to draw her ire. The rage ended in abrupt silence, chased by a scattering of soft weeping from the rooms down the hall. Eleanor rolled from the bed, her footsteps muted clicks as she crept across the threadbare carpet to listen by the doorway. She flinched as the door to the Madame's rooms slammed shut. Puzzled by the sudden cacophony, she leaned back against the wall, narrowly avoiding Rose as she barreled into the room.

The woman almost looked rattled, her dishwater hair in violent disarray, her single gray eye wide as she beckoned Eleanor with a quick jerk of her two fingers. "Come. I need your help."

Rose requesting anything was enough to pull her off the wall. Eleanor followed her, darting a nervous glance as she passed The Madame's closed door. It was pointless to ask Rose questions, and the speed of their descent through the carnal house wound a wire of nervous tension around her spine before she saw the open basement door. Why couldn't it have been an issue with one of the girls? She wasn't eager for another encounter with its occupant.

Next to the door was an omen in the innocuous form of a bucket of water and cloth. Unease wound tighter as Rose paused her descent long enough to jerk her head for Eleanor to go ahead of her.

Eleanor's jaw tightened. "What did she do to him?"

"Nothing worse than she did to you," said Rose.

"Then you should have no problem cleaning him up then," Eleanor snapped. Why did Rose want to drag her down there? To commiserate with another of The Madame's prisoners? Her neck pinched at the faint memory of pain. The wild man was barely cognizant on her first visit, she could only imagine what more darkness and a beating had done to his faculties.

The knuckles of Rose's hand whitened as she picked up the bucket, her jerky motions sloshing liquid onto her gray bleached skirts. "He won't calm in my presence."

Eleanor hazarded a wild guess. "Because you helped put him down there?"

"Yes," Rose hissed. She pushed her scarred visage close to Eleanor's face, forcing her back a step as she spoke in low, lilting tones. "Not all of us have the luxury of healing from The Madame's anger if we dare to disobey."

Sparest truth, spoken in a voice barely above a whisper, and despite herself, empathy hooked its claws into Eleanor. She swallowed at the lump forming in her throat. "What would you have me do?"

"Your presence might be enough to soothe him," said Rose. She moved behind Eleanor, pressing across the small of her back to move her forward.

"That confident in my abilities to soothe the savage beast?" A breathy panic laced her words.

"He didn't kill you last time."

Eleanor refrained from mentioning the bite because she would be unwilling to explain why. Instead, she allowed Rose to maneuver their awkward descent down the stairs, drawing up short at the bloodied chain stretched taut to the darkest corner of the room. She could hear his rattling growl from the shadows. The putrid taste of fear tinged with sour dread flooded her mouth as she managed the last few steps without Rose nudging her forward.

"Do you even know his name?"

"The Madame only calls him Wolf," said Rose. The rattling growl dropped to a warning octave at the sound of her voice.

That wasn't his name. Eleanor wondered if The Madame called him that out of spite.

Rose dropped down another step behind her "We need to clean him up—"

The chain went slack, their only warning before he flew out of the shadows, so fast the sound of metal chased after him. He rammed into the stairs and swiped at Rose. The normally unruffled servant scrambled back a step, her bucket losing most of its water to the thirsty stones below. A grim determination settled on her features; she hovered just out of his reach as he frothed and snapped at her, his face a bloody ruin after The Madame's ministrations. He was so focused on Rose, he ignored the closer, more accessible Eleanor.

Eleanor sucked on her teeth. "Well, he doesn't like you, does he?"

Rose's gaze shot to her, but she said nothing.

"Give it to me," she said, holding out a hand. Rose clutched the near empty bucket to her, a note of hesitation in the pinched lines bracketing her mouth.

"This was a mistake," she said. "He's too violent."

Eleanor flexed the muscles of her spine. Her tail whipped forward so that the poisonous barb smacked the step inches from Rose's bare feet. It was a move she practiced as soon as her body was healed enough to move. "I'll take my chances."

Rose handed off the bucket without a flinch of acknowledgement. "I'll keep The Madame occupied." She slid up the stairs without a backward glance. Eleanor turned. The wild man had returned to the shadows the second her tail came down. Rose might have lost her survival instinct, but the wild man recognized the danger of Eleanor's poison. Her shoulders slumped as she sought him out in the dark corners.

"I won't hurt you," she said. How odd that the tables had turned to make her the bigger monster. Her abused body throbbed at the thought. No, they weren't monsters. They were victims of this house and the monster who lived here. But that didn't make the wild man any less dangerous, and a wounded animal was more likely to lash out if he felt cornered by her approach. How could she coax him out?

Eleanor sank down, folding her spindly legs beneath her as she let her tail droop, nonthreatening behind her. "When I was little, I hated pain," she said. "I would yowl and caterwaul at the tiniest slip of a sliver in my finger. My mother—" The moisture evaporated from her mouth. Eleanor licked her lips as she unpacked the memory, fragile as the ancient moldering books her mother kept in the lockbox under her bed. "When I was being particularly awful, my mother would pull me into her lap and tell me an old story, from before the Gate, about a creature called a lion who had a thorn in his paw." A tear slid down her face as she spoke. "The lion was very ferocious. He snapped at everyone who came close, until no one would come near enough to help him."

The chain rustled as the wild man emerged from the shadows. Her story faltered as she got a good look at him. She didn't think it was possible to hate The Madame more than she already did. Eleanor swallowed at the tightness in her throat. "The lion was miserable. No one would help him remove the thorn from his paw, until a small soft voice spoke up."

"And the lion beheld a mouse," he rasped.

Eleanor's jaw went slack. She shook herself as he limped to her and slumped too fast to the ground. "You're...strangely calm for a man beaten within an inch of his life."

The wild man looked at her, his eyes still a feral yellow that sent her instincts rioting. "There is lucidity in pain," he said. "But this is nothing."

How could he say that? The bruises that riddled his torso were so deep they were bloody blooms beneath the surface of his skin. "May I clean you up?"

He rolled his shoulder in a careless shrug. The action tore one of his bruises open in a fine trickle of blood that dripped down his shoulder. The sight of him broke something in Eleanor, something she didn't know she had left after her time in the carnal house. Tears dripped down her chin as she wrung out the cloth and gently swabbed at a dried cut on his cheek. "What's your name?"

One yellow eye rolled to look at her. "Tell me more about your mother," he said.

He appeared to be as forthcoming with pertinent information as Rose. Eleanor bit the inside of her cheek as the crusted blood on his cheek broke with a fresh spill. Was she really helping here, or was she making it worse? He caught her wrist as she began to pull away. "Please?"

Eleanor released a shaky breath and continued to clean his wounds. "She loved the old stories. She had a book of fables and myths from before the Gate that she kept under her bed like precious treasure. Half the pages were burnt, but she said it was one of the most important possession she owned." Her throat tightened at the memory of her mother's singsong voice, rich as dancing sun motes. "She used to tell us stories of talking animals and the children of foolhardy gods." The muscles of her chest clenched so tight she couldn't breathe. The last sight of her mother's tear-stained face, her gentle spirit broken with resignation as they dragged Eleanor away. Her mother did nothing to stop it, bed ridden by the same sickness that stole the lives of her sisters, helpless as her tainted daughter was torn from their home.

"I don't remember my mother," he said. "If I had sisters, or brothers. I remember nothing of home." His head tilted up as he spoke, his feral gaze staring sightless through the ceiling. Eleanor thought he was slipping away when he finally spoke. "It's Kai."

She bit back a small smile. "Did you know Kai means 'beautiful' in the old tongue?" Another gift of her mother's books, a thousand pieces of useless lingering knowledge.

"I knew beautiful once," said Kai. He frowned down at the bruises on the backs of his knuckles. "Every thought, every memory is fleeting as smoke in the wind, except that one." His fingers curled, stretching the bruises into violet-red starbursts. "Every time the dark rises, it's an anchor around my neck. Or is it a life raft?" He turned to her, his expression lost and forlorn. "I can't remember who I am anymore."

A new tear spilled down her cheek, chilled by the damp air of the basement. "I'm sorry Kai." Her cloth was saturated with blood, his face still a mess, but there was no more water in her bucket. If she fetched more, would The Madame catch her? She bit her lip in indecision as she rose. Kai snagged her wrist once more, his grip surprisingly gentle.

"If you escape this place, take me with you," he said, "Or burn it on your way out."

Eleanor nodded, unable to tell him that neither of them were likely to escape before they died.

The Madame was in better spirits when Eleanor was readied for service that evening, which only heightened Eleanor's sense of unease. She was paid a personal visit as Rose helped her dress for the evening. Her face heavily done up for the evening's business, The Madame sauntered into the room. Her cloying perfume clogged Eleanor's nostrils, making it difficult not to sneeze. She froze as the Madame seized her chin.

"I'm going out this evening on business. There will be no incidents evening, is that clear?"

Eleanor swallowed hard and nodded.

Rose coughed behind them. "Will her potential patron be coming tonight?"

The Madame took a drag from her cigarette and blew the smoke over her shoulder. "They haven't responded yet. But remain open to new possibilities."

Rose didn't say anything to that.

Eleanor was positioned at the same station as last time, though Lord Harkham apparently hadn't kept his mouth shut. The room was quieter tonight, and not a single patron glanced her way. It was a situation she both wanted and dreaded. If she couldn't snare the attention of a client, she was nothing more than a decorative flower, pinned to the wall—pretty and useless. Worry beat a fevered note in her pulse as the long hours of the evening stretched before her.

The air shifted, weighted and anxious like a long-held breath.

Eleanor looked up, brows creased as she tried to pinpoint the feeling. The remaining occupants of the room appeared oblivious to it, continuing their playful exchange until the front door of the Nightingale House opened. The women and men froze. Not a temporary stillness; it was as though they had turned to statues of living stone.

Their faces were caught in an unnatural mixture of flirtatious smiles, their eyes too wide and over bright with fear. As one, their gaze slid to the lord entering the house, leading the way with a metal-tipped cane that announced each step with a deep throbbing vibration she felt shiver up from the tips of her legs. Eleanor found she didn't have to resist the urge to bolt, her limbs frozen in place like the others. Her heartbeat exploded as adrenaline and terror chased and tangled in her veins. The newcomer stepped into the parlor, and she knew he was responsible for their state by the power that sloughed off him, pulsing and dark. She wanted to cringe and curl away from that endless black, certain if she could she'd start screaming and never stop.

"Ssssss-" Rose hissed, choked and strained, forcing the sound through her frozen lips.

The newcomer turned to her, the light revealing his handsome face, tainted by a distracted rage.

"Oh." He straightened, rolling his shoulders and cracking his neck.

His features smoothed, and the awful pressure dissipated. Eleanor felt mobility return to her limbs, but didn't move, watching the lord. The entire room watched him like prey focused on every movement of a predator in front of them.

"My apologies, my mind dwelt on unpleasant matters," said the newcomer, nodding to the other gentlemen present.

They bowed their heads, murmuring dismissals of the incident, but they quickly dispersed with their chosen partners, leaving a handful of women in the room aside from Eleanor. Rose approached him, her smooth mask in place, but Eleanor could see her hands locked behind her back, knuckles tight and pale.

"Lord Vashon," she said, "We didn't expect you this evening."

"I did not expect to be here this evening," said the lord,

placing his cane against the wall as he shrugged free of his overcoat.

His maroon vest and cravat were immaculate, but dried blood dotted the cuffs of his white shirt. The other girls fidgeted; there were no alluring smiles for Lord Vashon. An undercurrent of fear stroked Eleanor's nerves with velvet claws.

"I received a missive from your madame. Consider this my answer," said Lord Vashon. "What did she have to offer?"

Her spine straightened at his words. Missive? Offering? Did it mean her, or The Madame's other unusual acquisition in the cellar, or both? She banished the thoughts as Lord Vashon unbuttoned his blood-stained cuffs and rolled up his sleeves.

"Come now, little Rose, I require distraction." The low undertone of his voice held a dangerous hunger that made the remaining girls shiver and curl into themselves.

Rose's mask didn't waver, but her fingers tightened so much Eleanor would be surprised if there was an ounce of blood left in her pale digits.

"The Madame is not here-"

"Ah, but you run the house in her stead," said Lord Vashon.

He stepped closer to her, the movement abrupt and fluid as the two fingers he slid down the ruined side of Rose's face. "I know we've had such fun together, darling, but I must insist."

A small sound escaped Rose, the soft, wounded keening of a trapped animal. Eleanor gaped at them. Her relationship with Rose was on strange footing, but the implication behind Vashon's words and Rose's reaction sent a chill through her as she grappled with indecision. If she interfered, she could make it worse for Rose, but if she did nothing, she feared what the lord would do. The other women abandoned all pretense, curling into shivering heaps of gauzy cloth as the lord turned to face them. Eleanor hadn't moved, and it was her stillness that drew his attention.

She felt an internal caress of her senses, invisible and intrusive as it invaded her thoughts, rifling through them. She'd felt a sensation like this before, both similar and vastly different. Eleanor clenched her jaw and shoved the memory deep within her mind. Her hands slid down to grip her chair as Lord Vashon took two gliding steps toward her, possessing all the casual menace of an advancing snake.

"You are new," he said.

He dropped down to his haunches before her, tilting his head this way and that as he studied her. For all her new bulk, Eleanor suddenly felt very small. However, as his gaze roved over her, that frightening smile shifted, replaced by curiosity that smoothed the cruel lines of his face, revealing a handsome countenance, the sort of features that drew the appreciate eye. Eleanor couldn't help but fall prey to the habit herself, studying him in turn. His face was a collection of pleasing features; the masculine line of his jaw, the near silvery color of his grey eyes, a long, straight nose, though there was a cruel set to his mouth, like a warning flag. The sort of beauty that came with a poisonous strike, something she could relate to.

A grin softened his mouth. He must have heard her errant thought.

"I'd like a room for myself and Miss Eleanor," he said.

Had The Madame told him her name or had he plucked the knowledge from her mind? By his secretive smile, she knew he'd leave her guessing. It was the sort of charm that could make her forget why she was here, though she couldn't dismiss Rose's grim expression as Vashon led her to another room.

He didn't touch her. Not once. Instead he lounged on the bed as she sat on a backless chair across from him. Silver eyes watched her as that fluttering plucking sensation filled her head, somehow far more intimate than nudity.

Vashon's gloved fingers absently traced the outline of his lips as he stared. She wondered what he saw when he looked at her, wondered what he could possibly find so fascinating. When he finally spoke, his words buzzed between her ears until he finally took leave of her. Rose came to fetch her soon after. Too incredulous to react, she followed Rose without a word, silent as the woman tugged the pins from her hair and guided her into the steaming tub of water. The heat soothed the numb shock from her system, allowing the words to finally pour out of her.

"He offered me a place in his household," said Eleanor. Rose braced her arms against the tub. Her single eye was full of ghosts.

"Don't accept," she whispered. The silence went taut before Rose spun and slashed an arm across the vanity.

"Stop!" Eleanor reached for her as bottles of perfume smashed in cloying bursts of liquid and shattered glass. Powder and rogue tins clattered as they spilled their contents in puffs of colored dust. The act was abrupt and violent, but Rose never made a sound as she gripped the edges of the vanity with white burning knuckles. The sound was negligible, more than one insistent lord smashed a glass here or broke a chair there in the heat of the moment, but the action was out of character for the stony Rose.

Eleanor stared at her, at the cruel scars that pulled and marred her features. "He did that to you, didn't he?"

Rose didn't look at her, but her head inclined in answer.

Eleanor looked away. "Why?"

Rose stared at her ruined reflection in the mirror. "Because he was bored."

The truth of those murmured words made the bile crawl up Eleanor's throat. The more pieces of Rose's past she uncovered, the more she understood the woman's mercurial nature. How long before Vashon grew bored with her? Worse, Eleanor doubted she could refuse his offer, without inviting his inevitable ire.

Vashon visited her throughout the week, his charming demeanor hard to resist, but Eleanor couldn't forget Rose's admission. What made their relationship stranger was the lack of physical contact. It worried her at first, as much as she was relieved, but Vashon didn't touch her beyond the cursory contact.

Nothing intimate, nothing to push her in that direction. She didn't understand why. Why wouldn't he touch her? What did he ultimately want from her?

To her further confusion, on the third day, Vashon came earlier in the afternoon. He arrived hours before evening service began and demanded an audience with The Madame in her rooms. He didn't come alone.

The girls watched the pair with wide eyed curiosity, Eleanor included, as Vashon stationed his unusual servant on one of the backless chairs. A necessary accommodation for the large wings that emerged from the youth's back, beautiful mottled wings. Eleanor wondered if they were as soft as they looked.

"Sit, don't move," said Vashon. He cast a winsome smile and bowed his head at her as she approached. "Hello lovely Eleanor. I'm afraid I have some business to discuss with the Madame today."

He left the boy there, legs sprawled out, his body as still as the others had been when Vashon arrived that first night. Eleanor doubted he could move an inch without Vashon's say so. The girls began to cluster nearby, whispering to one another as they looked over Vashon's servant with wondering, hungry gazes.

They drew back with a collective hiss as those beautiful wings began to weep, a rain of feathers that melted to nothing seconds after they hit the ground. The whispers scattered as the girls scurried to their rooms, spooked by the boy and his weeping wings. Eleanor remained, enthralled by the sight.

"Are you an angel?"

The boy startled, his wings snapping wide as his gaze shot up to meet hers. Eleanor's pulse tripped. His eyes were full of storms, stunning and dark, threatening to sweep her away. "*No,*" he said, his voice soft. There was a beautiful, echoing lilt to his voice that soothed her wounded heart. "*Why would you think that?*"

Eleanor folded her hands in front of her to keep from fidgeting. "My mother, she used to tell me stories about them." A feather brushed past her legs, still tangible. She bent down to snag it, thrilled by the velvet texture as she slipped it between her fingers. "They were protectors, I think, or agents of wrath. Her stories were a little contradictory in the details."

"*You... you remember your mother?*" That storm-shrouded gaze was focused on her now with frightening intensity.

She stared at him, willing herself to answer, but the words dried up on her tongue.

The Madame's door opened. Vashon emerged, in a swirl of cigarette smoke, rebuttoning his cuffs "Thank you for another memorable bargaining session, Madame. I shall see you this evening."

"The Nightingale Carnal House thanks you for your patronage once again," said The Madame, her voice surprisingly breathy. "I see you hovering out there. Come here, girl."

"To this evening," Vashon murmured to her as she passed. Eleanor's gaze jerked up to his, a flash of quicksilver, like the Trickster's of her bedtime stories. The boy's wings rustled. Vashon's attention turned to him with a flash of chilling anger. "I thought I told you not to move, Lyre."

"Don't keep me waiting," The Madame snapped, the threat of her anger propelling Eleanor's steps forward as Vashon advanced on his servant. She didn't want to look away, but she didn't dare watch, unwilling to witness a possible preview of her future. Eleanor closed the Madame's door behind her.

"There you are Little Mouse," said The Madame, her tone far too pleasant.

Eleanor braced herself. "You asked to see me, Madame?"

The Madame's cigarette holder clicked against her teeth. "The gracious Lord Vashon has paid a handsome fee to secure your services, and your services alone for the next several nights."

Cold flushed through her. A high-pitched ringing filled her ears, as if The Madame had cuffed the back of her head. "He did?"

The Madame chuckled without humor. "Far more than your troublesome hide is worth."

"Why would he do that?" Eleanor's voice cracked into a whisper. "He didn't touch me." The confession mortified her, but it was suddenly vital she understood Vashon's intent.

"Oh, he won't," said The Madame, sucking in a lungful of smoke, she exhaled in a stream. "Not one for intimacy, that one. He has other tastes."

Eleanor swallowed hard, the muscles of the throat frozen. "What does he want with me?"

"I find his choice baffling, Little Mouse, but he has paid well for you, so you will entertain him until he grows bored."

Rose's scarred face flashed through her thoughts. Eleanor shuddered.

The Madame often grumbled about her confusion at exactly what Vashon found so fascinating about Eleanor, but she kept his boredom at bay as the days trickled by just the same. He bought another week, then another. Sometimes, Lyre and his weeping wings would accompany him, though the servant's intensity made the other patrons and girls uneasy. Eleanor found Lyre's presence oddly comforting. She didn't herself understand what Vashon found so intriguing about her, but it helped to have another overwhelming presence in the room. Often, he would ask her to tell him about the other girls in the house, claiming he liked the sound of her voice. Sometimes, they sat in silence, while the fluttering shuffle of Vashon's magic caressed her thoughts. Occasionally, he would sit them both in the common room, his gaze wandering over the other women in detached observation before focusing on her with an intensity that mentally stripped her naked. Though she would never call his attention sexual, the sessions left her wrung out, within and without. Each night, after he left, Eleanor would sink into the bath Rose had waiting for her, as a quiet knot unwound inside her chest. Somehow, she would survive this.

The problem was the other girls. Vashon terrified them, though they knew his visits weren't physical. The nights he sat with them all, they barely moved for fear of his attention. When they found out Eleanor didn't have to service the other lords due to Vashon's patronage, their attitudes turned hostile. They would pull her hair as she passed by, tear at her clothes, ruin the cosmetics on her vanity, and a dozen other petty little crimes. She tolerated their harassment because their actions were nothing, little jealousies easily brushed aside. However, she hadn't anticipated Vashon's reaction to their treatment of her.

His mood was darker than usual that evening. He arrived earlier than most of the other patrons, accompanied by Lyre who stationed by the door like an elegant statue. It was just as well; they were alone since Lyre's presence tended to spook the other lords worse than Vashon did. Despite his apparent ire, he chose the parlor for tonight's session, so that the girls had nothing to do but lounge around or hide in their rooms. Some of them hid, but most had grown accustomed to Lord Vashon by then since he left them alone.

Eleanor was attempting to fix a tear in her skirts that 'accidentally' snagged as she passed by one of the girls sitting by the entrance. It was a small thing, a nothing incident she didn't even think of as Vashon rifled through her mind, an action she'd grown used to as he did so with each visit. She didn't know what he was searching for, but it didn't seem to frustrate him that he couldn't find it. However, this time, he stiffened. His gaze shifted to the girls strewn about the couches like decorative pillows.

"You think you are better than her," he remarked in a voice of whiskey and smoke, humming with dark excitement as he stopped behind her chair.

Eleanor froze. The sudden change in his demeanor caused her instincts to scream, she wanted to lash out, strike at him with claws or the sharp barbed tip of her tail, but she could feel his will pinning her down. Her gaze found Lyre's, his expression worried and tense though he appeared to be as helpless as she was. Vashon examined the others as he reached down to tilt her jaw to the side. He lifted Eleanor's hands to observe the claws at her fingertips. Through his physical scrutiny, she could feel the intrusion into her mind, far more invasive than before. Previously it plucked at her thoughts and memories, this time it dug into her mind, taking away her control. Tension bloomed through her, rising from her throat in a stifled cry as he forced her to look up into his eyes, twin chips of cold silver. He smiled.

"You are nothing but meat and gristle, encased in a pretty dress," he said. Dread washed through her. He wasn't speaking to her but to them. They could sense the danger, she could see it in their terrified faces, but they were frozen in place, unable to move.

There was a subtle shift in her mind, a tightening noose around her senses. Her sight fractured into unfocused shapes and colors. Eleanor cried out, but no sound escaped her locked throat. She could feel her limbs moving without her consent, her awareness of everything muffled. Forced underwater, unable to drown. Trapped in a cage of flesh and bone, her mind screamed and thrashed as her body moved without her.

The violation was unlike any horror she'd experienced. Time fractured, as reality lost its shape, each second flowed like liquid eternity, her mind adrift without an anchor. She felt her limbs twisting in a grotesque spectacle, felt blood drip, warm and salty-sweet from her lips, her tail whip and strike but at what, at who, she couldn't tell. Muffled shrieks and screams assaulted her ears. Inside her head, she sobbed, trying to shut it out, to become stone.

When the blinding hood finally lifted, she found her body curled backward, her claws dipping and swirling in the blood that coated the floor. Eleanor blinked, drawing breath as her vision slowly refocused. Blood dripped down the walls and streaked the parlor settees and chairs. It was eerily quiet except for her hard, panting breaths and soft sobbing from the other room. She turned her head and met the vacant eyes of one of the women, her body torn open, flesh peeled off her like petals to expose the meat beneath. Beyond her, there were others, unrecognizable, their bodies twisted into elaborate shapes that lost definition as her vision mercifully unfocused. Eleanor stared without seeing, acutely aware of the blood that dripped from her fingers, that painted her skin.

A cry wrenched from her throat as she collapsed, scuttling through the gore until she hit the opposite wall. She held up her blood slicked hands, choking on her sobs.

"They are beneath you," said Lord Vashon. He sat on one of the chairs, observing Eleanor with a thoughtful expression.

The lord rose to his feet; he sauntered over to her, carelessly stepping around the remains. Eleanor flinched from him, disgust and fear raging in her as he circled her.

"You mourn them, but they hated you," said Lord Vashon. "The servants of my house will welcome you like family. You would make a perfect addition to the house. Little Rose, I would like to purchase this one." Rose cowered on the floor behind him

Heat rose up her neck as ice solidified in her stomach. Vashon would take her home, and he would break her a piece at a time. He would violate her in ways she didn't know existed. Her stomach heaved. She lurched to the side, vomiting a thick, brackish- brown liquid onto the floor, like old blood. Eleanor backed away from it, trying to banish the horrid thought as her eyes slid to the body on the floor. What else had he forced her to do? She couldn't remember the exact details, a fact for which she was grateful. She couldn't even remember the girls' name. More than anything she wished she couldn't remember her own.

"No," said Rose.

Eleanor's head jerked up at the word. Lord Vashon turned to the scarred girl with a deceptively casual smile.

"I beg your pardon"

Rose used the chair to drag herself to her feet, her knuckles turning white as she faced him. "You owe the Madame compensation for this" she said, nodding to the women on the floor. "You will speak to the Madame first before any such bargain is struck. Take your leave, Lord Vashon."

The lord closed the distance between them. His smile turned vicious. "Where did you find such pluck, Little Rose?" His fingers danced up her scarred arm. "I thought we peeled it out of you ages ago."

She shuddered but remained on her feet. "Go, or I will report you to the council of lords."

Lord Vashon laughed. "Then I shall consult the Madame first. I am sure you will hear of it. Come along Lyre."

Until that moment, Eleanor had allowed herself to forget he was there. A glimpse of his horrified expression amplified the toxic loathing and shame that churned inside her. The lord shrugged on his coat over his blood spotted clothing, pulling on black leather gloves that concealed his stained fingernails. He nodded to Eleanor as he took up his cane. "Until next time."

He hummed as he departed the carnal house. Neither Rose nor Eleanor moved until they could no longer hear the thump of his cane on the alley stones.

Eleanor began to shake, coated in filth, unclean inside and out. She couldn't take her eyes off the body until Rose's voice snapped at her.

"Get up. Go fill the tub. Get in it." Those short, sharp sentences spurred Eleanor into action. Every joint of her body ached as she half crawled across the floor, hesitating at the wide expanse of smeared blood congealing on the floor.

"Go!" Rose snarled.

Eleanor flinched, forcing herself to move through it. She gagged at the cold, sticky wetness, wanting nothing more than to sink into the tub and never leave.

It wasn't until she curled up in the lukewarmswirling red water that she unraveled. Her frame shook as she sobbed, covering her mouth with her forearm. She couldn't touch her mouth with her hands, not yet. They weren't clean enough. They would never be clean enough.

Rose came for her eventually, saying nothing as she knelt beside the tub. She said nothing as she drained and refilled it, taking a cloth to scrub Eleanor's skin. Bit by bit, she scoured the blood away. Eleanor remembered Vashon's stained fingernails as she stared at the blood now caked beneath her own.

"Did he use me to peel the flesh off that girl?"

Rose's hand stilled at her words. "Yes."

Eleanor hugged herself hard to stop the tremble in her limbs. Part of her wanted to hug Rose, awash in the horrified realization that this was likely exactly what Vashon did to her, though she'd survived. Was that better, or worse? "That's what he'll do to me." If she was lucky, she'd die. She could still feel the blood dripping from her fingers.

"No," Rose hissed. Her fingers bit into Eleanor's arm. "That will not happen."

Her throat felt tight, so very tight. "You think the Madame won't sell?"

The silence was truth enough. The Madame didn't protect Rose, and she wouldn't protect her. It didn't matter that Lord Vashon killed one or all of her girls; to the Madame, they were stock to be replenished.

Eleanor knew she wouldn't survive Vashon's house. She wouldn't survive here. She had to run.

UNRAVELING

 10 

AZURE

Wallach's office remained silent after her third knock. Azzy frowned at the closed door. He usually told her if business called him elsewhere.

"There you are." Cherise approached her at a brisk walk. The head servant was agitated today, her plumes of smoke an opaque bluish-white that spun around her fidgeting hands in little swirls. "Come, eat. There's not much time."

Azzy picked up on the woman's nervous energy. Her whispers murmured too soft for her to pick up their warning. She could chafe over the Maven's chokehold later. "What's wrong?"

"A summons came from the House of Lords during the night," said Cherise. "Safiya's trial has been set."

"But we knew that was coming."

Cherise's smoke shimmered. "It should have been tied up for weeks in bureaucratic technicalities. The case is over a decade old. Someone pushed this forward."

Azzy didn't need to ask who. The true question was why? What did Vashon have to gain by pushing Safiya's trial forward, other than a distraction? Perhaps the Maven wasn't the only one playing chess on a life and death scale. "Where's Wallach?"

"At the House of Lords. He asked that I escort you there after breakfast."

"Me? What for?" She knew little of political machinations and far less about the laws of Avergard than any member of this household.

"Part of your training," said Cherise. "He'll explain more once we get there, Azzy, but he stressed the matter was urgent."

The head servant hustled her through a sparse breakfast of porridge and fresh fruit, hovering over her to ensure Azzy consumed every bite. Satisfied, Cherise dragged her to a room off the main hall Azzy had never entered before to outfit her in a simple formal dress suit that bore Wallach's house crest.

"You represent your household at the House of Lords," said Cherise as she tugged at Azzy's hem. "This is also a form of protection." She tapped the crest embroidered on Azzy's sleeve. "Every citizen of Avergard recognizes whose crest this is,but try not to draw any attention to yourself." Cherise sighed, a billow of smoke rolling out from her nostrils. "If you can help it, Azzy."

Worry coursed through her as Cherise led her toward the front gate. Howl was safely tucked away with Morglint, the Maven was nowhere to be seen, and Azzy was about to leave the safety of the grounds for the first time since Wallach brought her to Safiya's cell. Anticipation made her skin itch as they passed through the gate. Because she was aware of it, she sensed the moment the Maven's leash snapped as the whispers flooded into her mind. Azzy braced herself, startled by the level of clarity, a true physical sign of her training. Pieces of information drifted through her as they walked along the main street.

Azzy frowned. The street was unusually quiet, even for this early hour. Cool moisture slid along her skin as Cherise's smoke enveloped her.

"It's too quiet," said Azzy. The head servant was stiff beside her, tension framed the rigid lines of her body.

"We're being followed," Cherise whispered between clenched teeth. A flash of metal appeared in her free hand.

"I thought you said the crest protects us," said Azzy, her eyes trained on the wicked blade in her companion's hand.

"Some idiots need a harder lesson," said Cherise. She gently untangled herself from Azzy, both women relying on their extra senses to maneuver the streets under the cover of smoke.

Azzy wished she hadn't left Howl behind. An extra set of teeth wouldn't hurt to dissuade whoever followed them. The streets of Avergard seemed to be a constant buzz of activity between the night and day markets. Now they were near empty; a few scattered merchants hustled from stall to stall, their heads down in a resolute manner that telegraphed their fear. They were being stalked by a lord.

The whispers simmered, snaring her attention. She turned her head, as the quiet nudge she'd felt before solidified to an invisible chord, connected directly to her gut. Azzy stared in the direction of the cord, a frighteningly strong urge to follow the connection to its end, though she knew the destination. The Way of Heavenly Delights called to her, a siren song that twitched through the muscles of her legs. All she had to do was follow it and see what waited at the other end.

Cherise hissed at her side. Their cover of smoke blew apart as a wave of dizziness slammed into Azzy. The whispers surged and bounced through her mind as she fought to regain her equilibrium. Too late, she grasped their warning as an elbow clipped the side of her head.

She managed not to blackout, but she lost her balance. The impact jarred through her bones as her knees hit the cobblestone street. She ducked the first pair of rough hands that reached for her but failed to evade the second. Her stomach dropped as they hauled her to her feet, a hot pinpoint of pain pressed to her throat.

Lord Brusker held Cherise pinned against an empty stall. Her knife was embedded in the lord's arm, but it wasn't enough to halt the murderous intent that burned in his face. Azzy's stomach rolled. She kept perfectly still as the man holding her pressed his blade deeper into her throat. A trickle of blood slid down her neck, rapidly cooling in the morning air. Her captor reeked of spoiled beer and unwashed male. Brusker glanced at Azzy long enough to sneer his recognition. A dark finger of dread scraped along her spine as she realized she wasn't the target of this encounter.

Cherise bucked against his hold as Brusker rucked up her skirts, snarling in his face. He shoved a hand over her mouth, pulling back with a yelp a moment later where she bit him. Her last encounter with the lord may have been a shock, but Cherise's rage was at the fore now. Another wave of Brusker's disorienting magic washed over them. Cherise swayed, her disorientation enough for Brusker to slap her across the face.

Azzy bit down on her tongue as the world spun. She hadn't gotten a dose of Brusker's magic before, and now she understood how it disabled the lady of smoke. It was the prick of the knife that broke through, a shock to her system as her blood soaked into the collar of her dress. Azzy focused on Brusker as he loomed over Cherise.

"You'll pay for that humiliation, wench. And when I am finished, I will dump your body on Wallach's lawn for him to find."

The burn of the blade at her throat flushed through Azzy in a wave of hot rage. It sizzled through her veins, the taste of heat bubbling up her throat. The whispers coiled around her until the pressure of the blade fell away, their quiet murmurs wrapping her in a cocoon, quieting her mind as she studied the three men. The one who held her was still heavily inebriated from a night of drinking. The other hovered nearby by, equally drunk. They only needed a little push to succumb to an unconscious stupor. Magic, life—it all sparked with the same flare of light and fire, a simple thing to exchange her influence of one over the other. She tilted them over the edge. They collapsed to the ground as she swept past them, following the unmistakable fiery cord of Brusker's magic. Her steps seemed to carry her further than they should, allowing her to reach the lord in seconds. Brusker was too occupied with Cherise to notice her until Azzy grabbed his arm.

He went to swing at her. Azzy found the thread of his devious magic wrapped around Cherise, and she pulled it free. It unraveled at her touch. Brusker gasped and fell to the ground, writhing as she stood over him. There were dozens of frayed threads in his mind. A thousand little shames of terrible deeds done to women in dark corners. She began to pull them free. Brusker screamed.

The air tore open a few feet away. Azzy paid it little attention, her focus on Brusker as she shredded thread after thread.

"Azzy, stop!" Wallach's hands clamped onto her shoulders, breaking her concentration.

She sucked in a breath, her awareness widening. Petyr cradled an unconscious Cherise in his arms. Lord Brusker trembled at her feet. Wallach ignored him, pulling away from the three downed men. He led her through Petyr's portal, emerging in the familiar confines of the servant's dining room. Petyr carried the disoriented Cherise out of the room as Wallach rounded on Azzy.

"What happened?" he said, his voice tight with anger and worry.

Azzy resisted the urge to flinch though she knew the anger was not for her. "They were following us as soon as we left the front gate. It was a set up. The streets were nearly empty."

"I'll tear out his throat," Wallach snarled. The lord blew out a breath and shook his head, quick as ever to douse any visage of anger. "What did you do to Brusker? I've never seen that before."

She frowned at his incredulous expression. "I broke through his magic. It was the only thing I could think to do—"

"Azzy," said Wallach, a strangled note in his voice. "You didn't just break it, you unraveled it as if it never existed. I could feel the absence of it when I arrived. He'll never use that magic again." He paused. "What else did you do to him?"

"I just—I just kept pulling at the threads, the different women he hurt," said Azzy, unsure of how to explain what she saw.

"His memories," said Wallach. He rubbed a hand over his tired face. "When I got there, I got the barest taste, but it was enough."

"What do you mean?"

Wallach stared at her. "Your magic tastes like the Gate."

Recognition pinged through her thoughts. This wasn't the first time she had heard of the Gate, and she still didn't have a grasp of what it meant. "What is the Gate?"

Wallach knit his fingers together. "The Gate is what happened to this world, Azzy."

"But that's, I thought—" Her voice sputtered and broke. There was a note of panic in her voice. She didn't know the full significance of the gate, but she knew who came through it.

Wallach winced. "Now?" He pulled the glove off his right hand as the mouth opened on his palm and spat ink. His face paled as he read the message. "We've run out of time." His expression was somber as he looked at her. "Safiya stands trial within the hour. I need you with me."

"I can't do anything for her," said Azzy. The muffled whispers in her head buzzed, reeling from the burst of the half revelations Wallach had given her.

"You can. I need you to read the lords, Azure," said Wallach. "You need to tell me whose mind is no longer their own."

THE TRIAL

II

AZURE

The House of Lords shivered beneath her feet. Not a single lord appeared concerned by the tremor as they settled into their cushioned, high-backed chairs. Did anyone else in the city notice, or was the entire populace of Avergard so wrapped up in their individual lives they didn't see their city coming apart at the seams?

Azzy sat beside Wallach on a much sparser version, one of sturdy, unfinished wood, sanded to a smooth finish. Lord Brusker was notably absent. She kept her hands tucked under thighs to keep from fidgeting, wishing she could hide in Petyr's hidden pocket of reality. He hovered nearby, close enough for Azzy to feel the crackle of air, his presence hidden by Wallach's aura.

She swallowed at the heaviness of it. Azzy hadn't known how much he kept it under wraps in his household. How much he protected the rest of them from it, but here in the House of Lords, he needed to be the nastiest winnowrook in the nest. By flaunting it, he effectively tossed a blanket over her. Anyone trying to get a feel for her would only get a face full of Wallach's magic, and it stung. That didn't mean they didn't try.

More than once, a lord peered hard at her, before their expression broke in a retch.

"Why do they bother?" The attention unnerved her. She wasn't the only servant in attendance. Far from it, many of the lords had one or more in attendance. As Azzy took in the room, she realized many of them served the same sort of function she did, scanning the lords from downcast gazes.

"Information is the highest form of currency," said Wallach. "The lords of Avergard are a vicious lot of despots who rule with an iron fist, but that sort of leadership leads to an awful lot of boredom. Nothing is worse than an idle aristocracy with magic."

Wallach explained that the House of Lords was one of the glorious old buildings of Avergard, a relic of the city that once occupied the space before the advent of the Gate. It was a repurposed, elegant monument of masonry, replete with marble columns and statues of gods and monsters from a long-dead era. The lords sat in a horseshoe pattern around a central podium, their seats on raised tiers to afford everyone a full view of those who stood trial. Wallach sat at the very back, high above the others. The significance of that placement wasn't lost. Directly across from him, on the opposite end of the half circle, sat Vashon.

A servant of the House carried a tray to the table at the center of the room. Aside from the ream of documents there was a string of what looked like dull, white, lumpy stones.

"What is that?"

"Evidence," said Wallach, his voice tight.

Azzy stared until recognition clicked. Teeth, it was a string of teeth, taken from the Snatcher's Safiya killed. Why had she held onto that souvenir? Why had Safiya carried it on her person, as if begging to be caught if she came in sniffing distance of the city?

"Why didn't she wait until the caravan was beyond city limits?"

"Her desire for revenge wore out her patience," said Wallach. Azzy wondered if given a chance, would she have exacted revenge on Elder Prast and his cronies? Could she have slipped into their houses while they slept and ripped their teeth from their shattered skulls? Even after they burned her mother and threatened Armin more than once, she had done nothing. Instead, she led her brother into disaster trying to save the same people who threw him into the waiting arms of the Snatchers. Azzy survived, but she failed to requite the wrongs done to her family. The one man she had killed, Windham, had been more accidental than intentional. Part of her envied Safiya.

The massive wooden doors opened. Guards led Safiya into the chamber by her elbows, her chained wrists dangling in front of her. A formal robe hung off her frame, thinned by her confinement. It gave her a waifish appearance until her tiger-gold eyes flashed with open hostility. Safiya's gaze immediately traveled to the top tier, where Vashon and Wallach sat. Azzy glanced between the lords, wondering what the witch saw in their expressions. Both maintained an outward mask to conceal their emotions, but the eyes gave them away. Wallach's brimmed with worry, while Vashon's were eager.

One of the lower lords stood to read Safiya's crimes. Azzy tuned him out. As Lennon explained over dinner the other night, Avergard was a city that possessed few laws, but the ones they had were resolute. If someone were fool enough to be caught returning to the city after they committed one of those few crimes, the lords did what any ruling body would do to keep the populace in line. They made an example of the criminal. There were no pardons for self-defense or justified vengeance, no limitations to the length of time between crime and punishment. If he was correct, why did they bother to present evidence at all? It wasn't a trial if there was only one verdict, yet Lennon insisted the show was more important than the result. The lords needed the populace to see them as a fair, if strict, ruling body.

"After hearing the evidence, the House of Lords cast their vote for guilty or not guilty," said the speaker. "Those for 'not guilty'"

Aside from Wallach, there were a surprising number of hands. He must have called in every favor he had.

"Those for guilty."

Azzy was not surprised by the greater number. Wallach warned her it would be the case, but this is where he told her to pay attention. She sat back in her chair, letting the whispers wash through her as she listened to what they told her. A slight inhale was the only cue Wallach needed from her. He shifted in front of her, his jaw set as his hands gripped the armrests hard enough for the wood to whine. Azzy reached behind her, and let Petyr guide her into the crackling dark. Not a single lord looked their way, their attention rapt on the show taking place center stage. Most of them *couldn't* look away if they wanted to. *I need to know whose minds are no longer their own.*

The speaker rapped his podium with a gavel, the sound muffled but audible in Petyr's null space. "The House of Lords finds Safiya Sabhayar guilty for the murder of two dozen merchant citizens within the city limits. The sentence is death by beheading, which will be carried out in two days' time, one hour after dawn."

He rapped the gavel once again, signaling the end of the trial. It had taken less than twenty minutes to judge and sentence Safiya. She hadn't been given the opportunity to speak once.

The guards were coming up behind her. The House of Lords began to empty. Safiya looked up at Wallach, the vitality drained out of her as Azzy looked on, noting the smudges of exhaustion beneath her eyes as the guards seized her. She couldn't see Wallach's face, but she could read the tension in his body. They both knew how this trial would end, but the two-day window was an unforeseen pitfall. If Wallach attempted to free her, with the conviction hanging over her head, he would be sheltering, not a criminal, but a convicted murder. There would be nowhere safe for Safiya in the city and if they caught her outside it, they would just drag her back.

The moment the guards pulled her from the podium, Petyr grabbed Azzy's wrist. "Come on, we need to see who's waiting for her." This was the second half of their task. Wallach stayed where he was as the other lords chatted or left. He needed to be seen there, because the other one was conspicuously absent.

Vashon was already at Safiya's cell as Petyr drew them to a stop, further away than they had dared when Wallach was with them. Without Wallach's smothering influence, it would be harder to hide from someone like Vashon. The lord held a roll of parchment in his hands and said nothing as the guards pushed the witch back into her cell.

"Interesting *trial*," said Safiya.

"Did you expect any other result?"

"No," she said.

Vashon's smile held no malice. "Yes, I thought the teeth were a nice touch." Azzy shivered at the hint of admiration in his voice. Vashon tapped the parchment against the palm of his hand. "Do you want to live?"

"I don't want to die," said Safiya.

"I could buy out your sentence, right now," said Vashon. "You could become part of my household instead of walk to the executioner's block." Safiya stared at him. He held her sentencing in his hands, dangling the last hint of freedom.

Azzy could almost hear the witch's teeth grind despite the static of the null space. "What would the difference be?"

His mouth thinned to a white line at her insult.

"Goodbye, Vashon," she said.

He stepped closer to the bars, menace permeating the air around him. "You think Wallach will swoop to the rescue at the last moment? He's no saint to be idolized." He leaned even closer, his words a dark promise. "I will be there to watch your final walk, and when your head falls to the basket, I hope your shade will find peace while your savior wrings his hands and does nothing."

Azzy and Petyr exchanged an uneasy look. She knew they had a history, but what he said to Safiya hinted at something far more personal than she was privy to. "We can't leave her like this," said Azzy.

"We have to," said Petyr, though the agonized expression on his face said otherwise. "If we take her from here now, the entire House of Lords will come after Wallach."

She knew this, but her chest hurt at the sight of Safiya standing there, the formal robe from her trial limp on her frame, her face lifted to watch water drip from the walls. Azzy swallowed the lump in her throat and forced herself to follow Petyr.

Wallach waited for them in the empty House of Lords. There was no one to witness as the lord rose and entered a tear in the air, though Azzy wondered if any of the lords waited outside to see him emerge. What would they think when he didn't?

It was enough to make her head hurt. Wallach had to watch every move he made like this, every hour of the day.

Wallach waited to press them for information until they emerged from the null space. "What did you sense?"

"Nearly everyone who raised their hand," said Azzy. Petyr had described Vashon's gift of mental manipulation like a puppeteer pulling strings. That was exactly what it felt like in her mind as if she could reach out and pluck them.

"He went to visit her after," said Petyr, a note of disgust in his voice. "Offered to buy her freedom if she became his lady."

Wallach didn't outwardly react, but Azzy felt the pressure even through her now limited perception.

"Wallach," she said softly. His jaw flexed. The pressure eased.

"I'm sorry. It's been a long day, though it is far from over. Go change and take a rest if you wish."

Azzy retreated to her room, exhaustion dogging her heels. She opened the door to her room.

The Maven greeted her, her features so tight, the outer layer appeared to crack. "I'm afraid we've run out of time, pet."

 12 

AZURE

Azzy circled the Maven, spooked when the hidden face tracked her movements. "Run out of time to do what?" She didn't have the patience for more riddles and half-truths

"You must be ready," said the Maven, "or they will overwhelm you."

"Who will?" This was the most frustrating part of the training; The vague threats and odd words the Maven never explained.

The Maven answered with a blow to her chest that sent her flying into a wall. The impact knocked the air from her lungs. She rolled out of the way a second too slow. A long line of pain cut down her side.

"I've coddled and coaxed you along," said the Maven. "It's time to push." Her mask cracked further at the words, the edges of a terrifying grin peeking through. Azzy scuttled away until her back hit the door.

"Why didn't you push before?"

"It wasn't time," said the Maven.

She blurred and disappeared, and Azzy's eyes went wide as she dove on instinct. The Maven's lethal arm sliced over her head. If it had connected, it would have ripped through her neck. If this kept up, one falter would end her.

"Stop, this is too much," said Azzy.

Dying would solve nothing, help nobody. She had to survive her training to put it to use. She yelped as she failed to completely dodge another blow, a hot line that burned across her shoulder.

"Defend yourself," the Maven yelled. She continued her

pursuit, and Azzy had no doubt in her mind the Maven, unlike Wallach, would kill her if she failed to perform.

She tried to concentrate, listening to the whispers. But despite her attempts, the Maven charged her head on and slammed her against the wall. Azzy grabbed her wrists, straining to push the Maven back.

"Like a butterfly under glass," said the Maven, pinning her in place.

Azzy had no room for rebuttal, all her energy diverted to keeping the Maven from crushing her. Sweat popped on her brow, and the Maven's claws inched toward her chest.

"If I reach you," said the Maven, "I will wrap my hand around your heart and squeeze, pop it like a piece of overripe fruit. You must stop me, Azzy, or die trying." Her tone was too calm for the situation, but Azzy knew she was deadly serious.

"You'll die, and there will be no one to rescue your loved ones from their personal hells," said the Maven.

The pressure built, Azzy was losing, inch by inch. Her frustration mounted. She survived Winnowrooks and Snatcher's hooks, monsters that consumed whole cities, and a plunge into an endless body of water. Azzy screamed as she mentally pulled on the whispers with everything she had.

Something snapped inside.

Azzy hissed as pain shot through her skull. The whispers exploded inside her mind, a roaring cacophony that drowned out her thoughts. She sank into them, letting go completely as her perception of the world shifted.

The Maven stood in front of her, her power like clumps of knotted string in Azzy's mind. She reached in and gripped a single loose thread and pulled. The Maven collapsed to the ground, blood pouring from her nose.

Azzy drew back, mortified at what she'd done. The Maven clapped from her prostrate position. "Well done. How do you feel?"

As if something had shifted internally. The whispers ebbed and flowed within her, a constant stream of information. She tried to recall the healing rune she'd used on her chest in Morglint's tent. The rune snapped in place with ease, the wounds given to her by the Maven disappearing in a blink.

The Maven smiled. "I think it's time you followed the pull."

"To the Way of Heavenly Delights," she whispered.

The Maven gave her a secretive smile. "Take the boy with you." She pointed at the walls. Azzy wondered if she meant that in a literal sense until she moved forward, revealing a gap where the walls appeared to overlap, wide enough for her to squeeze through. Had that passage always been there? The Maven seemed to move unseen through Wallach's house, but if she used a gap in the walls, it diminished some of the woman's eerie mystique. What reason lay behind revealing the gap to Azzy now left her thoughtful. The Maven's words snagged her attention once more. "We have reached a confluence of events, little one. It is time to see them through."

13

AZURE

The spare space between the walls pressed around her. Protruding nails and splinters of aged wood stroked the exposed skin on her arms with a promise of pain if she shifted too far one way or another. Azzy fought to keep her breathing even, her gaze locked to the faint outline of Howl as he padded with careless grace in front of her. The barest hint of light broke through the empty spaces between floorboards and wall panels, but there were sections so dark she had to chance curling her fingers into the fur of his flank. The act slowed their progress as she had to shuffle sideways to avoid scraping her shoulders, but Howl remained patient and steady. She trusted him to lead her out while he relied upon her to keep them from discovery.

On cue, the whispers kicked up. Azzy's hand shot out and gripped a tuft of fur on the big cat's back. The clumsy motion cost her, a streak of fire burning across the top of her forearm. An inaudible growl rumbled through Howl's chest as the scent of her blood bloomed in the closed space. Azzy hoped the sound was too low to be heard by the presence that hovered on the other side of the wall. Not Wallach or Cherise, thank goodness, or the scant hint of blood would have given them away, but the whispers remained cautious, and the person on the other side of the wall appeared to pause their actions.

Azzy squeezed her eyes shut and held her breath, the sound of her heartbeat far too loud in her ears until she slowly shoved it down and focused on the buzz of information that filtered to her from the swarming whispers. Her thoughts filled with cool shadows and the safety of warm dark places, and Azzy knew Petyr hovered on the other side of the wall. Not exactly a threat, but they couldn't risk discovery, not now, not when the pull was so strong that even this small pause made the strain so great, she grew nauseous the longer they stayed.

The floorboards creaked as Petyr took a step forward and placed a hand on the wall. She could sense his confusion and curiosity, and more, his hesitation, as if he too could feel the weight of the night, the calm before tomorrow's storm.

Azzy didn't dare make a sound, but her lips shaped the words 'let me go' over and over, a silent prayer as she stared through the darkness. Howl pressed back into her legs, shivering and stressed. He didn't enjoy enclosed spaces, but he'd been so brave for her. She released the stranglehold of her fingers and ran her hand along his back in a soothing touch. Her lungs burned from the effort to hold her breath this long, the darkness taking on a brownish quality as the lack of air made her vision waver, when, at last, Petyr pulled back from the wall and continued on his way.

Azzy sucked in a shaky breath and nearly pitched forward as Howl continued on. She didn't linger, the pull too strong to ignore. Time seemed to crawl as they moved through the walls. Azzy couldn't grasp the passage of time; it could have been minutes, it could have been hours, the crawlspace was a place where time didn't function as it should but dragged on the body and the mind until the need to be free of it was almost as strong as the pull she followed. It reminded her of the long, breathless run she took with Brixby through the empty upper half of Haven. An event that felt like a lifetime ago, when in reality it happened only weeks ago. How much had happened in that time? How much had she changed? Would Brixby even recognize her if he saw her again?

An anxious writhing feeling that hovered over her, its hot breath at her neck slickened her back with sweat until her thin shirt stuck to her, aggravating the sensation until Azzy wanted to tear her clothes from her body for an inch of relief.

Howl's pace suddenly quickened to the point Azzy had to rush forward to keep up. She didn't tell him to slow, too wound up by the overbearing closeness of the space, but she paid for the pace with the warning bite of sharp points scraping the skin of her arms raw. She understood why Howl rushed forward as the caress of cool fresh air brushed her face, a lifeline she desperately grasped through the final stretch of that pinched dark space. Howl stopped so fast she smacked into his backside. He gave a soft affronted yowl as he pawed at the sealed entrance.

"Let me through," said Azzy, her voice whisper-soft. They were at the edges of the house now, far from any space the others would occupy, but she didn't trust her voice would escape notice. She felt rather than saw the blur of agitated air as Howl condensed his bulk to his far slighter human body. His hands gently gripped her elbows as he flowed around her so that she had access to whatever obstacle blocked their escape. Her fingers traced the outline of stone, relieved to find the mortar seal long disintegrated to the point where one good shove from her shoulder dislodged it.

Azzy would have pitched straight to the ground if Howl hadn't caught her, holding her up by the elbows until she managed to get her feet under her properly and clamber free of the house. Howl followed a moment behind after a fluid shift to his other form allowed him to clear the exit with a single leap. Free of the house, the pressing need for stealth loosened its stranglehold. He landed in the grass beside her, a thunderous purr rumbling through his chest as he kneaded the grass with his paws.

"I feel the same," said Azzy, a ghost of a smile touching her mouth before the pull drew on her hard enough that she gasped. Her head jerked up in the direction of the Way of Heavenly Delights, the whispers buzzing as that invisible tether went taut.

Howl pushed his massive head up against her palm, a contact that eased some of the pressure so she could draw breath. Azzy pressed a hand to her chest as the muscles around her heart tightened to the point of pain. She didn't need the whispers to prod her into action, not when danger plucked the unseen cord, though she was certain who she would find at the other end. A thousand hopes burst and withered in her thoughts, fighting for dominance until Azzy clamped down on her twisting desires. Who waited in the Way of Heavenly Delights? Her brother was under Vashon's thumb, tucked away in the lord's estate. What if it was Brixby? Or Kai? A shiver went through the muscles of her jaw. Don't overthink it,

Morglint's words of wisdom centered her as Azzy and Howl walked through the wild growth between the house and the outer wall until they found the gap.

Girl and lynx emerged into a wide alley, the bustling night market heedless of the two as merchants and customers continued their endless dance. A light rain fell, cooling the raw heat of her scraped skin. Howl lifted his face to the rain, the tufts of his ears flicking back and forth as droplets gathered in his whiskers. He sneezed and shook his great head. Azzy untied the cloak from her waist and held it out to him.

"Just until we get to the Way of Heavenly Delights," she whispered.

She was aware the patrons of the night market wouldn't tolerate a creature like Howl moving among them. Howl sneezed a sigh and blurred. Azzy kept an eye on the alley mouth as Howl donned the cloak, tying it tight to keep his scantily clothed state low key.

His smaller hand slid into hers, his grasp tight. A glance at his face found his pupils blown wide. Azzy smoothed his hair away from his face with her free hand.

"You don't have to come," she said softly.

"Yes, I do," said Howl, with a confidence that belied his shaking body.

The moment echoed another, so similar and yet so different, and the vise around her heart cinched tighter. A tear spilled from her unaltered eye. The situation may be different, but the choice remained the same. She couldn't seem to kick the habit of leading those she loved to ruin.

"We'll watch out for each other," said Azzy, her voice calm and steady despite the wobble in her soul.

This time would be different, she thought with a conviction that bore down on her shoulders like a sudden weight. *I am different now. I will not allow for Howl to fall.* He didn't let go of her as she took the lead, pressing close to her as she led him into the current of the night market. The press of bodies and cacophony of scents had to be doubly troubling to his senses, suppressed as they were in human form. She could hear his shallow pants as he followed close enough to clip her heels, though she didn't admonish him for it. She was grateful for his presence, grateful to have someone who relied on her so that she couldn't succumb to her own fear.

Walking through the night market presented a different tension than that of the crawl space, though both were equally oppressive. She could feel the gazes on them, assessing, tasting, as patrons and merchants sensed them pass by. Some gazes lingered longer than others, but Azzy kept her head down, following the quivering tether with a dogged concentration that carried her forward in an unerringly straight line until the crow abruptly thinned. She swore she could feel the difference in the paving stones beneath their feet as they entered the Way of Heavenly Delights. The quality of the air changed as the array of scents from the market dwindled away, replaced by something sickly sweet that left a smoky, bitter aftertaste at the back of her throat.

The whispers writhed in her thoughts, picking up notes of pain and desperation that permeated the stones beneath her feet and oozed from the mildewed walls of the carnal houses. The Way of Heavenly Delights sighed with lost innocence, full of ghosts and shades from a thousand broken bright things. Unease simmered through her veins. She recognized the despair that flavored the atmosphere of the district as the same that clung with wraith-like tenacity to Cherise and echoed in the scarred woman's eyes.

Shadows were deeper here— the warm glow that spilled from the carnal house doorways possessed the same allure as a predator dangling a beacon in the dark to lure prey into their maw. Azzy's whispers faltered, the ambient sense of danger momentarily overwhelming her before she could focus on the tether once more. The others were right to warn her away from here. She didn't begrudge them for trying to keep her safe, but she found herself wishing for the safety net of Wallach's overwhelming power or Cherise's veil of smoke. Even with the reassuring presence of Howl at her back, Azzy keenly understood her vulnerability, the sense of exposure grating like steel wool across her nerves as she forced herself to move. It was all too tempting to remain poised at the district entrance until dawn broke.

Her muscles were so tight each step jolted through her bones, but she ignored the clench in her jaw and dragged herself and

Howl along the tether. They shrank and darted amid the deep shadows between the squatting carnal houses when the wind abruptly shifted.

"Somethings burning," said Howl, his tone rigid.

A shiver of dread ran through her connection. Azzy burst into a run, the fear nipping at her heels, spurring her on as Howl stumbled after her. They saw the glow of the fire, pulsing and defiant against the gloom before they saw the carnal house aflame. Azzy's steps stuttered as the windows of the building burst with a spat of heat and glass into the eerie silence of the night. There were no screams. No shouts of alarm, only the hiss and pop of burning wood and a familiar pressure that locked her breath in her lungs. She yanked Howl back against her when he ran forward.

"You must stay here," she said, not recognizing the tone of her voice.

Howl looked up at her, wild and wide-eyed. "But Azzy—"

"You can't," she rasped. Her heart threatened to burst from her chest. "Please, stay here, wait for me."

A lie, she knew he could hear it in her voice by the stark expression on her face, but she wouldn't risk him. And she couldn't promise her return. Her resolve threatened to crumble at the lost look on his face.

"Promise me you'll go back to Cherise."

Tears spilled down his face. "Azzy, no."

"Promise me."

Time was a stone that threatened to choke her, but she took those few precious moments to extract his promise. He nodded, his jaw set, unwilling or unable to give voice to his answer. It was enough. She leaned in to press a kiss to his forehead. He held onto her hand until she finally pulled away. Azzy didn't look back as she rushed, headlong, into the burning carnal house.

14

ELEANOR

Pain finally dragged Eleanor from the blessed numbness of sleep. The ache had settled into her bones with the familiarity of an old friend. The oily fog that clung to her mind informed her Rose must have slipped a few laudanum drops into her cup last night. She was too grateful for the respite to be angry. What did that say to her state of mind?

A broken chuckle clawed at her throat at the thought. A laughable notion, the ravaged edges of her mind were raw, oozing, an open wound that had begun to fester. The pain that radiated through her body a further reminder of that moment Vashon slid the razor of his influence through her, taking her over, sealing her away. Her tears burned hot on her skin as they slid along her temples. The chuckle broke on a whimper. Eleanor clapped her bruised hands over her mouth to contain the scream that beat against her palms. If she let it out, she didn't think she'd ever stop.

The snap and crackle of muscles contorting beyond their limits, as Vashon pulled her strings in a stilted macabre dance. The low whistle of rent air when her tail whipped forward, the resistance of tearing flesh, the coppery tang of blood as it hit her face, dripped into her mouth.

Eleanor rolled off the bed as her stomach heaved. Her weakened limbs barely supported her as she snagged the washing basin off the nightstand, careless of the tepid water that splashed her face as she clutched the bowl and retched. The pulpy contents of her stomach smelled of rot and ruin, she heaved until there was nothing but bile and the sour taste of acid coating the back of her throat.

A hand rubbed between her shoulder blades. She hadn't heard

Rose come in but knew the girl was the only one who would approach her now. She rolled away from the foul smell of vomit, breathing hard as she shivered in her damp nightgown. Her hair was a matted tangle of sweat and dried viscera. The world throbbed at the edges, and for the barest moment, Eleanor wished she never left that mental box Vashon had shoved her in. That her memory was muddled haze of the incident was a cold comfort. Before awareness set in and she stood in a room of dead women. Eleanor shivered harder. She caught Rose's eye, the lone, lost look that mirrored her own.

"He said he wouldn't take control." There were a dozen unspoken things she could have said in that moment. Eleanor hated that these were the ones that spilled from her mouth, a helpless hatred of what she'd done, what he made her do. She swore there was still dried blood under her fingernails, despite Rose's vigorous scrubbing.

Rose lifted her unmaimed shoulder. "He's a lord of Avergard."

She'd expected it. She knew it was coming. So why did she think she could evade it? Warned by the whispers of the other girls, by the Madame's avarice, by the scars that twisted Rose's body. But she'd clung to the hope, after surviving so many days without incident, believed she fascinated him enough that he would leave her unscathed.

He might still intend to bring her to his estate, taking her from one Hell to bring her to another. Eleanor closed her eyes, remembering the lapse in Lyre's stony expression as Vashon stole her will.

"He reimbursed the Madame for the girls," said Rose, "and he made an offer for you."

Eleanor froze. Heat and ice flushed through her as Rose's words turned over in her mind until her skin crawled with the conflicting sensations. "No, no."

"Eleanor," said Rose. She didn't have to tell her the Madame's answer.

Eleanor sat up despite the black spots that threatened her vision and she grabbed Rose's arm. "I will slit my throat before he comes back," she hissed.

"You know I will do everything I can to prevent that," said

Rose. Despite everything she now knew of the woman, Eleanor had to remember, the only side Rose was on was her own. Rose tried to tug her arm free of Eleanor's grasp, but she wasn't done with the Madame's servant.

"Why do you stay here?" It was an honest question. Rose was treated as a disposable object by the Madame, and though she'd saved Eleanor more than once, there was an almost sycophantic attachment there.

Rose's apathetic expression remained. "Where else would I go?"

"Come with me," said Eleanor. Rose stood, still as stone. Her expression unchanging as she held her breath. The only sign of movement was her fingers, curling into the palm of her hand until her knuckles burned white from the strain.

"No," said Rose. The hollowed look in her singular eye was all the worse for the flat answer. Eleanor released her, swallowing the tightness in her throat. Rose was well and truly broken, she saw no future, no other possibilities, nothing but the cold comfort of misery given to her by the Madame because it was all she had left. But Eleanor didn't cry for the girl, she knew better than that. She said nothing else about her plans, because if pressed Rose would tell. Even this small slip might be too much, but there were other secrets the girl had kept for reasons unknown. It was best to say nothing more than try to puzzle through Rose's twisted sense of loyalty.

"I'll draw you a bath," said Rose. And while Eleanor desperately wanted to scrub the violence of last night from her skin, the underlying reason made her empty stomach clench. Rose had to prepare her for Vashon's return, but it didn't matter. She would be gone by then.

Rose took the bowl of vomit with her as she left, another small mercy as the air slowly cleared of the lingering scent of sick. Eleanor inhaled the semi-fresh air through an open mouth and schemed. Rose wouldn't come with her nor was it likely that she could convince the few girls who'd survived Vashon, sequestered safe in their rooms.

She wished she'd asked Rose when the lord intended to come for her, though if he remained true to form, he wouldn't return until later in the evening. That gave her the remains of the day to prepare. There was little to hold her here, no worldly possessions to reclaim. A warmer outfit and any food she could snag would be enough, and with so few of them left, she would have an easier time moving through the house undeterred.

She dug her nails deep into the taut flesh around her elbows. When had the person she'd become shifted so far from the girl who loved to read the stories from her mother's weathered books? Tears flowed, as Eleanor mourned that girl. She'd died when a monster burst from her skin. Was it the bone-deep invasion of magic that twisted her into the monster? Or was this form what lived inside her, all these years, waiting to come out? Those ponderings would break her worse than Rose.

"Your bath is ready," Rose broke into Eleanor's thoughts. She stood in the doorway, wiping her hands dry on a worn rag. Eleanor pulled herself up on unsteady limbs. Rose caught her as she staggered forward, taking her weight as Eleanor fought the tremors that threatened to collapse her legs out from under her. She couldn't reconcile Rose's actions with the girl's morals. Eleanor let the girl lead her to the steaming tub, not so much easing as collapsing into it as water sloshed onto the floor. Rose said nothing of Eleanor's apparent weakness as she scooped cups of hot water over her hair. Eleanor closed her eyes as the heat performed quiet miracles on her strained muscles until a soft moan drifted from her throat as she sank deep into the water. The warmth soothed the soreness; the water rinsed the sins away from her skin. At some point, Rose left her to her own devices. Eleanor used the time to solidify the details of her plan. She sat in the water until the steam began to chill, leaving cool dew droplets on her arms as her fingertips puckered.

Eleanor crawled from the tub in another heave of tepid water, wrapping herself in the coarse towel Rose left her, her shaking limbs muted. The bath served its purpose, invigorating her. Refreshed, she stalked past her room. Most of the other chambers stood dark and silent, a hall of temporary mausoleums until the Madame restocked. Eleanor ignored the tightness in her throat as she pushed open the first door. Her mother once said there was no honor in pilfering the dead, an ideology Eleanor once followed without question, but what did the dead need with pretty dresses and sweet-smelling perfumes? Despite this, she avoided the carefully laid out trinkets on the vanity, gifts from former patrons, a painstakingly constructed display to show the previous occupant's desirability, her worth.

So much effort to lessen the inherent misery of her life. Eleanor's hand shook as she opened the dresser drawers. Most of the clothing they were allowed in the carnal house didn't approach decency, but they were granted a plainclothes outfit for off days and the rare occasion when they earned a chance to accompany the Madame to market. Eleanor knew these details from the common room gossip but had never and would never earn such *privileges*. Her lip curled in a sneer that quickly fell. *As if I am so much better than they were? As if I am any less used and twisted inside?*

The plainclothes gown was a muddied brown, a coarse, practical, wool shift that would keep her warm enough. She let the towel fall, careful not to glance at her body in the vanity mirror as she pulled the dress over her head, tugging it in place over her lower half. The hem rose a little high, so the dark carapace of her legs was visible when she moved. It made her uncomfortable, but it was probably the best she would find. Eleanor finally chanced a look in the mirror, at the lean, hollow-cheeked woman she didn't recognize but for the fire in her dark eyes. She clutched the edge of the vanity hard enough that the wood splintered at the edges, driving slivers of wood into the tender pads of her fingers. She dismissed the prick of pain. One of the delicate perfume bottles toppled over with a clink. Eleanor set it upright. Even though she couldn't remember the name of the girl whose dress she wore. She met her own gaze in the mirror once more. The girl hadn't remembered her own name either in the end, burned away by the sickness of magic—renamed, rebranded until she was nothing but a shell used by the Madame's patrons.

It didn't matter what her name was here because the girl she'd been had died long ago, but Eleanor knew herself, and she wouldn't let the Madame, Vashon, or anyone take that from her. She paused as she left the room, staring at the chalk nameplate on the door. Kitty, a sing-song name for the patrons to croon, easy to remember. Eleanor swiped her fingers through it with a vehemence that surprised her. She stalked from room to room, smearing the names until she'd released the dead from the names that chained them here. She hoped whatever waited for them beyond, they either found a semblance of peace or nothing at all, because nothing was better than more misery.

Eleanor stood in the empty common room, at the cracked walls and stains that spoke of the horror and shame these girls lived every day and turned her back on it all. It was time to get the keys to the basement.

She moved through the silent house with as much stealth as she could muster, hoping the Madame remained passed out. Perhaps the loss of so many of her girls in such brutal fashion affected even the Madame's black heart, through Eleanor doubted it. She crept down the stairs, easing over the steps that creaked until she made it to the first floor. Without the general noise of the girls, the house sighed around her, a melancholy accompaniment to the wind that blew through the district. Eleanor folded her hands into her skirts as she wandered the floor. The Madame's parlor door was shut though she thought she scented the familiar pipe smoke. If the Madame was chasing a high, so much the better for Eleanor's plans. She held her breath as she eased past the door. There was still no sign of Rose, but the keyring hung on the hook, another small blessing. Eleanor didn't question it. She squeezed the keys together to maintain their silence as she lifted the ring free and kept her steady pace down the hall.

The day was further along than she realized as she reached the front half of the house, the shadows deeper as the natural light began to fade. Anxiety fluttered in her chest as she approached the basement door. This would be the hard part. She gritted her teeth as she held the lock tight, testing and discarding with slow, deliberate motions to keep the silence until she found the right one. Eleanor slowly released a breath as she eased the lock free and set it on the floor.

She opened the door with the same nail-biting slowness, but that didn't stop the squeal of the hinge. Eleanor froze, the sound cut off in the space of a second, but it had cracked through the house like a banshee's wail. She clutched the door, trembling, waiting, as her heart battered against her ribs. The Madame's door remained closed. Rose didn't appear.

The man in the basement remained silent.

That was more unnerving than the rest. How he had howled and screamed before, his cries unheeded or worse, the Madame would answer them. Had she finally broken him? Was he dead?

Eleanor swallowed hard and carefully shifted her ungainly limbs through the narrow opening. It was just wide enough for her bulk to slip through without provoking the hinge. Urgency pushed her forward as she struggled not to make a sound. Her hands clutched the railing, ignoring the splinters of worn wood that dug into her palms. By the time she reached the landing, the silence had left her nerves strung taut, alert to every hint of sound in the dark.

"Are you there?" Her voice was barely a whisper. The dark pulsed against her open eyes as her vision began to pick up heat. She could see the faint outline of the man, cowering against the wall across from her. After staring a few moments longer, she could perceive the slight lift and fall of his chest. He still breathed. "I'm going to get you out of here."

She released her firm grasp on the keys, the soft clink of metal muted in the cloying darkness of the basement. A snarl tore the air. Eleanor peered through the dark, her tail twitching. Not cowering. He was crouched there, a predator's crouch, and she'd wandered into striking distance. Eleanor scrambled back as he launched himself at her. She thought the chains would stop him until the curious lack of noise registered. She swallowed a strangled yelp as he slammed down on her, pushing her down painfully onto the stairs. The clicking of teeth far too sharp for any ordinary mouth sounded far too close to her face as saliva dripped on her cheek. A feral sound ripped from his chest, nothing near human. Fear wicked off her skin. Eleanor whimpered, trying to force her body into action. She wasn't a helpless human woman, not anymore, and when her brain finally caught up, she bucked, whipping her tail hard enough to knock him off her. Eleanor wasted no time scuttling backward up the stairs, away from the scream of vicious rage as he bounced off the concrete floor.

Beneath the instinctual fear that drove her back, Eleanor mourned her failure to save him. She didn't know what state his body was in, but his mind was gone. He would kill her if he caught her again.

She scrambled backward up the uneven stairs, scraped and scared, though he didn't follow. His growl rose, low and menacing from the dark, but he didn't pursue her. She only had a moment to interpret the significance of that before the basement door swung back, and the Madame seized her by the back of her dress.

Eleanor went airborne with a shriek. Her body crashed hard against the opposite wall, her head snapping back with a crack that blurred her vision as she slid to the floor. The Madam sat coiled across from her, her dark hair in disarray as her shoulders heaved.

"Vile little bitch," she snapped. Eleanor flinched as the coils of the Madame's insectile lower half rolled forward, closing the distance for the Madame to strike her. Braced as she was, the impact shot a starburst of pain through her cheek. The Madame's body curled around her. She could feel the pressure inside as her bones whined, the internal snap and pop of flesh stressed to the breaking point. Her vision wobbled at the edges as her head rolled to the side. Rose lay a few feet away, her blond hair streaked red, her face pulped like so much meat. Her lone eye stared sightlessly at Eleanor, who might have thought the girl dead if her ragged breath didn't whistle through her shattered nose.

Eleanor mouthed her name, trying to evince some response, but her blank expression didn't change. She'd checked out, after giving Eleanor away. Eleanor couldn't summon her anger at the girl's betrayal, not when she stared at the shredded visage of her face. A sob bubbled in her throat. She had failed to convince Rose to come with her, she'd failed to save the man in the basement, and she'd failed to escape. The Nightingale House would soak up her blood in its floorboards until she was another specter trapped in the woodgrain.

The front opened as the shadow of Vashon poured in, stretching and stretching, but she couldn't move herself to avoid it. It fell over her toes; she swore she could feel the temperature drop where it touched her.

"What's this now?" His voice rolled over her, deceptively calm. She could feel the anger simmering beneath it as he recognized her, his mind feathering against hers, the light, gentle to the point that it confused her. He set his cane against the wall as he took a step toward them.

"What have you done?" Her body quaked at those words. In her mind, she shied away, burrowing further into herself, unable to physically flee from the pressure that built in the air.

"I did as I saw fit with what's mine," the Madame hissed.

"But she is not yours," Vashon countered in the same smooth, silk voice he used on the room of girls before he wrought their deaths.

The coils of the Madame's lower half drew in tight, a reaction that betrayed the venom in her voice.

"*Good*." Eleanor let the vicious thought slip through. After everything she'd been through, she deserved to see the Madame's fear.

"Yes, you do," Vashon murmured. Anger tainted her satisfaction, that he could see her thoughts so easily, but she was too tired to resist him and too tired to feel ashamed by her desire. She gazed up to find Vashon studying her, his expression somber. "Do you want her pain?"

"What?" The Madame shrieked. She tried to flee, but Vashon held up a hand. The Madame froze, her spine bent at an awkward angle. She didn't so much as blink, he'd completely ensnared her body and mind.

Eleanor stared at him, the edges of her vision crackling like dead leaves. It hurt to keep her eyes open. She wanted to rest, but the desire for recompense, to payback every slight brought upon her merely for existing, was a searing cold weight in her chest.

"Yes," she rasped. Vashon smiled. She wanted to regret her choice but found she could not. His polished shoes moved passed her, careless of the blood that pooled around her as he searched the house for what he wanted. She knew what he wanted, could feel him ruffle and pluck the knowledge from her mind as he went. The Madame remained frozen, her face an exaggerated mask of fear as her unblinking gaze slowly slid to stare at Eleanor.

Vashon returned and handed two items to the Madame, who accepted them with jerky, tightly controlled movements. Eleanor didn't want to watch, but she couldn't look away. She wanted to close her eyes, yet they remained open. Open as the Madame poured the lamp oil over her own head. Open as the oil cascaded down her tangled black hair, soaked into her blood-spattered silk robe. The oil dripped down her face like tears. Vashon leaned against the wall, his pose casual as the Madame held up the box of matches.

A high keening noise poured through the Madame's translucent teeth as she fought Vashon's influence with everything she had, but her fingers plucked a match free and struck it against the textured side. Eleanor's eyes widened, her exhaustion melting away in dread as the match flared. No, this isn't what she wanted. This wasn't what she wanted.

"Mama, no," Rose sobbed.

"Wait, stop," Eleanor gasped. She struggled to sit up. Vashon didn't acknowledge either of them, his gaze glued to that single dancing flame.

The Madame pressed the lit match to her oil streaked cheek. The fire flashed over her, swarming her. Vashon kept his hold on her until her skin began to blacken and bubble. Eleanor knew the instant he released her, as the woman's agonized cries pounded into her skull. The Madame staggered forward, clutching at the walls as she burned. Still alive, but senseless from pain, aware as the flames consumed her, the Madame slapped against the walls of the hallway, clutching at paintings and wall hangings, feeding the eager flames until half the hallway was lit up.

Vashon hovered over Eleanor. She wanted to shrink from him, horrified at what he'd done, at herself that she weakened enough to want it. She whimpered as he slid his arms under her, lifting her with such care her thoughts scrambled. What did he want from her? She was terrified of the answer. Her body hung limp, her awareness a tenuous thing. The heat of the fire was a distant sensation that licked at the edge of her sense. Her arms swung as he turned to carry her from the carnal house. Madame Murmur's screams finally ceased. The Nightingale House burned. Rose stared up at her from the floor, her breathing labored, but still very alive.

Rose didn't deserve her pity. She didn't. There was barely anything human left in the girl. The Madame was dead. She could be free. But Eleanor knew, Rose wouldn't move as the carnal house burned around her. She had allowed the Madame to die, but she couldn't leave Rose there. It was a matter of Eleanor's own humanity.

Eleanor gave a cry and writhed out of Vashon's arms in a jarring tumble to the floor that hit every aching part of her. He crouched down beside her, frowning at her as if she were a petulant child.

"That was rather senseless, yes?" He smoothed a hand down the side of her face. "Please do not do it again." He wouldn't let her do it again. She could feel him, a serpent coiling around her mind, ready to draw in tight.

A feral snarl rent the air. Vashon whipped around with a frown a second before the wild man leapt on his back. Eleanor somehow found the strength to roll to her side as the two of them crashed through the burning hall. Vashon shouted, his expression one of pure shock as the wild man seized his fine shirt front and slammed him against the wall. Vashon bared his teeth, his grey eyes narrowed in concentration until the wild man knocked his head forward into Vashon's nose.

"Lyre!" Vashon sputtered as he struggled to keep the wild man from his throat. "Lyre!"

The flames writhed as a rush of wings filled the air. Eleanor's gaze slid to the doorway where Lyre stood, his expression stark at the sight of her. She wanted to tell him not to look, to run, but his face went slack as Vashon slid on his mind like a glove.

Lyre jerked forward.

"Dispose of this one. We really must be on our way," said Vashon. He spoke for her benefit, a child showing off his toys. Bile pooled in her mouth as Lyre faced the panting wild man. Her ears popped as pressure-filled the air. Vashon wanted her to see this too, she couldn't look away if she tried, which was why neither of them saw Rose as she grabbed the lord of Avergard's ankle and drove her blade straight down through his booted foot.

Vashon roared with pain and rage, backhanding Rose as he snarled an order under his breath that made Lyre twitch. The pressure in the air doubled to the point of pain.

An awareness settled over her, a coolness that trickled through her veins. Eleanor gasped, shocked by its familiarity, one that had faded to a dream. A figure stood in the doorway, her wide-eyed gaze soaking up the scene as Lyre's wings spread until their tips brushed the scorched walls. The flames shied away from his feathers.

The woman darted forward, moving in front of Lyre without a moment of hesitation. She clapped her hands over his mouth. Lyre startled violently; his wings clapped hard enough to smother the fire in their immediate vicinity, though the smoke remained, burning Eleanor's eyes as it choked her lungs.

"Not like this." Her soft voice filled the sudden silence. Tears pricked at Eleanor's eyes. She recognized that voice, dreamt of it during those first days before the Nightingale House leeched the hope from her soul. She couldn't see Lyre's expression, but she saw the wild man as he rose to his knees, the naked relief that smoothed the feral lines from his face. He felt the same pang of recognition she did, but the girl didn't take her gaze off Lyre. She didn't flinch as Lyre grabbed her shoulders, digging his fingers into her, but he didn't move her, his wings twitching through the agonizing encounter until Vashon's awed whisper reached their ears.

"The sister."

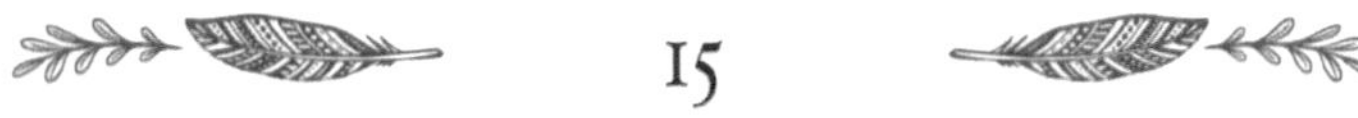

15

AZURE

Azzy thought her heart might burst from her chest. Her gaze locked with Armin, his storm-shroud eyes disoriented, confused, and afraid. He didn't know her, didn't recognize her, but her words stalled him. They touched something lost and forgotten that she could see him worrying, an unhealed wound festering beneath the surface.

Kai hovered behind her. It hurt to see the feral pain in his eyes, one of the wretched collars gouging into his neck, eating away at his sanity. She longed to go to him, but she couldn't look away from her brother, not now, with danger dancing on tiptoes along her nerves. The stench of burning meat and boiled blood singed her nostrils as it told her the story of what happened here. Between her brother, Kai, and the two injured women on the floor, she felt pulled in a dozen directions.

She longed to help them all, she didn't know if she could save any of them. The weight of choice sank to her core, a smothering lodestone that held her in place, torn between a dozen pathways. Above all her choices, her awareness of the injured Vashon fizzed as the whispers spooled in her head—a strange constant murmur of noise like the buzzing of a giant swarm. A disconcerting sensation but one that didn't overwhelm her senses.

Vashon's expression changed as he noticed her, the haughty anger seeping into dangerous curiosity before a shade of wonder stole over his face as he rose to his full height.

"The sister," he said with a tone verging on reverence.

The swarm of whispers buzzed louder, drowning out the alarmed spin of her thoughts. Armin's reaction was far more intense. His eyes went wild as his grip on her shoulders deepened to bruising intensity before he shoved her away and spun back on Vashon.

"Per-"

Vashon sneered and closed his hand into a fist. Armin's knees crashed to the ground. Azzy reached for him when Kai's arm wrapped around her waist. He dragged her back as Armin surged to his feet, teeth bared. Vashon tightened his fist. Her brother's steps staggered. Vashon's gaze shifted to her, and Azzy stiffened at the sensation of invisible hands crawling through her mind. The whispers surged.

A trickle of blood flowed from Vashon's nose and his hold on Armin snapped. The brilliant, mottled wings on his back beat once as her brother tackled the lord. Azzy's sense of danger screamed, but Kai didn't give her an inch, his gaze set on the open door. No, no, this couldn't be happening. She had to save her brother. She couldn't leave him to Vashon.

"No, wait, please," she cried, twisting in Kai's grip.

She framed his face, caught between the fear for her brother and the ache at seeing Kai again. He stilled, leaning into her touch with a whimper that made her chest grow tight. Armin couldn't stall Vashon for long. The moment swelled as the choice loomed. Azzy's expression crumpled as she sobbed. Her hands swept down to grip Kai's forearms, anchoring them both to the present.

"Help me save the girls," she said.

The words cut at her lips, but she hadn't known what she was walking into when she followed the pull here. Kai reluctantly pulled back from her grasp to lift the injured blonde woman in his arms. Caught between fire and blood, Azzy made the impossible choice as she approached the dark-haired woman. She didn't register the woman's scorpid lower half until she shifted her legs beneath her blood-stained dress. Azzy wasn't sure what level of ferocity she would encounter, but when she locked onto the woman's bleak gaze, a frisson of awareness coursed through her. She knew this woman. Azzy stared, transfixed as she tried to place where she knew her from when the memory bubbled up through the swarming whispers, the scared face as magic ravaged her body and mind.

"It's you," said Azzy.

The scorpid woman swallowed, her voice course due to her injured throat as she spoke. "You're real," she rasped. Tears streaked her bruised face.

Shock fizzed through her senses, but she couldn't stop to process it all. Not when Armin fought so fiercely to keep Vashon from her, she had to find another way.

"Can you move?"

The girl nodded and hissed in pain as Azzy helped her to stand. Azzy took as much of the girl's surprisingly slight weight as she could as they made for the door. She paused at the entrance, torn by the desire to save her brother and her need to get the others to safety. She came face to face with him at last only to leave him behind once again. Azzy coughed, her body succumbing to the smoke despite the disquiet in her mind. The scorpid girl's head lolled on her shoulder. Armin looked up amid the struggle, though surely the distraction would cost him. Their gazes locked, filled with unspoken longing and a thousand words forgotten but never gone.

Vashon hooked a leg over Armin's and flipped him sideways.

"Go," the scorpid girl rasped. "Go before he seizes your mind."

Azzy turned away. It cost her. Each step cost her, but she kept moving forward until she saw a familiar four-legged shape prowling the shadows. Howl must have been too anxious to maintain his human shape. The cape tangled around his neck like a smock.

"Howl!" The lynx darted forward and pressed his furry bulk to her legs. His body shook with the strength of his purrs as he rubbed his cheeks against her, completely unperturbed by the scorpid woman.

"Help me, please," she said. Howl blurred, quickly pulled the cape down as he shored up the injured scorpid woman's other side.

"You have interesting friends," said the woman, her expression relaxed as they fled the burning carnal house. A buzz of power nipped at Azzy's senses. The swarm of whispers hissed a warning. She didn't look back but doubled their steps. They were far from safe. Kai shuffled forward several feet ahead of her, her first good look at his emaciated form as he limped with the other girl dangling from his arms.

The Way of Heavenly Delights had finally noticed the carnal house fire. The streets began to fill with curious lords pulled from their illicit activities. They weren't safe. They couldn't be seen.

"Howl, we need to, we need to duck into an alley or something—"

Kai collapsed to his knees, spilling the injured woman in his arms onto the unforgiving stones as he clutched at his head. Faces began to turn from the fire, to look, to stare, distracted anew as power shook the building so hard part of the top floor collapsed in on itself. The victor would emerge soon. They had to get off the street.

"Take her," she told Howl as she rushed to Kai's side. The gaunt lines of his face hurt to look at, and she couldn't shake the feeling she'd failed him too. "Kai?"

"Not here," he said, his voice rough and strained from long disuse. "Not here, not here. Can't be here. This city is death. Death Below. Death rises. It *yearns*." Her skin prickled at his words, far too similar to the malevolent whispers of the Pit. In the smoky glow of the streetlamps, Kai's irises were a dull yellow and mindless. He couldn't stay like this. The collar's spikes were encrusted with old blood as they dug into his neck, the wounds blackened and oozing. She didn't know who snapped the foul thing on him, but she had to pry it free, even if it meant carting him in wolf form through the streets of Avergard.

"I'm going to take this off," she said. Part of her wanted to rip it free, but she hesitated, the whispers filtering through her mind. She had to proceed with caution. The streets grew more crowded with each second, pressing in on them. She couldn't do this here. Kai's hands gripped her wrist. She met his gaze, bright yellow wolf eyes stared back.

"Azzy?" He said her name with a shock of wonder. The right side of her face was wet from the tears that fell freely from her unaltered eye. He moved into her, wrapping her arms around him as he pressed his face into the crook of her neck. He inhaled deeply, and his body shook against her as recognition set in. Azzy gripped him tightly, fervently returning his embrace.

The scent of smoke and misery clung to him, his ordinarily light brown skin ashen and streaked with filth. She stroked his back, the muscles twitching and relaxing under her touch. She was all too aware of the passing seconds, of the curious faces that peered in their direction, of the silence that filled the carnal house as it burned. Urgency pricked at her nerves. They had to move. They couldn't stay here. Kai's hold on her tightened as if he sensed her anxiety, afraid she would flee from him like startled prey.

"We have to move," she breathed. Howl hovered nearby, supporting the scorpid woman, while the other woman lay unconscious on the street.

"I—I can't," Kai sobbed against her neck. Azzy lifted her arms to the collar around his neck. He jerked away from her with a hiss.

"Let me take it off," she said. She fought to keep her tone calm and soothing, but anxiety crept in at the edges. Kai's trembling grew worse, but he shook his head hard, an act that made the spikes dig in. He winced.

"You can't, can't take it off, not here, not here," he gulped air between words as if he were drowning.

"Come on then," said Azzy, trying to lift his body from the ground. His head fell back as he looked at her, reaching up to stroke her cheek with unsteady hands.

"Go," he whispered. Azzy shook her head. She already tore herself away from her brother, she couldn't lose Kai too. Not after she'd found him again. Desperation ate away at the last of her calm, her movements more frantic as she tried to lift and drag Kai to the nearby alley, somewhere, anywhere other than the open street. The door to the burning carnal house blew out onto the street with an explosive crack that made them all flinch. A disheveled Vashon strode from the entrance, dragging an unconscious Armin in his wake by the hinge of one wing, the other bent at an odd angle.

Azzy stifled her sob as the lord of Avergard dropped her brother at his feet and began to scan the crowd. The whispers surged, the murmuring hive coalescing around her mind. Protecting her, she realized. Her heart tripped in her chest. If he saw them, everything she'd sacrificed tonight would be for naught.

A figure shifted in front of her, blocking them from Vashon's view. "Grab the other one and bring her to my shop."

Azzy's heart stalled in her chest as the familiar voice poured over her, a balm to her fevered thoughts. "You boy, follow them."

Howl hesitated, watching her face. She barely had the faculties to nod ascent, as the figure leaned in and waved a vial under Kai's nose.

Kai's eyes rolled back in his head, and Brixby was there to catch him. Strength surged through her limbs as she met his warm gaze. "You must get up, Azzy."

She inhaled a sob of relief, overwhelmed as she struggled to stand. Brixby lifted Kai over his shoulder with a grunt of effort. Azzy reached out and pinched the back of his shirt between her fingers as if to convince herself he was real. The cloth beneath in her grip was soft and warm from his body heat. Her breath came in harsh pants as she held onto his shirt like a lifeline, following her long-lost guardian into the narrow doorway of a nearby shop, where a long haired stranger, face unseen, had carried the unconscious scarred woman. The two of them had disappeared further into the building before Azzy crossed the threshold. Her knees went weak as the familiar sights and smells of an apothecary shop enclosed around her. She finally released Brixby's shirt as he carried the unconscious Kai through another doorway.

Brixby paused for only a moment to look at her. "I must attend my patients. Once I get them stable, we'll talk."

"Go," she said, her heart thumped painfully against her ribs.

He nodded. "Nuin, are they ready?"

Azzy startled as another figure emerged from the other room, wiping the blood from their long delicate fingers.

"They're settled, for now, Oswin, but the two women have severe injuries. And the other..." The lilting voice trailed over as they clicked their teeth to their tongue. Their violet gaze settled on Azzy, filled with a warmth that echoed her guardian's. "Why don't I prepare some tea for your ward?"

Brixby gave her shoulders a gentle squeeze as he extricated himself from her grip. "Thank you, Nuin."

Azzy wanted to help, but exhaustion pulled at her bones. She hadn't slept since the Maven came after her, pushing her to her limits to break through. She still wasn't sure if the Maven was an enemy or an ally, and she wasn't eager to put herself within spitting distance of the enigmatic figure so soon.

Slowly she turned to take in the rows and rows of glass bottles, packets of dried plants, the mortar and pestle still full of some half-crushed powder, as if she interrupted Brixby in the middle of work with another of her problems. She trailed a hand over the wooden cutting block as she ached for another time, another place. If she closed her eyes, the fragrant scent of drying flowers nearly took her there, but she could never go back. She could never reclaim it.

Azzy registered footsteps approaching her a moment before Brixby grabbed her shoulders and crushed her to him. The embrace broke something inside her, a stone shaken loose from the dam of everything she'd kept at bay, the flood of fear and pain washing through her as she clung to Brixby, solid and real, unable to stop her sobs. He held her through it, an anchor that kept her from being swept away.

"I thought you were dead," said Azzy. "A ghost haunting me."

She sniffled, trying to ease the tight muscles of her chest, her relief and wonder palpable as the immense weight of worry fractured. Armin was still in danger, Kai was out of head, and Safiya was set to die in less than two days' time, but as the whispers moved through her mind, she felt something shift. The tether went slack as she followed the pull to its end, all the pieces aligned.

"My poor girl, I'm so sorry," said Brixby. He pulled back just enough to swipe away her tears with his calloused thumb. His other hand gently touched the corner of her altered eye, his expression somber. "You've been through so much, Azure."

She took a steadying breath even as she reached up and held his hand to her cheek. She looked him over as he did the same to her. Her guardian had a few more nicks and scars on his arms, his hair longer, styled in dreadlocks he pulled back into a high tail.

After so long underground, the sun had darkened his complexion to a rich brown that made his light eyes even more brilliant.

"I'm going to look in on the others. I'll be right back," he said.

Azzy sat hard on the workbench stool, her whole body sagging though her nerves still hummed. What if Vashon found them here? How could she defend this place, and those she loved, against him?

A muted thump startled her. Azzy hadn't even heard Nuin approach as they set a steaming mug down on the workbench in front of her. Nuin drew up another stool and gracefully sat next to her with a bowl and washcloth, their expression patient as they wet the cloth.

"I'm going to wash off the blood, little one," they said.

Azzy studied the stranger as they gently lifted the cloth and dabbed at the dried blood on her arms and neck with slow, deliberate movements. They were tall, possibly taller than Wallach, fine black hair pulled back to the nape of their neck in a simple style that contrasted to the delicate silk robe they wore. There was a golden undertone to their light skin, their features androgynous, angular and beautiful, from their long, tip-tilted nose, and pointed chin, high aristocratic cheekbones, and full, lush lips. There was power in their violet eyes, and Azzy realized with a start she was looking at a lord of Avergard.

Nuin went still. "No harm will come to you here," they said, their rich voice almost hypnotic. "Vashon won't find you."

Her eyes widened. "How?"

Nuin smiled, the effect devastating. "Call it my specialty."

Azzy fell silent, unsettled but relieved. She lifted the mug, the grassy scent of the tea and the warmth of the mug soothing her nerves before she even took a sip. Lord of Avergard they may be, Nuin didn't seem to mind the menial task of cleaning her up.

"How do you know Brixby?" She saw it then, the glow that filled Nuin's face at the mention of her guardian.

"I bought him at auction," they said, a simple answer that spurred another dozen questions.

Brixby ducked his head through the doorway. "I need another set of hands."

Nuin jumped to their feet, flowing across the room with

soundless grace, Azzy on their heels. The other room proved to be an infirmary; the others laid in cots. On the far one by the wall, Kai slept, Howl curled in lynx form at his feet. She knew her friend would keep a watch over Kai as they helped the women.

Brixby had already managed to bandage and stabilize the blonde, but the scorpid woman lay deathly still, far too pale from blood loss.

"Pin your sleeves," said Brixby. "I need someone to hold while I work." Azzy knew what he meant. Her injuries were severe enough; he needed to sew her up inside.

"Let me wash up," said Nuin, rolling back their silk sleeves.

Azzy knelt beside the scorpid woman's cot. She'd saved her life and left her to the mercy of the Snatchers. No, as Morglint said, there were things beyond her control, things she couldn't take all the blame for; she couldn't save this woman from the Snatchers, not then, when she knew so little about herself and how her magic worked. Brixby and Nuin's voices murmured with low urgency behind her as she lowered a hand to the woman's chest. Her heartbeat was faint, sluggish, as if the effort to keep beating was too great to manage. The whispers threaded through the contact, probing, exploring the extent of the woman's injuries. It was astonishing she lasted this long.

Azzy lifted one of Brixby's blades from the nearby tray and dragged a quick-burning line across the tip of her finger. Silence fell behind her as she pulled the symbol from memory, the broken rune Morglint taught her in that tent, which felt like years ago now. She pieced it together in her mind, saw where it needed to be altered, fixed, completed. Heat gathered in her chest as her mind dropped into the center of her milling whispers, where they slid around her, guiding her, as pressure built. Her hand shook as the blood flowed, inked itself on the woman's skin. The pressure popped as it snapped into place. The woman sucked in a breath as the symbol sank in and disappeared, the wet sound of mending tissue and crackling bones filled the sucking silence.

Azzy rocked back on her heels, the cut on her finger still dripping as the scorpid woman opened her eyes. They stared at one another for a long silent moment before the woman sighed and fell asleep. Azzy didn't dare look at Brixby as she turned to the other, the blonde. The power was still there, brimming beneath her skin, but Azzy could feel the drain on her body in a way she hadn't before as if the knowledge and conscious effort created new limitations. Brixby's hand stopped her.

"You're going to collapse," he said, his tone calm despite the worry in his eyes. Azzy wanted to push through, she would push through. Howl gave a warning growl from the other cot. She didn't see the vial until the sickly-sweet scent clogged her nose. The whispers settled as a sweet fog rolled through her mind and dragged her down.

THE LONG WAY BACK

 16 

AZURE

Azzy woke to find Howl curled up on her feet, his human form clothed in the ill-fitting cloak that twisted up around his neck. He looked even younger asleep; his lax expression still bore the soft curves of a child's face. By her estimate, he couldn't be older than twelve but was probably younger than that. He'd pulled his gangly legs tight to his chest, the position so cat-like she smiled.

She eased out from under him as she took inventory of the other cots. The blonde woman was still there, heavily bandaged and unconscious, but clearly not in the same critical life or death situation as her companion. The scorpid woman was so heavily beaten her body's natural healing was shot. Azzy held her breath as she looked at the last cot, but it was empty. Nervous energy fluttered under her skin. Her bittersweet reunion with Armin stole something of the moment that could have been between them, so focused on her brother she hadn't given Kai the reaction of her heart.

Azzy entered the main workshop to find Brixby and Nuin sitting side by side as they drank tea. The way Nuin leaned into Brixby made Azzy feel as if she had intruded on a private moment between them, but Nuin was quick to notice her.

"Ah, she's awake," they said. "Promise not to overextend yourself in the next few minutes and I'll brew you some tea."

"You better not even try it," Brixby muttered into his mug.

She wanted to cry and laugh. How she had missed him! Her emotions were a mixed cluster of highs and lows, equally intense as she leaned against the work bench. "Where's Kai?"

Brixby frowned. "The two-kind? He's in bad shape Azzy. I

moved him to the inner yard to give him air but he's not healing like he should be either. He needs to shift. I don't know who put that collar on him, but he resisted my attempts to remove it."

"We can't remove it," said Azzy. She had a theory of who put the collar on him, though she hadn't worked out the why and the how of it either. The only one who could answer her was Kai. "Could you show me to the inner yard?"

Nuin raised a brow. Brixby got to his feet. "Are you sure?" That steady sea green gaze met hers. It was a gentle question, one borne of worry for her. He'd stopped her last night to keep her from burning herself out, but he trusted her to take care of herself.

"Yes," she said. He nodded once and beckoned for her to follow. Azzy burned to ask him questions about this shop, about Nuin, and what happened to him after she fled from the Snatchers, but Kai was suffering. She should have seen to him immediately after the scorpid woman. Her body was still stiff from the healing, an exertion she hadn't expected when her previous episodes seemed so effortless, but Wallach warned her that knowledge gave magic shape and boundaries.

Brixby led her back through the makeshift infirmary to a door that opened out into an enclosed garden, rows of herbs and flowers planted in neat pathways for purpose over aesthetic. Kai knelt in the center of the garden, hands braced on his knees, with his face lifted to the sun.

"Be careful, Azzy," was all Brixby said before he shut the door behind her.

She kept her steps slow and soft as she approached him, but she knew he could hear her by the tilt of his head. The muscles of his back began to twitch. The closer she drew, the more injuries she noted. Where had he been? Who did this to him? Her chest went tight as she laid a hand on his shoulder and he flinched at her touch. Kai looked up, the wolf staring through his eyes. Azzy kept her hand on his shoulder as she moved around him. His complexion looked gray under the sunlight, bruised beneath his eyes and the hollows of his cheeks. He swayed slightly as he sat there, as if the very effort of sitting up right was too much, but the collar dug into his neck with each minute shift of his body.

She couldn't wait for answers. The moment her hands touched it he snatched at her wrists, his grip painful as his breath came in sharp pants.

"No, I have to find her. I have to…."

"Who do you have to find?"

"Azure," Kai panted. "Must find her. Warn her. *They rise.*" Each word cost him, until he gasped between them, unable to catch a breath. His fingers curled into fists over his thighs as his arms shook. It hurt to see him like this, senseless that she stood in front of him.

She knelt across from him and gently cover his hands with hers. "You found her," she said. His gaze flickered over her face, unseeing, but his ragged breathing eased. He looked down at their hands. A tear slid down his cheek.

"Failed her. Failed them all. So dark," he said. "Out."

That he formed words was miraculous. Azzy slowly reached for the collar again. He caught her hand and pressed it against his cheek.

"The witch," he breathed.

"I know," said Azzy. Had they arrived in Avergard together and been separated somehow? Why had Kai followed her here, to this city that was so dangerous for him? "Why didn't you stay in the woods?"

"Azzy," said Kai. He closed his eyes as he rubbed his cheek into her palm. Was that his reason or did he finally realize she sat in front of him?

"I need you to trust me," she said. He stilled. His throat worked.

The yellow of his eyes burned as they opened to slits. "This is real?"

"Yes," said Azzy, her voice roughened by the tightness in her throat. "Please, please let me take this off you?"

His gaze finally focused on her face. Kai shifted forward before she could react, cradling her face as he brushed his lips along her brow, down her nose, across each cheek, gently exploring the planes of her face before he rubbed his cheek against hers and tucked his chin into the crook of her neck, his arms loosely wrapped around her back. Azzy slid her arms over his back, running her hands in soothing circles until the tension drained out of him.

She kept one hand on his back as she lifted the other to the collar. "I met a little boy who is a lynx. He calls himself two-kind, says that two bodies share one soul and shift seamlessly between them." She nicked her finger on one of the many jagged edges of the collar, splitting her concentration as she spoke. "He told me, the longer someone like him is forced into one shape or the other, the more they forgot how to change their shape at will." Kai twitched at the scent of her blood, but she kept her hand firm on his back. Her bloodied finger began to trace the runes of the collar where they flared and disappeared from the metal.

"Wait," Kai gasped, his gaze fleetingly lucid as he looked up at her. She froze, the barest inch left to unravel before the ugly collar fell free. "Safiya placed it on me."

"This won't hurt her, I promise you," said Azzy.

His shaking hand reached up to brush his knuckles along her cheek. "And you?"

She captured his hand. "I won't do that to you again," she whispered. "Will you let me remove it?"

He nodded, his gaze shifting, going distant from one second to the next.

The collar fell to the ground between them. The shift was instant. The wolf whined, his massive head still resting on her shoulder. Azzy closed her eyes as she continued to run her hand in circles along his back.

"I'm sorry I didn't find you sooner," she said. He pressed his nose into her ear, whining low in his throat. The sound broke her heart twice over. She held the wolf close, breathing hard through the desire to sob. Her short respite in Wallach's household had lulled her into a false sense of safety. So quickly, she'd forgotten how to handle the constant sense of danger, the ebb and flow of loss and survival that constituted her life. Or was it that the taste of safety, of partial peace, made it so much worse?

Kai shifted to settle his head on her lap, still whining as she stroked the coarse fur of his back. She stayed with him, until the whine finally gave way to deep breaths as he found rest at last. She was loathed to move, soaking in the combined warmth of the sun and Kai, worried if she moved an inch, he would wake to find her. The door to the shop opened and Brixby emerged, Howl on his heels, and a mug of tea in his hands. Howl froze at the sight of the wolf, his gaze flickering between Kai and Azzy as he approached on tip toe. He settled on a patch of grass a few feet away, on his haunches, ready to spring away if Kai moved.

Brixby sat on the stones beside Azzy and handed her the tea. He picked up the dead collar, turning it over in his hands as Azzy took a tentative sip. A different taste than last night, somehow cool and hot at the same time. Each sip seemed to send a pulse of renewed energy through her.

"Nuin is a master with teas," said Brixby. He traced the smooth length of metal where the runes had been and released a long breath. Azzy worried what his reaction would be, but when he looked up his gaze brimmed with warm pride. "You've figured yourself out at last."

Azzy laughed, Kai stirring with a grumble as he shifted his head to her knee. She gently stroked between his ears. "Yes," she said.

Brixby nodded to the crouching Howl. "Your young friend speaks quite highly of you."

"Does he now?" Howl ducked his head when she glanced his way, his cheeks tinged pink. "He's a good friend," she said, her voice soft. Howl inched closer.

"He told me you serve in the House of Seven Smiles," said Brixby.

Azzy inhaled through her nose. "There are worse places to be."

Brixby's long dark fingers tapped the stones beneath him. "Will you be returning to his house?"

She looked at her guardian, uncertain of the intention in his question. Brixby saw her expression and shook his head.

"Nuin and I could shelter you here," he said. "You don't have to go back."

She thought of Cherise, Lenin, and Petyr, loyal to a fault, who welcomed her into their little family. Of Wallach, so closed off, yet so desperate to redeem himself, unable to see himself as anything other than a monster. She thought of the Maven's smirking face, lurking the halls of house, unknown, unseen, pulling the strings....

"I have to," said Azzy.

"Then we shall return you formally," said Nuin from the garden doorway. They sipped their own tea, their glossy black hair loose and long down to their waist. "It will guarantee the safety of the others through the market."

"The others?"

Nuin arched a brow. "I can hide them here, but if Vashon is looking for them, he will only extend me the courtesy of another lord until his patience runs out." They took another sip of tea. "Collectively, they will be safest in Wallach's household."

Nuin was an even more unusual lord than Wallach, seemingly content in the confines of a small apothecary shop in the Way of Heavenly Delights, and Azzy knew why as their gaze slid to Brixby. They told Azzy they bought Brixby at auction, but it was clear to her that her guardian was not a servant here.

"I shall go check over the others," said Nuin. "I doubt most of them are in any shape to be moved just yet." They winked at Azzy as they drifted back into the house.

Azzy smiled and reached for Brixby's hand. "What happened to you, after I ran?"

Her guardian's shoulders fell. "I did everything I could to delay the inevitable."

She gave his hand a squeeze. "You couldn't stop it, no one could."

He raised his brows, catching her gaze. "I'm not so certain of that now."

Azzy shook her head. "I can't stop the change, but-," she bit the inside of her lip. "I think I can do something."

Brixby turned over her hand to look at her injured fingertip. The bleeding had stopped but the cut was still there. He made a face and pulled a vial from one of his numerous pockets, dabbing the cut with a drop of cool liquid that burned. "I spoke to Eleanor while you slept, a very illuminating conversation."

Azzy blinked at him. "The scorpid woman calls herself Eleanor?"

"No, her name is Eleanor," said Brixby. He withdrew a length of gauze and dressed the wound. "Her memory is intact. She said you were the one who pulled her through the fever."

Azzy swallowed. "I didn't think she remembered me."

"She didn't just remember you," said Brixby, giving a tug to the end of the gauze bandage. "There was a connection. She knew you were in the city."

"I didn't know she was here," said Azzy. Or had she? The eponymous pull she followed hadn't led her to one person. She'd felt a tug to the Way of Heavenly Delights since that first day Cherise brought her to market. Maybe it wasn't an individual connection that brought her here, but all of them, though she couldn't shake the sense that her arrival last night wasn't a coincidence. The Maven hadn't pushed her to the brink in the encounters until yesterday. A confluence of events, those were her words.

Azzy stiffened. "What time is it?"

"Still early in the morning," said Brixby. "You didn't sleep long after sunrise, and the others woke before dawn."

Safiya's execution was set for the following dawn. There was still time, not a great deal of it, but there was still time. Azzy rubbed her face as the familiar weight of urgency settled on her shoulders. She couldn't wait for the others to recover. She had to return to Wallach before he did something reckless, except she had no plan to offer him. Frustration created a knot beneath her brow, an ache she couldn't ease.

Cool fingertips pressed to her temples. Azzy startled as Nuin tapped the side of her head. She hadn't heard or sensed them approach, distracted by pain, but neither Howl nor Kai reacted. Brixby appeared amused over his mug of tea.

"You have too much tension for one so young," said Nuin. The coolness spread beneath her skin; the ache faded.

"Thank you," said Azzy.

"There's too much weight here," said Nuin, gently tapping her skull. "You can't carry the weight of the sky alone." They gathered the empty mugs and retreated into the house.

"Nuin's right," said Brixby. "We'll help you find Armin."

"There's someone else," said Azzy. "She's almost out of time."

Brixby frowned. "Tell me."

"She set to be executed tomorrow," said Azzy. A flicker of surprise crossed Brixby's expression.

"What do you *need* to help her?"

Azzy lifted her hands in a helpless gesture. "I can't get to her."

Brixby sat back and steepled his hands. "You need to get into the prison." He bowed his head to her. "That I can do."

Azzy gaped at him. "How?"

Her guardian gave her a long look. Right, he was an apothecary. "Honestly, Azzy, are you so bent on doing this yourself that you've forgotten how to ask for help?"

"Every time I ask for help, someone I care about is caught in the crossfire," said Azzy. Her hand stroked through Kai's fur.

Brixby sighed as he clambered to his feet. He leaned over to pinch her chin. "But it is their decision to walk into fire."

It took some convincing for Howl to remain behind. She avoided a fight with Kai through the convenience of his exhaustion. Brixby slipped her into Avergard's prison with laughable ease. He tossed a cloak over her shoulders and called her his apprentice. That was all it took to get her inside. Brixby went about his business, attending to the prisoners to keep up the ruse while Azzy followed the tug and pull of her whispers until she found the witch's cell.

She hadn't spoken face to face with Safiya since their bargain in the woods, though she'd watched two separate encounters that made her feel like a voyeur to the witch's plight. Safiya rose to her feet, her expression incredulous before Azzy drew back her hood.

"You shouldn't be here," Safiya hissed, her gaze darting along the empty hall. Who was she looking for? Vashon? Or Wallach? The hint of disappointment in her gaze spoke of the latter.

"I came with the apothecary," said Azzy.

The witch's mouth pressed into a thin line. "They do want their prisoners healthy to the end."

Azzy wrapped her hands around the bar. "I can't save you."

Safiya's smile was bittersweet. "I never wanted you to try, Azure." Because the witch had a plan. Azzy could see the glint in her gaze. Safiya had weeks to think her way out of her predicament.

"I think," said Azzy, "that you could have escaped this cell at any time."

Safiya's smile widened to a grin. "Ah, but I would still be a wanted woman with a death sentence over my head."

"What will you do?"

Safiya shrugged. "According to the good citizens of Avergard, I must die tomorrow."

"If you won't tell me your plan," said Azzy, "at least tell us how we can help."

"Us?" A frown marred her brow.

"Wallach will tear down this prison stone by stone before they have the chance to bring you to the block."

Safiya scoffed until she realized Azzy was serious. "He can't," she said, her tone anxious. "He would ruin everything. Ruin himself," she said, the words coming faster and faster. "I can't let him do that. Not for me."

"Then tell me how we keep him from doing that," said Azzy. The witch held her stare for so long Azzy wasn't sure her plea worked, but Safiya approached the bars and gripped her hands.

"I'll need you once the ax falls."

Nuin greeted them at the door on their return, a concerned expression on the lord's beautiful face.

"He started pacing as soon as he woke. The boy stayed with him, even though the wolf makes him nervous."

Azzy nodded and rushed past them to the inner garden. Howl wasn't the only one keeping watch over the restless wolf. The scorpid woman, Eleanor, occupied the far corner of the garden.

Howl didn't seem put off by the woman's insectile appendages, pressing against her legs in lynx form, his feline eyes trained on the wolf. Kai rushed to her side as soon as Azzy entered, nearly knocking her off her feet as he brushed against her. He limped as he paced, as he ran, his hind leg slightly crooked. She set a hand on his back to still his movements. He trembled under her touch.

His soft whines began to fill the air.

"The Madame kept him chained in the basement," said Eleanor, folding her arms over herself. Her eyes were haunted as she spoke. "I don't know how he got there, but he got worse every day."

Kept alone, in the dark, unable to shift, it had to be Kai's worst nightmare. Azzy hated that she hadn't tried to find him sooner, that she hadn't followed the pull before last night. This was so much worse than the damage done by the collar alone. What had that imprisonment done to his mind? Could she ever help him find his way back?

"Howl?"

The boy shimmered to human at her call. Kai turned against her legs with a snarl. Azzy gripped his fur with both hands to stay upright. Howl cringed but managed to keep his human form. "I can't talk to him, Azzy. He's too wild inside."

More animal than human. Her fingers tightened their grip on his fur. Kai began whining again, rocking back and forth on his bad leg though it had to hurt him. No, an animal wouldn't act like this unless there was something else wrong, something that interfered with the natural instincts to avoid discomfort to an injured body part.

"Could-," she stopped, swallowing at the hard lump in her throat. "Could you leave us alone?"

Eleanor nodded, though Howl hesitated until she took his hand and led him inside. Kai trembled hard against her legs as they passed, his fear a palpable thing as Howl sniffed the air.

The wolf moved with Azzy as she brought them to the center of the garden once again, easing him to the ground with his head in her lap. The high canine whines didn't cease though his body went lax on the ground beside her. She buried her face in his ruff, uncertain she could undo what had been done to him. It wasn't a matter of fixing him, but a matter of helping him find the way back. Azzy took a steadying breath and sank into the stream of whispers that flowed through her mind.

The whispers stirred around her, pushing and pulling her forward, as they followed the sound of Kai's distress deep, deeper, into the pitch dark.

She heard his labored breathing in the dark.

Kai?

His awareness shifted, tightened, closed off from her. *He was alone in the suffocating darkness, trapped beneath the ground.*

No. You're here, with me. Azzy reached for him. He jerked back.

Not real, not real. I'm going to die here and never see her again.

Her heart ached. She kept moving forward until her seeking hands found him, pulling him forward. He quaked against her.

She's gone, gone, gone. I couldn't keep her safe. Couldn't find her.

Kai, come back to me. She couldn't pull him through, not on her own, not if he didn't want to come back. *Why couldn't you stay in the woods? Stay free?* It was a stray thought she hadn't meant for him to see. She knew he'd come seeking her but didn't understand why. They'd relied on each other to survive the dangers of the Above, a bond forged from necessity over choice. She'd forced him into a human shape, uncertain if he could shift naturally like Howl or if he'd forgotten how. Could she even help him relearn something that should be instinct? She couldn't even help him out of the dark.

Had to find her. Must keep her safe. I can't leave here. My leg can't heal. I failed her again.

It was like trying to soothe a raw, exposed nerve. Her touch seemed to do more damage than good. What good was she here? She had this power to unmake magic, to pull memory from the ether, and find the true nature of things, but there was no magic in Kai's trauma and pain, a mental cage woven from his recent imprisonment. How long had he been down there, collared in the dark?

You didn't fail me. Azzy wished she could see his face, but the human side was buried beneath the wolf. It was possible she could recreate the cord she made when they journeyed through the Below, but she didn't want to trap him in one form, reliant on another to shift.

I failed. Couldn't protect mine. Couldn't find her. Lost in the dark.

His thoughts grew more scattered, drifting away from her. He'd called her 'mine'. In the quiet of her mind, she mourned the loss. She hadn't dared to let herself think of him in such terms, so uncertain of her emotions, of his, but Kai was certain. He'd followed her to a city of monsters.

Yours. She pushed the thought to him, a final attempt before she pulled back. Maybe she could reach him one day, when they weren't constrained by time. She would think of some way to help him.

She stared across the empty garden, her hands still buried in his fur. How could she even think of leaving him like this? Except, she didn't know how to reach him. Despite the bond between them, she knew next to nothing about the wolf. The smattering of knowledge she'd gleaned from their time together wasn't enough to wade through the chaotic tangle of thought and memory. She didn't know how to navigate it. She wasn't even sure where to begin.

"There is a thread there, you need only to follow it down." Lord Nuin's voice was soft, but she stiffened, unsure when they'd come in. One fine brow lifted at her expression. "I will not be dismissed in my own house."

"I'm sorry," she said. Her voice wavered. Nuin approached her, and gracefully lowered to the ground. Their hands found hers, gently unclenching her white-knuckled grip from Kai's fur.

"Who do you apologize to, young Azure? My illustrious person or the wolf?" There was no admonishment in Nuin's tone. A sad smile lit their face, one that spoke of loss and heartache.

"I don't know how to help him," Azzy whispered.

"Close your eyes," they said, knitting their fingers together as they spoke.

Azzy inhaled sharply through her nose as a tugging sensation filled her veins.

"Do you see it?"

She tilted her head at the sound of Nuin's smooth voice. The whispers flitted around in her mind, cowed by their presence. The tugging sensation lessened, until Azzy floated in the quiet darkness behind her closed eyelids.

"A thin shining cord, gossamer as spider silk, one connects to the other," their voice coiled around her, as the image flickered into existence inside her mind. "Follow it down."

She didn't hesitate, following the cord into the dark, wandering until something moved just beyond the range of her senses.

"Kai," she whispered. The figure stilled. "Come back to me." The cord went taut. Kai latched onto her. "Azzy," He repeated her name like a prayer. She tensed, holding her breath as she gave a gentle mental tug. Relief surged as he responded to her pull. Slowly, Azzy raised him from the dark. She opened her eyes to find the two of them were alone once again. Kai shuddered and rolled to his feet. The bright yellow of his irises had cooled to a molten honey-gold.

Howl opened the garden door, dropping down in a crouch next to Azzy. "I can hear him now."

"What is he saying?"

Howl frowned. "Something about a cord."

Azzy took a deep breath. "I won't bind him."

Kai answered with a wolfish sneeze.

"Azzy," said Howl, "He can't shift without help. He doesn't remember how. But he—uh, he wants to be human." Howl's cheeks turned bright red.

Azzy pursed her lips at Kai. "What did you say to him?"

Howl shook himself. "I can teach him, but it will take time."

Azzy worried her lip. Time was against them. When was it not? She removed the gauzed bandage from her finger. Her blood had dried to a dark brown. It only took a nudge to wake it up as she pulled the gauze apart and began to braid the pieces together. She thought of the collar's runes as she worked, filtering them through the whispers in her mind. She didn't want to tie Kai's life to hers, not when her death could mean his and vice versa. The blood shimmied and flowed through the forming cord, forming what she wanted within the woven fabric like living ink. The runes snapped into place. Azzy stood and fastened the cord around Kai's neck. His body shimmered as his shape condensed.

Kai wrapped human arms around her waist and pressed his face to her stomach. Sweat coated his skin, but his body no longer shook. His hands splayed against her back.

"You found me," said Azzy.

THE EXECUTION

17

AZURE

The door to Wallach's estate opened to the lord himself, his face white with barely suppressed anger before he took in the gaggle of tired and injured, led by the serene, smiling Nuin. Bafflement quickly became the predominant feature on his face as Azzy slid to the front next to Nuin, her arm around Kai's waist.

An hour ago, Brixby and Nuin held the man down and rebroke his leg. There was a purpose to the break, but Kai's scream of pain still echoed in her ear. They'd used what Brixby referred to as the latent energy of the shift to reset and heal the injured leg. Kai still had a limp, but that was because the leg was still tender rather than crooked. Howl supported Kai on his other side, while Brixby carried the unconscious Rose, who had yet to wake.

Nuin broke the silence with an elegant bow. "My lord Wallach, we seem to have found your lost lambs wandering through the Way of Heavenly Delights. Your servant informed us she grew lost wandering the market and requested an escort home."

Wallach returned the bow, lifting a brow at Nuin's carefully worded greeting. "I am not one to abstain from formalities. Allow me to invite you in, Lord Oferrie."

"Please, I prefer to be addressed as Nuin. Do you have any sort of infirmary in your house, Lord Wallach?"

Wallach cleared his throat. "My head servant will help you set something up. Cherise!"

The lady of smoke drifted into the entrance hall, her incredulous gaze barely visible through the plumes of smoke. She stole a glance at Azzy, who shook her head. "Yes, my lord?"

"Could you please help our guests set up an infirmary in one of the upstairs rooms?"

Cherise took in the state of the others, lingering on the unconscious Rose. "This way, please."

Most of them followed her until only Azzy and Kai remained. The wolf refused to leave her side again. Wallach waited until the others were well out of earshot before, he rounded on her.

"Where have you been?" He hissed; his anger throttled, but enough to increase the pressure of the air.

Kai growled under his breath, the sound deeper than a human could make. Wallach's gaze narrowed on the man.

"Another two-kind? Is this what drew you to the flesh district, Azzy?" Wallach slapped a hand against the wall. "I told you it was too dangerous to go.

"I spoke with Safiya," said Azzy.

It was if she'd physically slapped him. He took a step away from her, incredulous. "Her execution is set for an hour after dawn."

"Yes," said Azzy, "and she needs us to be there."

The muscles of Wallach's jaw flexed as he ground his teeth. "You don't need to placate me this way. I worried for your safety. It was ill-conceived to go to the district alone."

"I wasn't alone," said Azzy. "Howl was with me."

Wallach pinched the bridge of his nose. "So you went with a child to the flesh district, full of Snatchers who would snap up a boy like Howl in a blink, and carnal houses that would bury you so deep I'd never find you?"

"I had to," said Azzy. Kai leaned his head on her shoulder, lending her strength. "My brother was there."

Wallach stared at her. He began to pace, tugging on his beard. "Did you encounter any lords?"

"Lord Vashon." She swallowed, knowing how much her admission could reveal.

"How did you get away?"

Azzy opened her mouth to answer and stopped. By all rights, she shouldn't have escaped. The odds were against her. If Kai hadn't broken free, if Vashon wasn't distracted by the injured Eleanor, if Brixby hadn't seen her a moment before he closed his shop door, they wouldn't have escaped. The Maven's insidious whisper dripped through her mind, a confluence of events.

"I'm not sure," she said. The Maven was nowhere to be seen. Normally she hovered nearby, unnoticed by the others. She wondered if the Maven had followed them somehow, despite all her precautions against that very occurrence, manipulating events from the shadows. Her absence also meant that Azzy couldn't reveal her to Wallach. Another problem Azzy pushed aside as Safiya's execution loomed.

"Then *how* doesn't matter," said Wallach. "Will Vashon come after you?"

She almost repeated herself. "I think Nuin will stop that from happening," she said.

Wallach nodded. "Nuin's a minor lord, but their illusions are more useful than some of the bombastic powers the lords boast." He nodded to the hall where the others had disappeared to. "Who are the others?"

"Eleanor and Rose are from the Nightingale Carnal House," said Azzy. She didn't mention her other connection to Eleanor. It would only distract Wallach. "Brixby is my guardian from Haven."

That made Wallach's brows rise to his hairline. "Is he like you and your brother?"

"No," said Azzy. "But he's very resourceful." A mild statement. She still hadn't gotten the story of how Brixby went from the auction block to a free apothecary working beside a smitten lord of Avergard.

"And who is this?"

"Kai," she said.

"Your explanations are growing more succinct, Azzy," said Wallach.

"Is it really important where he came from?"

Wallach blinked, an odd expression crossing his face. "No, no it's not." He cleared his throat and straightened the lapels of his jacket. "Tell me about Safiya's plan."

The paved stone square outside the Avergard prison was more packed than she'd ever seen the night market despite the hour of the day. Wallach told her that public executions were not as common an occurrence as one might believe in a city full of monsters with a loose grasp of morality. Rather, they were used as demonstrations, a brutally constructed reminder that while there weren't many defining laws in Avergard, they were absolute, and violations were punished with lethal efficiency.

Safiya, no matter how justified her actions, broke the law when she killed the Snatchers within the city's outer grounds. If she'd wanted to exact her vengeance after the Snatchers were well on the road, it wouldn't even be considered a crime. From what she knew of the cunning witch, the fact she couldn't contain her rage long enough to exploit that loophole said something to the nature of the Snatcher's crimes.

The gathered crowd was already wound up, shouting jeers that made Wallach's gloved hands clench with the creak of strained leather. Azzy knew he had to be as unsettled by this as she was. People gave the Lord of Seven Smiles a wide berth, which gave her an excellent view of the podium that lead to the executioner's block. The black-clad executioner was already in place, sharpening the head of his ax to razor-thin perfection. Beheading seemed a rather barbaric style of punishment for the city but considering the regenerative power many of its citizens possessed, removing the head was likely the easiest and most permanent option.

Kai restlessly shifted from one foot to the other, his expression remote as he watched the crowd beside her. She had wanted him to stay at the estate and rest, even threatened to have Brixby put him under, but Kai insisted he come with her. He was far more lucid now, but the press of people clearly unsettled him, evoking that claustrophobic feeling. He growled quietly under his breath, widening the circle around them by another foot. Between Wallach and Kai, there would have been a spotlight of interest had it not been for Petyr. People moved away from them on instinct, but they couldn't see what they were moving away from. Petyr muddled their perception until they could have been giving space to a pile of trash rather than the Lord of Seven Smiles. It kept the more dangerous gazes from turning their way.

A hush fell over the crowd as the prison doors swung open. There was a beat of silence as Safiya was led out, her face slack, amber eyes blank. The guards prodded and pulled her toward the block, her steps slow and sluggish. Azzy doubted the witch managed a wink of sleep. The first time Safiya's steps faltered, the jeers began again. Azzy ignored them as she scanned the crowd. It took her several long moments to find him. Even when she had, it wasn't Vashon she spotted first but Armin, who stood beside the lord with his head bowed. From where she stood, she could see his wings bound to his back. She swallowed, forcing herself to look away from her brother to the lord who brought him here. Vashon watched the proceedings, his face a mask of nonchalance, but the eager light in his eyes gave him away. He came for blood.

Azzy pressed her lips together hard and shifted further behind Wallach. She could easily say it was because she didn't want Vashon to see her, but he was enraptured by the spectacle of Safiya's walk to the block. Azzy didn't want Armin to see her. If she searched for it, she could feel the faint connection between them, but he didn't remember her. The lack of connection hurt to see, and the sight of her confused him more than anything. She didn't know the depth of Vashon's hold on her brother, and she didn't want to test its loyalty.

Her attention swiveled back to the executioner's block as Safiya was pushed up the last few steps. The witch was shoved hard to her knees. Azzy tried to catch her eye, searching for the sign Safiya told her to look for. With the press of power around her, her whispers remained muted, slowly stirring as the guard yanked the witch's hands down and tied her in place.

"Come on, come one," she muttered under her breath. Lord Wallach went still beside her. The air crackled around him as the executioner pushed aside the red mass of Safiya's hair.

"Azzy," said Wallach, his voice full of warning with an undercurrent of fear. His hands shook at his sides as he fought not to act.

"Wait."

The guard stood at the edge of the podium, reading a final decree of Safiya's crimes, punishable with death by beheading. He rolled up the sheaf of parchment he carried and gestured to the executioner, who pulled his hood down over his face.

"Azzy," Wallach hissed. The sound caused the short hairs on the back of her neck to stand on end.

"Trust her," said Azzy.

The ax raised high. Dread pooled in the pit of her stomach. Safiya's eyes were blank, empty, as if she'd already checked out. Azzy chanced a quick glance at Vashon, who watched the witch's face with predatory intent. What if she hadn't been the only one to visit Safiya yesterday? Azzy faltered. Wallach tensed at the taste of her fear. He surged forward as the ax fell.

The crowd cheered as blood spurt into the air. The witch's head fell neatly into the waiting basket, while blood gushed from the stump of her neck. Wallach froze in shock, the expression on his face as horrifying as the cheering crowd around them. Azzy dug her nails in the palms of her hand. The whispers tugged and teased inside her head. She finally managed to look away from the gruesome sight of the beheaded body. Her gaze found Vashon.

The lord stared at the body, his nostrils white, mouth set in a grim line. Molten rage flared in his silvery grey eyes.

Azzy turned to Petyr. "The alley, now." He nodded to her, the air blurring behind him as he vanished between spaces. She caught Wallach as he took another step toward the body on the block.

"There was no signal," Wallach spoke through his teeth. He looked ready to explode, with anger or grief, neither would be good for anyone nearby.

"Look at Vashon," she said. Wallach's fingers closed on her wrist, his grip hard enough to grind her bones together. Azzy flinched. "Please, look."

Wallach's nostrils flared, but he listened to her, his grip immediately slacking. He inhaled sharply when he caught sight of his rival. "He's looking for her."

A GOLEM OF BLOOD AND TEETH

18

AZURE

"*I'll need you once the ax falls.*"

Her mind flashed to her encounter with Safiya, the evening before the execution. Azzy itched to return to the others, but Safiya had asked her to remain a little longer. "I might need your help for this part."

When Azzy pressed the witch for more of her plan, Safiya held up the tooth she took from the mouth in Wallach's palm. Azzy turned the tooth over and over in her hand as they waited for full night to fall. The prison was silent and still, the deep dark set in.

"Tonight holds the darkness of a new moon, a time of deadly bargains and exchanges of blood for power," said Safiya. She knelt on the floor of her cell, her expression serene as she held out her hand for the tooth. Azzy dropped it in her palm, unable to stop her shudder as the witch pressed it point down into one palm.

Safiya clasped her hands in front of her, the tooth pressed between them, and she began to murmur a nonsense prayer. She had explained this to Azzy during their long wait. The point wasn't for any winsome deity to hear her, no, she needed the stir of words in the air. There was power in words, nonsense or not. Safiya murmured until the air buzzed against Azzy's skin. She could sense the build of magic in the cell. Safiya clamped her jaw tight for the next part as she shifted the tooth, so it stuck horizontally between her hands, the pointed ends indenting each of her palms. She held her breath and brought her palms together with a grunt.

Blood dripped down her wrists, thick and fast, wicked by the power buzzing in the air. It pocked against the dirt floor, a chorus of wet thuds, but the ground didn't absorb it. The puddle grew, wider and wider. Safiya began to whisper again, soft words, that Azzy strained to hear.

Memories , that is what the witch offered to the hungry power hovering around her; visions of her people who lived in warmer, moist lands, of the rage that burned in her for years, of her secret wishes during the years she spent alone in the wild wood. The whispers told Azzy the intent of the witch's words, but she chose not to listen to the details. Instead she looked on as Safiya poured her blood and her words onto the ground until she swayed from the loss.

Safiya opened her hands, letting the tooth fall into the blood. It dropped like a pebble into a well, the ripple of its passage spreading until the entire liquid surface stirred. Safiya ran her bloodied hands through the thickened air, scooped the buzzing power in her arms, her limbs shook from the effort. She shaped it there, a loose mass of conjured power which she shoved down into the pool of blood. The rippling liquid began to boil as Safiya set her open palms down on the writhing surface and pulled up. The liquid thickened and bulged before imploding in on itself as it spat out a figure that bore her face.

A golem of blood and teeth made in Safiya's image.

"Oh," said Azzy. It was solid plan. The likeness was exact, down to a faint scar above Safiya's lip.

"It's little better than a living doll, but it will serve its purpose," said Safiya as she stripped off her clothing. Azzy passed her the guard uniform she procured for Safiya earlier, allowing the woman to dress as she carefully maneuvered the golem into Safiya's old clothes.

"She's not made of glass," said the witch, shoving the golem's arm in a sleeve.

"She's faintly warm," said Azzy.

"It needs to be convincing," said Safiya. She carefully positioned the doll in the same pose she had been kneeling in on the floor. It was a clever choice. The guards wouldn't question the golem's listless expression or the stiff clumsiness of her limbs, she would appear as a woman who spent a sleepless night before her death kneeling on the floor of her cell.

"Go, Azzy. But remember you can't tell Wallach. You can't tell anyone."

They had to believe it was real. Staring at the golem's listless face, it wasn't too hard to convince herself.

Safiya slid under her cot to wait for the dawn

They had planned it down to wire. At least, that was what Safiya assured her, though Azzy held more than a few doubts the guards wouldn't notice the witch's sudden and complete compliance. The guards would take the golem from her cell. They would have no reason to shut the door behind them, leaving Safiya free to walk out, dressed in the guard's uniform.

Azzy worried over that last step. "You really think the other guards won't notice you?"

"I promise, they will be quite distracted by the festivities outside," said Safiya. "Executions are a merry old time."

The crowd was in prime form, celebrating the display of death as the guards shoved her golem onto the block. Their bloodlust made Azzy's skin crawl, but she couldn't let it distract her. Not when this moment was so critical to their success. As the axe swung down and Azzy clutched Wallach's arm, she searched for a hint of Vashon's magic.

In the mouth of the nearby alley, she caught sight of Safiya in the guard uniform, far closer than they'd agreed on. Did the witch sneak closer to see her own execution? The air tore behind her as Petyr emerged. Azzy could see his smile from across the crowd as he offered Safiya's his arm. A breath of relief crested through her.

She sensed the moment before Vashon struck. Azzy lurched away from Wallach, rushing for the alley at a dead run. She wouldn't get there in time. Azzy watched, unable to looked away, unable to stop it as Vashon slid behind Petyr and drove a blade through his chest.

Azzy shrieked. She couldn't stop, not when the scene continued to unfold. The distance seemed insurmountable. Each second that passed moved like honey through cloth. Safiya took a step back, blinded when Petyr's blood spattered across her face. Vashon moved with her, piercing her stomach as he drove her back into the alley wall. The witch gripped the blade, slowing its progress but unable to stop it. Vashon leaned into her, pitting his strength against hers, toying with her. Azzy was close enough to hear the words he spat in Safiya's face.

"You almost fooled me with those memories," said Vashon. The guard's helm fell off Safiya's head as she struggled, spilling her tangle of dark red hair. Vashon drove the blade in another inch. "But the rage wasn't strong enough. Nothing but a pale shadow of the real thing."

Safiya spat in his face and bared her teeth.

Vashon wiped her spit from his cheek with a flicker of anger in his expression. "Such a waste. You could have seen the dawn of a new world by my side."

Vashon pushed away from Safiya and flicked her blood off his blade in cold, careless movements. Petyr lay sprawled behind him, twitching as he bled out from the wound in his chest.

Safiya threw a punch that caught the lord in the jaw. Vashon skidded back a step, but the blood loss had already taken a toll, weakening her. Azzy finally reached them, skidding to a stop through a growing pool of blood.

"No!" At her cry, Vashon's attention snapped to her. Azzy's flesh crawled at the open fascination in his expression.

"You've come," Vashon breathed. He spread his arms as if welcoming her. His fingers twitched, but Azzy didn't move. Vashon hissed with delight. "You *are* immune."

Azzy shifted her stance and reached behind her. Her fingers brushed the warmth at her back. After so long apart, it was a small miracle to know, without fail, Kai would be there.

"May I?" She whispered the plea for his ears alone.

"Yes."

Azzy wrapped her fingers around the cord at Kai's neck. Vashon's mouth formed a perfect 'o'.

Kai the wolf sailed over her head and crashed into Vashon. Azzy rushed past them and dragged Petyr with her to reach Safiya.

"What are you doing?" The witch's voice slurred as she watched Azzy with glassy eyes.

"Shut up," Azzy snapped. She paled at how still Petyr was. No, she had to save them. She had to save them both. Azzy grabbed Safiya, falling deep into the whispers as she tried to keep them both from bleeding out. Her concentration broke as Kai yelped and skidded back, a nasty wound in his flank. Panic flared through her chest. Azzy didn't have the chance to react as Vashon pressed his sword to her throat.

"I wouldn't if I were you, unless you want to lose them all," said Vashon.

Safiya's head lolled on her shoulder. The witch was losing too much blood. Fear trapped her at a crossroads of indecision. Petyr was far too still in her lap.

Wallach appeared, poised to strike, his gaze flashing between the three of them. She hadn't noticed his approach, caught up in the chaos of the moment, but she sensed his presence now, the pressure boiling in the air, barely contained. Vashon slid the blade to Azzy's chest, directly over her heart. Kai snarled, but neither he nor Wallach could advance without Vashon striking her down.

No one made a sound. Azzy inhaled a breath. She focused on Vashon's sword, staring at the elegant metal hilt. The whispers went taut as she found a thread and pulled.

Vashon's blade slid free of its hilt, clattering over the stones. Kai ran at him again. Wallach ripped off his gloves as Vashon threw up his arms. Azzy screamed as Petyr jerked forward with ragdoll grace and took the impact from Kai for Vashon. Vashon dropped into a crouch with a smile of malicious glee.

"Finally going to get your hands dirty, Heinrich?"

Azzy clenched her jaw tight. She could feel Safiya slipping away. Vashon whipped forward and caught Wallach by the wrist, while Petyr's body kept Kai occupied with awful wooden movements.

Azzy pushed the fight out of her mind. She shifted Safiya further into her lap as her shaking hands began to trace a symbol on the bare, bloody skin of her midriff. It was the healing rune she used before, though her hands shook so bad she feared she would mess it up. Safiya hissed in a breath through her teeth as her wound flowed in reverse, as her tissues and organs knit back together, seamless as if the wound never was. Because it wasn't.

Her skin heated as blood flushed back through her veins as if she'd never bled for the golem. Because she hadn't.

Azzy looked up to meet Safiya's stark gaze as she whispered, "You're not human."

19

AZURE

zzy knew she'd risked too much when Wallach and Vashon both stopped mid-fight to stare at her. Wallach's expression was one of relief marred by worry, but Vashon's gaze held a strange child-like wonder tinged with predatory hunger. A shiver rippled under her skin, the exertion of magic weighed by the warnings slithering around inside her skull.

Safiya stiffened in her hold as the whispers inside her head rose to a wail. Vashon rammed his blade through the distracted Wallach's leg. The Lord of Seven Smiles stumbled, distracted as his opponent faced the two women.

Azzy knew Vashon was coming for her. Her muscles went taut, bracing for the blow, when Armin stepped between them.

"Let them go," her brother said, his voice full of a dozen muffled echoes that scattered between the bricks of the alley like dried leaves.

Where had he come from? Azzy hadn't perceived his arrival though his presence beat against her senses. Her pulse seized in her throat as Vashon sneered and pierced Armin's shoulder, using the blade to maneuver him out of the way. Armin hissed and clasped the weapon, baring his teeth as the edge bit into his palm.

"Let them go, and I'll stop resisting you," said Armin.

Azzy couldn't completely stifle a cry at his words, the sound choked and coarse as sand in her mouth. He didn't recognize her, not truly, but the connection between them fizzed with awareness. He knew she meant something to him, and that was enough.

"You barely resist me now," Vashon spat. He dug the blade in. Armin winced but didn't relent.

"Isn't it odd that your grand scheme has taken this long?" Azzy couldn't see her brother's expression as he spoke, but there was a lilting taunt in his tone. She swore she heard laughter among the echoes in his voice.

Vashon's nostrils flared. "You've only prolonged this miserable existence."

There was a beat of silence as Armin's grip tightened on the blade. Blood slid down his wrist before the flow reversed, swirling against his skin. Azzy stared at the droplet, transfixed, as the full breadth of Armin's transformation fell on her with suffocating force. The tension of the moment pooled as the blood on his wrist slid back towards the wound. The threat of violence shifted to a promise as the weeping feathers of Armin's wings stilled to a stop.

"Take his offer," said Wallach. The Lord of Seven Smiles had moved unseen, his hand now hovered directly behind Vashon's head, punctuating his threat with the click of unseen teeth.

Vashon heaved a sigh and plucked his blade free. "I feel I've done enough. Soon none of it will matter." He took out a handkerchief to wipe the blood from his weapon before he concealed it back in its innocuous cane sheath. Vashon offered Wallach a parting sneer. "The time has come old friend, to make amends with the past." He twitched two fingers at Armin, who jerked forward as tethered on invisible strings.

For the second time, Azzy watched her brother leave, but this time she made no move to stop him, stunned by the truth she'd glimpsed in that perilous moment. Armin didn't look back at her once. She stared after him, unable to move, unable to think beyond her own failure, as feathers began to rain once more, lingering as lord and servant shifted out of sight. Azzy swallowed a sob and crawled out from under the witch. The pave stoves were slick with split blood. She made her way to Petyr, who had collapsed to the ground as soon as Vashon left. She moved his head to her lap as her shaking hands traced the familiar rune on his chest. Nothing happened, not so much as a twitch in the depleted reserves of her magic. She moved her hands over and over, ignoring the obvious until Safiya gently grabbed her wrists.

"You have such strength inside you, Azure," said the witch, "but even you can't bring back the dead."

Azzy's vision blurred. Petyr's blood cooled against her skin. She couldn't save him. "I'm so sorry," she whispered. Kai's head nudged her shoulder. She leaned into him, burying her face in his ruff as Wallach knelt on the other side of his fallen servant, mindless of the filth on the ground. He pressed his bare hand to the man's still face.

"Rest, my friend," said Wallach.

Safiya staggered to her feet. "We have to go."

"I know," said Wallach.

He lifted Petyr in his arms. Safiya offered Azzy a hand up as a familiar tear formed in the air. Wallach had consumed the last of Petyr's magic to get them home. Azzy followed them, hedged in on either side by witch and wolf. How odd, to find herself reunited with the two who started on this path with her. The price had, indeed, been high. Azzy felt numb inside as they emerged into the servant's kitchen. A haze of smoke and chatter greeted them before the others caught sight of Petyr in Wallach's arms. The smoke peeled back from Cherise's stark face. A sob broke from her as she rushed forward. Lenin clutched his chest, his whorled face a mask of sorrow. Morglint stood away from the others, sadness craved into his uneven features. *One of their own*, the words resonated in Azzy's head as Wallach's servants surrounded them.

Azzy was new to their little family, but she keenly felt their loss. Kai's nose nudged her hand, still covered in Petyr's dried blood. She sucked in a breath at the contact, reminded of her responsibility to him as well. She retrieved the bundle of cloth Cherise set aside for him before she bent to place the cord back around his neck. The wounds of their battle were nothing more than faint shiny marks of healing skin. She wondered, if the result might have been different had Kai gotten the chance to help their fallen friend. Azzy shoved the thought aside. There was no use ruminating over what could have been. Kai shrugged into the overcoat, in Wallach's house colors. He tucked his hand under her chin, a gentle nudge until she forced herself to look up at him. Kai appeared utterly exhausted, but he touched his forehead to hers.

"This wasn't your fault," he said.

"You need to rest," she replied. She knew what happened wasn't her fault, but the guilt remained. She knew it wasn't over.

"Rest with me," said Kai.

The invitation was so very tempting, but as Azzy stood with her head resting against Kai's shoulder, she spotted the Maven. The knowledge of what they'd avoided in that alley haunted her.

The Maven leaned in the doorway of Wallach's study, her face impassive as Cherise and Lenin carried their dead companion past her. A spark of rage flared through Azzy at the sight of her, she felt the certainty in her bones that the Maven knew exactly what her brother had become. She was done with the Maven's machinations, done being the plaything of lords and nightmares.

"I'll come join you in a bit," she said to Kai, managing to keep her voice calm. "I need to talk to Wallach first."

Kai hesitated, his gaze sliding to where the Maven hovered, but he didn't give her away. "Be careful," he whispered to Azzy.

The Maven saw Azzy watching her, waggling her fingers with a small, secretive smile on her lips. Azzy walked away without acknowledging her. Everyone she cared about was under this roof but one person. The Maven had gone through a great deal of trouble to manipulate the pieces in play, but Azzy needed to see the whole board.

Azzy stalked from room to room until she found Wallach in the kitchen, conversing with Safiya, Nuin, and Brixby.

"I need to talk to you alone," she said, her tone terse, but she simply couldn't summon the energy to care.

Exhaustion nipped at her heels after she healed Safiya. Wallach frowned at her but followed without argument. She said nothing as she led him to his study, hoping the Maven hadn't caught on to her intentions and hightailed it elsewhere.

The Maven was crouched on Wallach's desk, rifling through his papers, content in her invisibility.

"What's this about, Azzy?"

The Maven ignored them. Azzy said nothing, letting the whispers guide her as she found the thread of the Maven's perception to others and pulled.

The Maven stiffened. Wallach saw her.

 20 

AZURE

The Maven's smile was cold and cruel as Wallach's attention shifted to her. He stared as if he'd never seen her before, though Azzy knew he must have sensed her from time to time. The Maven had been squatting in his house for years and Wallach was far to perceptive not to notice hints of her presence. But at the expression on his face, she realized the familiarity ran deeper.

"Well done, Child," said the Maven.

"You." Wallach ripped off the glove of his left hand, his expression hostile as the mouth on his palm split open. The Maven hissed and crawled backward off the desk. "You've been here this whole time?" The mouth in his palm gnashed causing the Maven to cringe.

"The time wasn't right," she said, her sing-song voice strained, the echo more obvious as her body shifted and flickered in a sporadic backward retreat that made Azzy dizzy to watch. "You weren't the one I needed, Henrich, but I knew you would find the one I did."

She dropped into a crouch, her back pressed against the wall as her mask flaked and cracked, revealing something alien underneath that Azzy had only glimpsed through the filter of her false face.

Azzy stared at her. "What are you?" She'd asked the question dozens of times, and though the Maven never answered, Azzy wondered if she might already know the answer. One she refused to acknowledge, though she didn't know why.

The Maven cocked her head, her expression expectant, as if

she sensed Azzy's inner turmoil, but it was Wallach that answered.

"She's a child of the Gate."

Azzy said nothing, could say nothing. The Gate was what destroyed this world, but through all her lessons, from both teachers, she'd come to understand so little about it and she'd played right into the Maven's plans. Embroiled by the need to save those she loved; she'd followed the pull at the Maven's urging. The Maven had pushed and led her along since she entered Wallach's home, and Azzy never gleaned to what purpose. Azzy never stopped to think how unlike herself it was, not to push, not to dig when the answer could mean so much to her survival.

The Maven laughed at her bewildered expression. "Oh child, you tried. But I've played this game much longer than you."

"Yet you never faced your opponents," said Wallach, "like a coward."

"Me, the coward," the Maven purred.

"How do you know her?" Azzy's whisper cracked as her whispers fed her bits and pieces, forming a picture that made her stomach clench.

"My, you have kept her ignorant, Heinrich," said the Maven as she shifted from one foot to the other, the swaying motion derailing Azzy's train of thought. "Afraid she will judge you for your past sins, Wallach?"

"Be silent," Wallach snarled.

"Do you fear she will turn away from you in disgust, despise you for the monster you truly are? The magic reflects one's fears, Wallach, it gives us the forms we choose."

Wallach's nostrils flared white. His gloved hand curled into a fist while his extended arm remained steady. His eyes brimmed with old pain. He might have held out on Azzy even then, his secrets held tight, if the floor didn't rock beneath them. Azzy caught herself on the desk as Wallach slid to keep his balance.

The Maven's expression shifted to one of solemn anger. "That fool. He'll have it open before day's end at this rate."

The color drained from Wallach's face. His hand dropped as he leaned hard against the wall. "I thought we had more time."

"Then you are the greater fool for it," The Maven spat. "I warned you once that your desire to bury the past would lead you afoul. Now your pride has set us upon the precipice of ruin, once again."

Azzy glanced between them, frustrated by them both in equal measure. Wallach appeared shell-shocked. She knew the Lord of Seven Smiles hated what he was, knew that he loathed the fear he inspired in others. There was an ageless strain of regret that had made her wonder more than once if Wallach remembered the man he'd been, though she never questioned what sort of man that might be.

She faced the Maven. Questions filled her mouth, eager as ink to spill, but she had to ask the right one, to peel back the layers of deception, intentional ones if she hoped to fill the numerous gaps in her knowledge. "Why did you bring me here?"

Wallach's wide-eyed gaze darted to her. In his mind, he'd stumbled upon her in the Snatcher's caravan, but Azzy knew the Maven had whispered and steered the events of the House of Seven Smiles for decades. It was by design that Wallach chose to meet the Snatcher's caravan outside the gates of Avergard before she and Morglint made their ill-planned attempt to escape. An intervention that saved both their lives, but the manipulation was clear. Wallach and Azzy were both pieces in the Maven's long game. Considering the abilities of those sheltered under his roof, Azzy doubted any member of the household was here by chance.

"Every door requires a lock and a key," said the Maven, swaying from side to side. "Poor Dierk, sweet lost lamb, believes the key is the answer. He plans to rid the world of our ilk, but we both know that keys open what locks seal away."

Wallach's shoulders slumped. He scrubbed a hand over his face, exhaustion evident in every line of his body. "Who is this key?"

The Maven's gaze slid to Azzy, and she knew. The little details she'd seen and surmised clicked into place, the dream of the pit in Vashon's house, Armin's voice reverberating through her bones as he spoke to the yawning pit. **Rise.** The tremors weren't an effect, but an answer.

Saliva pooled in her mouth as bile rose in her throat. "My brother," she whispered.

"Key," the Maven smiled.

Wallach stiffened. "And lock." He glanced at Azzy and away, his eyes full of shame though she didn't understand its source.

Azzy shifted to sit in a chair, unable to stand as dread slunk through her on clawed feet. "Dierk is Vashon?"

Wallach nodded in answer. The Maven cackled as she swayed.

"She's called you both by name," said Azzy. Wallach bowed his head. The Maven pushed off the wall, swaying closer.

"Because I was there, Child, we all were, when the first fool dared to let us in," she said as she spun and twisted around Azzy's chair. She dropped into a crouch, her long nails tapping along the top of Azzy's thighs. "They were the first ones we danced with as we entered this world, touched by our joy, changed forever, but I'll tell you a secret."

The Maven leaned in closer, her voice girlish as she spoke, a stage whisper meant for Wallach as much as it was meant for her. "Our touch burns away the memory in beautiful rebirth, but we wanted the first ones to remember, so they do."

Wallach's hand clamped down on the Maven's neck. She screamed as he flung her away. Her blood dripped from his palm where his teeth took their payment of flesh. Azzy said nothing as he stood there, shoulders heaving, his expression haunted by the sins of his past.

"Our country was ravaged by war. We were pinned between two nations tearing at one another that left thousands of our people dead. We stood to lose everything, our land, our people, everything. He promised us a weapon we could defend ourselves with. We were desperate." Wallach's shoulders heaved as he spoke, his pupils blown until the black eclipsed the dark blue of his irises.

"Ah, he gave you such interesting ideas to solve your little problem," the Maven laughed, as she clutched at the oozing wound on the back of her neck. "You followed him like an attentive flock of lambs. Raised on a pedestal like the false idols of old."

"There was an army about to raze our capitol city to the ground," said Wallach, "We didn't know what he would do to find the Gate."

"Liiiiiies," sang the Maven. She crept closer once more, but now she circled Wallach. "You knew, little lamb Wallach, you simply convinced yourself it didn't matter."

Azzy could hear the echo of screams in the Maven's voice, millions of agonized voices that spoke of a terrible truth. "What did he do?"

The Maven's smile was one of dark satisfaction. "Oh, their leader was a cunning one. He offered us such tributes, lured us to the Gate with the scent of death and spoiled flesh. A feast prepared for our arrival."

Wallach shuddered. "They were not tribute," he whispered, and Azzy saw the source of his shame. "They were innocents. Families, sheltering from the fighting outside the capital. By the time we realized what he was doing, it was too late."

"The flock left to wolves," said the Maven. She leaned against Wallach's back, her voice silken menace. "Their leader invited the armies to sack your precious city. Told them to slaughter your people. And you unlocked the doors for them. You could have warned them. There was time, wasn't there, for the city to evacuate. Instead you and Vashon stood by, as your false idol opened the Gate."

"He told us their lives wouldn't be given in vain," said Wallach. "We thought it was our only chance to save who was left."

"But then your leader realized the truth of his lovely promises. You watched him take the coward's escape. And when my brothers and sisters poured through the Gate to eat their fill, you saw the horror you'd invited in, and we made sure you remembered the sins etched in your bones for the long centuries of your life." The Maven spat those last words at him.

Azzy stared at Wallach. The Maven spoke as if the Gate opened a few years ago rather than centuries. Were all the lords of Avergard gifted with longevity and memory of the world that once was, or just Wallach and Vashon? The Maven seemed to hear her thoughts, her flaking face leering at Azzy from across the room.

"Only two poppets remember us, Child, but it doesn't take many to know better," said the Maven. "One wanted to forget, and the other wanted to fix what they broke. Can you guess which is which?"

Azzy didn't answer the barb. Wallach wouldn't even look at her. "How would opening the Gate again fix anything?"

"Oh, it won't," tittered the Maven. She gave a girlish giggle that amplified the ghoulish appearance of her face. "Poor lamb believes if he opens the way, we will return from whence we came, as if we would leave such tasty morsels. No, he will only invite more to the feast."

Azzy clutched at the arms of the chair. The Maven spoke of the predatory things that lurked in the pit and haunted her darkest nightmares, but her words didn't make sense. If the Children of the Gate had such monstrous appetites, how had they not consumed the city of Avergard yet? Cherise told her there were other cities, other settlements, and holdouts of civilization spread across the vast reaches of the world. Were the Children like the Maven? Predators who camouflaged themselves in plain sight?

"Where are the other Children of the Gate? Are they like you?"

The Maven's expression turned somber like the flip of a coin. "You are fortunate I am nothing like my brothers and sisters. I suppose you could call me the runt of the litter. And I like this world. I've found other sustenance to consume where my siblings gorged themselves until their cities fell."

A chill ran through Azzy. She remembered the whistling hollows above Haven, the sensation of eyes watching her through the eerie silence. The same silence she found in Caletum before she was nearly driven off a ledge that lead to a bottomless pit.

"Oh my god," said Azzy.

"We were once revered as gods," said the Maven with a shrug, "they prayed for us to take their sickness, to save them from death, unaware we gifted them both."

Azzy peered up at Wallach, who still wouldn't meet her gaze. "You were so incredulous when I told you I was from Below. You said it was impossible."

"Azzy," Wallach whispered. He stared hard at the floor as he spoke. "The Children of the Gate were insatiable. Two days after they came through, the war ended because there were no cities left. They tore through the largest populations of the world and left nightmare creatures and twisted beings in their wake. Nothing safe, nothing untouched. They crossed the oceans to new continents in a week's time. Within a month, global communications were nearly impossible. We made a choice."

"Such a terrible choice it was," said the Maven. She'd resumed her perch on the desk, a gargoyle in frayed silk, her hair a wild tangle around her body.

Wallach ignored her as he finally looked up, focusing solely on Azzy, his cobalt blue eyes bottomless as a still pond. "We constructed the cities Below to act as containment for the Children of the Gate. Two hundred thousand souls were commuted to each city through an impartial lottery."

"You said they were insatiable," said Azzy.

"Ah yes, well, he likes to downplay the bargain we made," said the Maven. "I gave them the means to ensnare my siblings, tether to them to the cities, where they had to curb their appetites or risk a slow starvation."

Azzy stared at them, the horror of the truth sinking its teeth into her throat until she couldn't breathe. "All those people," she gasped. She couldn't fathom the weight of such a decision, the desperation that would fuel such terrible reasoning. "How you could you agree to such a thing?"

Wallach visibly flinched at her words. "A devil's bargain, the sacrifice of a few for the survival of the many." His expression was haunted. Azzy couldn't recognize the man who'd condemned hundreds of thousands of people to a terrible fate, to the same man who took the broken and lost into his home. Was this Lord Wallach's idea of penance? Could those few he saved equate to the thousands he sentenced to die? Was he different from any of the other lords of Avergard, or nothing but another monster in a fine suit? One she now found herself tethered to, for good or ill.

"Please, you think man wasn't on the path to self-destruct? Humans killed their own indiscriminately, for power, for greed. The wars of man killed millions before we arrived, bodies left to waste and ruin. At least, we consume what we kill." The Maven shrugged, her expression nonchalant as her head swiveled back to Wallach. "We had a good run. Those tethers held for centuries—forced them to nibble away at their offered populations. But, eventually, they found their loop-hole." She gave Azzy another terrible smile.

"Don't you dare pin this on her," Wallach snapped.

"Her?" The Maven arched a brow. "*Her* they fear."

"Lock and key," said Azzy. "They sensed my brother."

The Maven's smile turned secretive. "Something like that, yes."

Wallach began to pace. "How close is he?"

"Far closer than he should be," said the Maven. She rolled her eyes. "You weren't the only one who thought we had more time. Somehow, he's made his Key more cooperative."

"This is my fault," said Azzy.

Wallach stopped to look at her face. "No—"

"Petyr was dying. Safiya was bleeding out. Vashon was going to take me, but Armin stopped him. He offered to go with Vashon freely if he let us go."

"And I encouraged it, Azzy," said Wallach.

The Maven fell silent.

Azzy clasped her hands in her lap as the whispers rose and fell through her thoughts like a swelling tide. "How do we stop him?"

"We cannot," said the Maven. Azzy looked up at the Maven's oddly somber expression. She jerked her chin at the pacing Wallach. "Don't you hate him for what he's done? Do you really think he's a monster worth saving?"

"Are you worth saving?"

The Maven threw back her head and laughed. "Not at all, Child, not for a long time."

Azzy looked at Wallach. There was a part of her that understood the hopeless desperation that propelled Wallach to sacrifice the innocents of a city for a chance to save his people. Under similar circumstances, what choice would she have made? How could she judge the measure of the man when she'd spent a life watching those around her do nothing to stop evil deeds because of fear, because they wanted to survive. She had a keen understanding of how the guilt of those decisions ate away at a person until there was nothing left to feel. What she couldn't reason was what happened after. How impartial could a lottery truly be when she'd seen firsthand the sort of power disparity that existed in Avergard. Wallach carried guilt, it was evident in how he treated his household, it tempered every decision he made, but did he understand the fate of those condemned to the Below? Could she trust such a man? Did she have a choice when the hour drew so late?

"It doesn't matter what I think," said Azzy. "We need him."

Wallach met her gaze at last, his expression conflicted.

"If we have any chance of stopping my brother, we need to go through Vashon," said Azzy.

"I will help you," said Wallach.

"No," said the Maven. "You will keep my siblings at bay while I lead the girl to her brother."

Wallach shook his head. "You can't take him alone. His servants are loyal to the bone."

"So are hers," said the Maven.

Azzy frowned. "I have no servants."

"Liiiiiie," said the Maven.

"Companions," said Wallach. "Sometimes, we choose who we follow."

The Maven scoffed. "The two-kind can resist Vashon with ease."

Azzy stiffened. "I'm not taking them." Kai's mind was still a mess, and Howl was a child. She refused to risk them.

"We might not have a choice," said Wallach.

"I won't ask this of them, not again." She asked so much of Howl already. Her reasons for not risking Kai were far more self-ish, but she couldn't, not when she finally found him again.

"I will need Safiya here," said Wallach.

"Yes, how convenient," said the Maven.

"I've already lost one of my own," snapped Wallach.

Azzy bit the inside of her cheek until it bled. She remembered Petyr's wide sightless eyes as his breath ceased. She could still feel his blood grow tacky and chill on her hands. She wanted to keep Kai and Howl far from this fight, but it wasn't fair to the others, to Wallach, or to them.

"I'll ask them," said Azzy. Another tremor rocked the house as she spoke.

"We don't have long," said the Maven. "We must do this tonight, or more of my brethren will flood this world until there is nothing left but bones and dust."

STOLEN MOMENTS

21

AZURE

Azzy curled up against Kai's side. She clung to this moment, a silent wish she could stay here, at his side, without the danger the loomed over them, tainting the peace between them. She wished she could have stolen a dozen more moments like this one before she had to ask that terrible question. Stalling, she said nothing, enjoying the warmth of his body against hers. She swallowed the tightness in her throat as she leaned forward to brush her lips against his cheek. He captured her there, cupping her face as his lips traced her nose, the curve of her brow, and her chin before they found her mouth.

"I dreamt of you, like this," he whispered against her lips.

The quiver in her chin gave her away. Kai opened his eyes. The wolf still slunk close to the surface, but he was calmer now. Azzy reached and fiddled with the cord around his neck. Would he run if she asked him? It would be better if he removed the cord and fled the city. Free to outrun whatever monsters came to devour them all. But she knew he wouldn't run, just as she knew his answer before she asked the question.

"We're going after my brother tonight," she said.

"Who else is coming with us?"

She pressed her forehead to his, unable to keep the pain from her face. "If I begged you to run, would you?"

"Only if you ran with me," he murmured.

Azzy's answering laugh broke with a sob. Kai wrapped his arms around her and let her quietly fall apart against his chest.

"That's the second time I've broken down in as many days," said Azzy. Kai gently pressed his mouth at the corner of her

"

altered eye. She was unable to shed tears but still aching from the need to.

"It's not a weakness to fear, or to cry," he said.

"Thank you," said Azzy. It was what she needed to hear.

Kai remained silent for a moment as his fingers traced her jaw. "Why do you wish for me to run?"

Azzy inhaled against the tightness in her chest, struggling to put into words what she felt for the man beside her. It was a connection she never had a moment to properly explore when their time together was spent tumbling from one danger to another. But she'd felt it when she stepped in front of the Snatcher's hook, and she could feel it there now, an invisible thread between them so akin yet vastly different to the thread she'd tied around her brother's finger so long ago. A connection that plucked through her awareness, solid as it was fragile, both precious and rare. She barely begun to scratch beneath the surface of it, and here they were about to tumble into danger again.

"Because it is my weakness. The thought of you free, and safe," she swallowed hard, "is easier to bear than the thought of your death."

Kai's hand stilled as he looked at her, an undefinable expression on his face.

"This has become so much bigger," said Azzy

Before she knew about the Gate and the insatiable Children that ravaged her world, before she knew about redeemable monsters and immortal lords, she followed a list of impossible tasks. The center of her world was a simple string, tied tight around her finger, around Armin's, as a physical symbol of their bond. The world was bigger now, so much bigger, and she had so much more to lose, but Azzy didn't regret the wonders she'd seen; the night markets, the dark heart of a poppy, the people she'd let into her heart, the sun on her face. She couldn't admit it to anyone else, but Kai understood what drove her better than anyone. "I need to save him, Kai."

"You will," he said.

She didn't want to leave the bed or the warmth of his side, but she still had to speak with the others.

"Try to get some rest," she said. His hand lingered, trailing across her cheek as she left with a silent promise to return.

She found the others in Wallach's makeshift infirmary. Safiya slept thanks to Nuin's tea. Brixby checked over the unconscious witch, but Azzy had sealed the worst of her wounds to keep her from bleeding out. She'd hoped to find the witch conscious, but perhaps it was better for her not to go through with this piece of her plan. Brixby's gaze caught hers as she entered, coming around to sit on the cot beside Howl and Eleanor as they played at cards. The younger two looked up as Azzy sat on the cot across from them.

"I am going after my brother tonight," she said, careful with her wording this time. Howl didn't react, but Eleanor shifted. She knew who Azzy had to go through first. A frown creased Brixby's brow.

"Not alone," he said.

Azzy shook her head. "Not alone, but I can't bring you," she said, careful not to look at Howl. He would scent her lie, but not the reasoning behind it. She didn't have to explain herself at all as Eleanor spoke.

"Vashon would shred our minds and turn us against one another," she said. A ripple of fear shivered through her limbs.

Brixby's eyes widened. "Who has a defense against that?"

"Wallach," said Azzy. She hesitated before she added. "And Kai."

Howl went still on the cot, but she wasn't done. Her loved ones needed to know what was coming, and she was going to ask something of Howl that was just as dangerous.

"The Children of the Gate are rising," she said. Brixby's gaze snapped to hers. The other two shared a glance of confusion.

Safiya coughed from her cot. "Please tell me that idiot doesn't think he can hold them off alone?"

Brixby turned a scowl on her. "How long have you been faking sleep?"

"Long enough," said the witch of the wood. Her face was wan, lined by exhaustion, but anger burned in her gaze. "Azzy?"

"Why do you think I'm here?"

Safiya cursed. Eleanor frowned at her. "I don't understand, why are we worried about children?"

Azzy told them in short, sharp words what she'd learned from Wallach and the Maven. She kept what she'd learned of Wallach's past to herself, unable to understand the context of those revelations amid the other horrible truths she'd learned.

"Damn," said Eleanor. "Here I thought we were through the worst of it."

"The worst is yet to come," said Azzy, "And that is why we are needed on two fronts." She tugged at the cuffs of her sleeve.

"I want you to stay here," she said to them.

Safiya struggled to sit up from the bed. "Like hell I will."

Azzy gave the witch a sharp look. "Not here like an invalid. Wallach will have his hands full. There isn't enough time to stop them from coming. We have to hold them off as they rise and he's one of the few who can."

Eleanor stood. "We can't follow you into Vashon's estate, but the rest of the city is vulnerable. Is Wallach really powerful enough to hold off something like—like that?"

"Yes," said Safiya, "but not for long." She looked mad enough to spit.

"Then that's where we will be," said Eleanor.

Azzy hesitated. "He needs to hold them off until I can reach Armin," she said. She hadn't shared the truth with Wallach and the Maven, not with so many secrets clogging the air between them. She didn't trust the Maven with the truth. Azzy glanced up to find Safiya watching her.

"If you can't reach him, kill him," said the witch.

"I won't do that," snapped Azzy.

"He would have killed us all in that alley and you know it," said Safiya.

It didn't surprise her that the witch sensed what she did. In the moment, Armin's rage bruised the air, a writhing, living thing prepared to break free and consume all its path. An energy so dreadfully similar to the Child that lurked in the silent city Below.

"That's not who he is," said Azzy. "I have to make him remember that."

Safiya scowled. "What if he doesn't?"

"He will," said Eleanor, her voice soft. "She can do this."

Azzy wished she shared that faith. She glanced around the room, taking in the scent of clean linen and wet herbs that lingered on the air. There was an elegance to the infirmary, the essence of the house's lord in the brightly colored tiles beneath their feet and the plush softness of the beds. An iron stove kept the room at a comfortable temperature. Despite the warmth and calm of the room, it was hard not to think of the chill room behind the far door, where Petyr laid on a plain metal table.

"How long can Wallach hold out?" If anyone had an honest gauge of his abilities, it would be his former pupil.

Safiya's jaw flexed. "I don't know."

"Can you bolster his abilities?" Azzy gnawed the inside of her cheek as she waited for the witch to answer.

"I'm nowhere near where I should be," she admitted.

"What if I gave you something?"

Safiya raised a brow. "I'm not taking your other eye."

"There has to be something else," said Azzy. She thought of how the Maven accessed those hazy buried memories. Would it be enough, broken as they were?

"That will not be necessary," said Brixby. "Nuin and I will help you reclaim your stamina." His expression left no room for argument.

"Excellent, more foul-tasting teas," the witch muttered as she fell back onto the bed.

Brixby ignored her as he watched her ward, his jaw tight. "You have come such a long way from Haven, but please remember you are not in this fight alone." Her guardian shifted forward to pull her into a tight hug. The scent of earth and herb so part of his essence it nearly toppled her grip on her emotions. "Your mother would be proud."

Azzy swallowed around the lump in her throat. She burned to ask Brixby about the memories the Maven dredged up, about what he knew of their mother and where they came from, but there were too many people in the room. There was another part of her, a small, cowardly part of her, afraid of his answer.

"Rest while you can, Azzy," said Brixby. "I'll see what Nuin can concoct for our young witch."

Howl cornered her as Azzy tried to leave, unable to completely hide the hurt in his expression as he grabbed the back of her shirt.

"You don't want me to come with you?"

Azzy pulled him into a hug, wishing the boy didn't have to fight at all, though she understood far more about his nature, and consequently Kai's, than she did before.

"You need to keep the others safe," she told him. "They can't sense what you can. I'm trusting you to protect them."

Howl rubbed his cheek against hers. "I will, I promise." Her heart hurt. Wallach would be in as much danger as they were, perhaps more, and she knew Howl wouldn't leave his side, no matter what. She caught Eleanor's gaze over Howl's shoulder. The scorpid woman nodded to her, easing some of Azzy's strain. She had to trust those she cared for would watch out for one another.

Their time was too limited for anything else. She watched as the group dispersed, Howl to find Wallach, Brixby to find Nuin, while Eleanor settled on the edge of Rose's cot. The scarred woman remained unconscious, a sleep so deep Nuin explained she might not wake up from it. Eleanor watch the sleeping woman's face with such a conflicted mix of emotions Azzy felt like a voyeur. From what the scorpid woman told her, Rose was partially responsible for Kai's imprisonment, but Azzy couldn't summon any anger towards the woman.

Rather than hover, she returned to Kai. He'd dozed off again while she was away. She stood in the doorway, committing the lines of his face to memory, worried by the deepened lines that bracketed his mouth, the exhaustion that bruised the skin beneath his eyes. He was still too pale, too thin, the bones of his leg still weak after Brixby helped reset them.

"I can feel you staring," he said. Azzy said nothing as she slid next to him. There was nothing she could say that would deter him. Instead, she traced the contours of his chest and wished there weren't so few moments left between them.

There was a conclusion to this evening she'd carefully danced around since her conversation with the Maven. Armin was a key. Azzy was a lock. A key could be used and then taken away, but a lock...a lock stayed with the door.

Azzy wasn't sure on which side of the door the lock needed to be.

22

ELEANOR

The world might be ending, but the night market was in full swing. The others didn't seem to think much of it as they threaded through the bustle of the market en route to their various destinations, but she found the crowded streets unsettling. Why hadn't Lord Wallach alerted the other lords? Or did they know and simply not care about what happened to the populace at large? That certainly seemed par for the course of the lords. When Eleanor scanned the night market crowd, she noticed a definite absence of excessive finery and arrogance. There was a palpable tension in the air, though she suspected that was due to the lord to one side and the lynx to the other. It should have been risky to have Howl's large lethal form beside her, but no one said a word when Wallach kept them company. The crowds parted like the river around a large rock. Wallach was very much the center of everyone's attention though not a single soul dared glance in their direction. Azzy's contingent slipped through without drawing a stray gaze.

Eleanor glanced up at the enigmatic lord, not sure what to make of him yet. He had a far different demeanor than the other lords she'd dealt with. His bearing was somber rather the haughty or aloof like the patrons of the carnal house. Nor was he like Vashon with his deceptive charm.

"How will we know if they're here?" she inquired.

Wallach's gait didn't slow, forcing Eleanor into an uncomfortable gait to keep up with his long strides. "We will know."

He came to an abrupt stop at the market's center. The effect was interesting. The crowd rippled back into a widening circle around the Lord of Seven Smiles. No longer in motion, more than a few patrons stole a furtive glance, a mix of fear and curiosity in their expressions. Though she was sure Howl gave the patrons of the night market a pause, the lord was in a category of his own. Eleanor could easily blend; dozens of scorpid women stood at the edges, watching the milling masses with hungry gazes. How different her fate would have been if the fever swept her memories and personality aside like debris on the tide. She would be one of those lean predators, waiting and watching for some fool to wander into her clutches. It was because she was watching the scorpid women that she noticed it first, simply because they did. Each of them frozen, the stillness of a predator sensing their fortunes had turned to prey. The scorpid women burst into movement, the motions jerky and abrupt as they looked around for the source of their unease.

She tugged on Wallach's sleeve and pointed to the ladies as they began to retreat into the shadows. "They're spooked."

Wallach sucked in a breath. "Brace yourselves."

"I'm not scared of them," said Eleanor.

"I meant for me," said Wallach. Shrugging off his jacket, he handed it off to Eleanor as he unbuttoned his vest. His jaw was set so tight she thought his teeth might crack. A line of worry grew deeper between his dark brows. What exactly was she supposed to brace for? If Wallach thought she hadn't seen a naked man before, Azzy hadn't been entirely honest about Eleanor's former occupation.

Wallach's shirt front puffed out as he removed his vest, as if a sudden draft of air shoved its way beneath the fabric. Except there was no wind. Wallach turned to untuck the back of his shirt from his trousers. Eleanor stared. Something moved beneath the fabric covering his shoulder blades. Howl took a step back to huddle in Eleanor's skirts as the space around them widened. A few people had stopped to stare in morbid fascination. She raised a brow and quietly accepted his vest as he proceeded to unbutton his shirt sleeves.

A hush fell over the crowd.

Eleanor wanted to snap at the lot of them to move along when a child fell into the wide circle surrounding Wallach. The boy didn't cry out. He didn't make a sound, not a cry, not the slap of his sticky hands on the stones, or the creak of his leather shoes scuffling across the ground as he scrambled to his feet. An oppressive silence settled around her shoulders, tangible as carded wool. It wasn't the hush of an entranced crowd but an unnatural silence that closed in around them, slowly choking off their air. Eleanor looked around. Realization swept through the crowd, evident in their varying expressions of confusion and fear. One of the merchants dropped the metal pot he'd been hawking. Eleanor watched it bounce in the void of silence until it rolled to a stop at the edge of Wallach's circle. The crowd heaved in on itself as the first threads of panic drew taut.

The low roaring hiss of a Lynx ripped through the air. It bounced off the stones, shredding the unnatural silence. Eleanor blinked at him in surprise. How could his voice break through when nothing else could? That singular noise shattered the voluminous tension that gripped the night market crowd. Cries and clatter filled the air, the spell of silence broken as the denizens of Avegard scattered into the night. Wallach handed Eleanor his gloves, unperturbed by the events as he continued to undress. Her gaze snagged on the palms of his hands. A mouth opened in each palm, tasting the air. Eleanor glimpsed rows of triangular teeth. Her lips parted in shocked understanding. She hadn't realized how literal Lord Wallach's moniker was until that moment. He didn't look at her as he slid off his shirt to reveal a well-toned physique, unmarred but for the seams of the mouths—one across his abdomen, another high on his chest near his throat. She chanced a curious glance and saw another two high up on his shoulder blades, mentally counting them off in her head.

Aside from their startling appearance and placement, she didn't see what all the fuss was about until the mouth on his abdomen split. Eleanor stared into the maw and fought for control of her bowels. Fear poured out of her, drawn by a physical force that hooked under her skin and ripped the emotion free. People couldn't help their reaction to Wallach, their very physiology betrayed them. Eleanor inhaled a breath and shifted her gaze to the man's face as she carefully accepted his shirt with a steady hand.

Wallach's gaze was locked on something unseen above them.

The unnatural silence slammed down again, submerging the near-empty night market in an eerie, noiseless void as Wallach widened his stance. He raised his hands, palms up so their mouths bit at the invading presence. Eleanor staggered as the weight of the air increased. The surrounding presence teased the edges of her senses, a nightmare that hovered at the edge of waking, the shape and size of it a frustratingly vague picture she couldn't pull together.

She knew by the movement of his chest that Wallach's energy already flagged, but Eleanor couldn't hear her own heartbeat in the choking silence. Howl paced, his gaze drawn upwards as well, though he didn't make a sound either. Eleanor wondered why until one of the stalls burst in a silent cloud of splintered wood. The presence swallowed up her shriek of surprise but for a split-second Eleanor caught the ripple of air around something solid and massive. Fortunate that the night market was nearly empty now, the last merchants scurrying away with their wares. She hoped the citizens of Avergard had enough sense to remain in their homes. Wallach shifted his stance, locking his knees, but she noticed the slight tremor in his legs. Worry tugged at her gut. The witch hadn't caught up to them yet. Wallach had to at least hold on until then.

Wallach shoved his hands upward. Eleanor quickly looked up and away as all seven of his mouths opened. Concentrated pressure slammed into her. She staggered as the air overhead shimmered. At first, Eleanor thought it was an aftereffect of Wallach's power, until her vision adjusted to the creature's size, the shifting of massive, invisible limbs, and realized the scope and scale of the Child hovering over Avergard. Her lips parted as the whimper slid from her throat, absorbed by the silence before it ever gained purchase. The pressure doubled, squeezing the air from her lungs as the rippling air began to gain color and shape. Eleanor couldn't tear her gaze away until Howl nearly knocked her over. She threaded her fingers in the lynx's fur, grateful for his presence. She risked a look at the lord, careful to avoid the mouth that evoked fear. She had plenty to spare.

Sweat streamed down Wallach's face and bare chest. His shoulders shook from strain as his knees bent another inch. It was as if he held up the weight of the sky. The Child hovered above them, a half-formed thing, beating them down with silence. Safiya slid across the stones in front of Wallach. She'd needed to time her entrance to coincide with the emptied market since she'd gone through a very public execution only yesterday.

The witch slapped her open palm to the ground, an audible sound that ricocheted through the vacant market, echoing off the stones. The Child appeared above them. Eleanor bit down hard on her tongue to hold back the scream.

The Children of the Gate were never meant to be seen. It didn't resemble any singular creature in memory. A hodge podge of limbs hefted its bulk above the ground, coated in skin that ran like melted wax, a dark rusted color like river clay or old blood. There was no face or features other than the mouth, the long, jagged maw drove off any lingering fears she held of Wallach's appearance. Despite the lack of eyes, she could feel the weight of its attention on them. Her mind couldn't wrap itself around the sight of the creature that leered down at them, but it pricked at those primal instincts of prey in the presence of a much larger predator. The desire to run was laughable. Where could she run, where could she possibly flee that this behemoth couldn't reach her? It was that cold, cruel logic that kept her from bolting even as the odds of her survival spiraled to nil.

Eleanor wondered why the Child hadn't attacked them yet, but as Wallach's outstretched arms shook from strain, she realized he truly was holding this massive creature at bay. Safiya said Wallach could hold them, but not for long. She prayed whatever Azzy had to do to stop this, she finished soon. The silence broke as a boom shook the air. The ground shook beneath them.

Eleanor, not knowing what caused her to do so, let her gaze drift to the heavens. A second Child of the Gate shimmered into view above her.

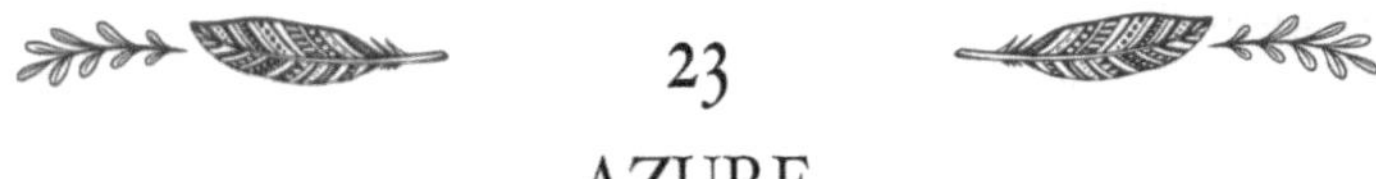

23

AZURE

They stood at the threshold of Vashon's estate when silence blanketed the city.

Kai slid his hand into Azzy's, a final touch of contact. She laced their fingers together, wishing they never left the warm bed at Wallach's estate.

"Let's go," said the Maven. The silence didn't affect her or Kai, but Azzy could feel the weight of it, far stronger than what she'd experience Below. It squatted between her shoulders, breathing down her neck like some great beast. Azzy wrapped her fingers around the cord, waiting for Kai's nod before she pulled it free. The change was uncontrolled and instantaneous.

Kai, the wolf, butted his head against her shoulder. She combed her fingers through the thick ruff of fur at his neck before they followed the Maven into Vashon's domain. Nothing attacked them as they crossed the wide expanse of decorative gardens to reach the front door. Where Wallach kept his estate immaculate, there were signs of decay here, clumps of dead shrubs, yellowed grass and shriveled flowers. The hint of rotted plant matter teased her senses. Kai's hackles rose.

The Maven shoved the doors open the second she reached them. She moved with that reptilian grace that raised the hair on Azzy's arms. The Maven was done with masks. Her true face would be burned into Azzy's memory until the day she died; a face that was not a face, a poor facsimile of one, as if the Maven had the barest idea of human features but couldn't grasp them. Her eyes were sunken pits in her skull, pushed so far into her misshapen skull they were nothing more than puckered, withered pits. The jagged gash of her mouth was an afterimage, a blur of teeth and shadows, the mouth of the demon that hovered in the dark corners of the room, beyond the edge of nightmares. Pallid corpse-like skin stretched tight over her knobby frame, her exaggerated joints giving her a boneless grace as she prowled through the halls of Vashon's estate. Wolf and girl brought up the rear. Kai scented the air as he entered, lips curling in a snarl over sharp canine teeth. The whispers surged in Azzy's mind, creating a swarm that protected her from Vashon's probing reach.

They had only crossed the threshold when they encountered the first of Vashon's servants. The female servant appeared from one blink to the next. Azzy recognized her two-toned face from her nightmares of this place. She braced herself as the seam that ran down the middle of her face began to split.

The Maven rose behind her. Spindle-thin fingers clamped down on either side of the girl's head. A whimper of shock slipped from her lips. There was a crunch and wet tear. Azzy bit the inside of her cheek. The girl's body dropped in a heap at her feet; her head rolled in a lazy circle several feet away.

"We have no time for theatrics," sneered the Maven.

A throbbing whistle rent the air as a spinning blade slid through the Maven's arm. Another servant appeared, a boy younger than her brother, his pale angelic face marred by the hatred that blazed in his dark eyes. Azzy barely had time to comprehend the volatile mix of youth and hatred when he charged at them, another blade raised high. There was no finesse in the attack, one Azzy managed to avoid with ease. This close, she could see he was painfully young, his movements careless and wide. His next swing left his defenses wide open.

"Wait, no," said Azzy, the words died on her lips as the boy's lips peeled back in an inhuman snarl. His vacant gaze swung towards her at the sound of her voice. There was nothing human left in that face. Kai saw it too. He took the open, tearing out the boy's throat in a quick, efficient movement.

The ground lurched beneath their feet. The Maven paled.

"We're out of time. Azzy, go! Run!"

Azzy stumbled into an unsteady run as the ground continued to buck and surge beneath her. The walls shook around her until she wondered if the whole estate would come down on top of her before she reached Armin. She followed the familiar route of her nightmares, until she skidded to a stop outside the room of the pit. Azzy couldn't catch her breath as she saw what waited for her.

Armin hovered in the air; his outstretched wings motionless as they wept feathers. His head was bowed as storms swirled in his eyes, transfixed on the mouth of the pit that heaved and breathed beneath him, a faint glow that steadily grew brighter with each passing second. Azzy took a step toward him when the knob of a cane smashed into her jaw.

The blow knocked her off her feet. Azzy crashed onto the floor as the taste of copper bloomed in her mouth. She spat a mouthful of blood on the marble floor and tried to lift herself up. A shoe pressed against her back, holding her down as invisible claws sank into her mind trying to shred their way through the swarm of whispers.

"Fascinating," said Vashon. Azzy gasped as he nudged her side hard enough to flip her over. He crouched down in his fine, blood-speckled suit and smoothed her hair out of her face to get a better look at her. "Such an elegant defense. I've never seen anything like it. Rather than try to keep me out, you invite me in and fill your mind with noise. It's absolutely deafening." His expression was akin to awe as his gloved fingers traced the curve of her cheekbone beneath her altered eye.

She let her other eye close, a motion that looked like a cringe to appeal to his need to dominate while she studied Vashon through the lens of her altered eye. His power was a massive, tangled knot at his core, flavored by the minds he'd touched, the memories he'd plucked and gathered like knickknacks for the parlor table. She could almost see it, the thread she needed to pull to unravel it all, when she stopped, listening to the swarm in her mind. Vashon's thumbnail dug into her cheek.

"What do you see through this, I wonder," he mused. "Do you see my weakness? My desires?"

"I see the truth," said Azzy, her words muddied by the pain in her jaw, though the bone wasn't broken. He frowned at her answer, reaching for her again when the Maven's clawed fingers slid over his shoulders.

"You haven't learned to play nice, Dierk," she hissed. Vashon slammed his elbow back, catching the Maven by surprise, but that move left him vulnerable as Kai barreled into him, knocking him off his feet. She let the others handle Vashon as she lurched to her feet and rushed to Armin.

He floated nearly two feet off the ground, too high for her to reach his face, but Azzy had another idea to get his attention. She took Kai's cord from her pocket, pulling a thread free from the braid. She lifted his limp hand and wrapped the string around it, once, twice, three times, so tight his finger paled at the pressure. Ritual, their life was full of them: in the horror of the feasts, in the moments Armin would sit her down to tame her unruly hair, in a knotted string to connect them. Azzy wrapped the string around her finger.

"I will always find you," she whispered.

Armin sucked in a breath. She caught him as he dropped, buffeted by his wings, their tied hands clasped together. He shuddered in her grip, the connection there, faint, where they pulled at the shreds of his memory. But it was there, where her brother hid the memory of her so not even the burning fever of the magic could touch it. A seed of memory she coaxed along until she found the roots buried deep. Armin's gaze focused on the string before his gaze shifted to her face. Recognition flared.

"Azzy?" His other hand touched her arm, her face, testing to see if she was real. "Azzy!" He pulled her into a tight hug. His wing brushed her cheek, soft as silk.

"I found you," she said.

Armin sobbed against her shoulder. From the corner of her eye, the glow of the pit gained a blinding brilliance. Azzy swallowed hard. It wasn't fair, not after she finally found her brother again. She held him tighter, watching over his shoulder as the Maven approached her.

"Vashon?" Azzy asked as Armin stiffened against her at the name.

The Maven shrugged. "Temporarily out of order," she said. "I can't take him out like you can."

"They'll need him," said Azzy, her voice soft. Armin tried to look at her, but she couldn't let him go. This was her last stolen moment. The Maven peered into the pit but said nothing as Azzy held her brother. She took a steadying breath as she pulled back, unwrapping the string from her finger. "Go to Lord Wallach's estate. Brixby's there."

Armin's eyes widened. "You found him—"

"Yes. I'll explain all of it later, but there's no time now," Azzy smiled up at him. "There's so much to say, but no time."

Armin paled as reality and memory crashed back around them.

"Azzy, why are you here? The pit, its--"

The Maven suddenly appeared beside him. "She's doing what all good siblings do and cleaning up your mess," she purred. She tapped his temple. Armin crashed to his knees, wings fluttering a frantic rhythm, but he didn't rise, couldn't rise.

"What did you do to me?" A note of panic threaded his voice.

Azzy yelped. "Stop! You didn't have to stun him."

The Maven shrugged. "The family reunion has to wait my dear. Unless you want to chat up your little brother while the Children devour the city?"

"Don't touch him again," Azzy snapped. She walked to the pit's edge, squinting into the bright light still rising from the depths. "How do I close it?"

"Oh child, don't you already know?" The Maven's smile was cruel.

Azzy froze. No, this couldn't be it. She *did* know. She'd suspected such an outcome when the Maven first mentioned a lock and key, but she'd refused to accept it. Not when she'd fought so hard, and so long to save her family. She stared down into the pit, horrified at the choice laid before her. A choice that was not a choice.

"Time to fulfill your purpose, child," the Maven whispered in her ear. Azzy couldn't move fast enough as the Maven's spindly fingers shoved her forward. Azzy tottered on the edge. Gravity twined around her, beckoning her down. She refused to leave the Maven here. Twisting at the waist gave her just enough leverage to snag the Maven's arm.

The Maven screeched as their combined weight took them off balance. Azzy used their awkward position to shove the Maven down, but there was no chance to pull herself back up. Her body spun as she fell backward into the pit. She caught one last glimpse of her brother, still trapped on the ground, as he screamed her name. The power in it was almost enough to hold her there, almost.

Kai raced across the room, leaping after her into the light.

Azzy plunged into brilliant white. The air throbbed and pulsed against her skin and beneath it as she fell. A distant roar of fury vibrated through to her bones. She felt a mental snap inside, locked in place, as the light evaporated, and Azzy free-fell through its absence. She was certain she would fall forever.

There was hard ground under her, sudden and solid, though she never felt the bruising sensation of impact. Azzy rolled over to avoid choking as her stomach heaved at the sudden cessation of movement. She had landed, but her body thought it was still falling. Her head spun. A wolf whined nearby.

Kai. Azzy's head lolled, her relief palpable at the sight of him. She hadn't wanted him to follow her but was grateful he was here. Where was here?

Azzy rolled onto her back and caught her breath at the sight of the sky above her. A patchwork of stars greeted her, a tapestry of mutilated heavens mashed together into an unsettling quilt. None of the stars looked like home. A loud roar echoed through the air, followed by a screech that made her sore muscles go tight. She knew where she was, though the Maven was nowhere to be seen. Azzy fell back, too stunned to move as she looked upon the shattered sky within the Gate.

EPILOGUE
ELEANOR

She knew they were about to die when Wallach collapsed. He slumped to the ground, unable to hold himself up as the Children of the Gate opened its mouth above them. Eleanor braced herself, prepared for a grisly death down the creature's gullet when the silence shattered.

The scream stretched on and on, a thousand agonized voices in harmony. The Children seized up, vanishing from sight as their presence rapidly dissipated.

"They left?" Eleanor looked around the empty Night Market, bewildered. What was scary enough to spook a Child of the Gate?

Safiya knelt beside Wallach. Her expression blanched as she clutched at the blue pendant around her neck. "She's gone."

Eleanor jerked as if slapped. "No. No, you're lying." She wanted to believe the witch lied, even as she felt the truth resonate through her.

"We have to find the boy," said Safiya.

How could they? If Azzy failed there was no chance of getting to her brother or helping him remember his humanity. Any minute the Children of the Gate would return to finish what they started. The sense of hopelessness swelled in her chest until Eleanor was certain her heart would crack from the pressure. It was finally too much. Eleanor clasped her hands over her chest, trying to keep the torrent of emotion at bay.

She froze. Above her, the air filled with the rush of wings.

Azzy Still Needs You

Did you enjoy Skin Curse? Reviews keep books alive . . .

Azzy needs you now! Help her by leaving your review on either GoodReads or the digital storefront of your choosing.

Azzy thanks you!

Acknowledgments

A massive thank you to the crew behind Midnight Tide Publishing, who gave this series a second chance to shine. We've been battered by the waves of industry these past few years, but it's been a blast to steer through the maelstrom with such fine company. And to my partner, through all our ups and downs, you've remained a solid rock, supporting all my endeavors and finding ways to make it work.

About the Author

Kristin Jacques is an award-winning author of fantasy fiction for teens and adults. She currently lives in a small town in Connecticut with her partner, kiddos, and two trash goblins who think they are cats. When not writing, she's usually reading, gaming, or catching some excellent b-horror movies. She is currently working on projects full of magic, mystery, and delight.

For more info:

Wattpad:<u>https://www.wattpad.com/user/krazydiamond</u>
Website: <u>http://www.kristinjacques.com/</u>

More Books You'll Love

If you enjoyed this story, please consider leaving a review.

Then check out more books from Midnight Tide Publishing!

The Fae Ingredient by Jason Bustard

Amandine loves to cook. As the scull for a noble house in the magical land of Beregoth, she watches and learns from grumpy old Chef Brutsche and his assistants and dreams of being a chef herself one day. After a new acquaintance has a peek into Chef's secret pantry, a mystery begins to unfold. Dark fae, old magic and a strange mushroom lead Amandine to try and discover the secrets of Chef's amazing food.

With the strange ingredient from Chef's pantry in hand, Amandine sets out, with the help of her friends, Gil, the baker's apprentice, and Fredderick, a mysterious noble youth with magical powers, to discover what it is and what the secretive Chef Brutsche does with it. Along the way she discovers that it may have a link to a local tribe of dark fae who are in a bad light with the nearby townsfolk and nobles. Are the Boglings really responsible for the recent problems plaguing the town of Stoneman? Will the key ingredient to one of Chef's signature dishes be lost forever? As Amandine struggles with these questions, she and her companions are flung into events that will test both their bravery and her cooking skills...

Available Now

The Stars Forgot Us by R.J. Garcia

Fifteen-year-old Jacob Kelly would love to go back to simpler times. Before his parents' divorce and the onset of his older brother's schizophrenia. But when he returns to his hometown, things feel off. After a series of strange occurrences in his new house, Jacob fears the house is haunted, or even worse, he is losing his mind.

To his surprise, Jacob discovers a mysterious teenage runaway, Sanctuary Daniels, living in the house. She reveals she has been kept by a figure known only as Mother, in a place where downstairs children are languishing prisoners, and upstairs children do Mother's bidding.

Both Jacob's investigation into Sanctuary's allegations and their budding romance are cut short when she is reclaimed by evil beings. Beings who unleash terror upon Jacob and his family. Now he must journey to a real haunted house to save his first love and fight for his life.

Available Now

Ephesus by Christis Christie

As a soul lost before it could live, Ephesus was gifted a special role—he must collect the dead.

Ephesus has known no other existence than reaping souls, experiencing life only from the shadows. Remaining separate was easy, until the day he meets a unique little girl with an ability she should not possess.

But can friendships be nurtured when life and death aren't meant to mingle beyond the point of passing? Ephesus must navigate the world fulfilling his purpose while also balancing his newfound curiosity of the girl's life. However, when a threat arises, will it mean their ruin?

Available Now